An Old Story of My Farming Days

Vol. I

by

Fritz Reuter

An Old Story of My Farming Days
Vol. I
by Fritz Reuter

Copyright © 2024

All Rights reserved.

No part of this publication may be reproduced, stored in a retrieval system, or transmitted in any form or by any means, electronic, mechanical, photocopying or Otherwise, without the written permission of the publisher.
The author/editor asserts the moral right to be identified as the author/editor of this work.

ISBN: 978-93-64286-38-1

Published by

DOUBLE 9 BOOKS

2/13-B, Ansari Road
Daryaganj, New Delhi – 110002
info@double9books.com
www.double9books.com
Tel. 011-40042856

This book is under public domain

ABOUT THE AUTHOR

Fritz Reuter (1810-1874) was a renowned German novelist and a pivotal figure in 19th-century German literature. He is especially noted for his writings in Low German (Plattdeutsch), which vividly portray the rural life and culture of Northern Germany, particularly Mecklenburg. Early Works: After his release, Reuter began his literary career. Major Works: Reuter's major contributions to literature include a series of novels and stories that depict rural Mecklenburg life with a blend of realism and humor. Notable works include: "Ut de Franzosentid" (During the French Period): A collection of stories set during the Napoleonic Wars. "Ut mine Festungstid" (During My Time in Prison): An autobiographical account of his imprisonment. "Ut mine Stromtid" (During My Apprenticeship): A semi-autobiographical novel regarded as one of his masterpieces. "In the Year '13: A Tale of Mecklenburg Life": A historical novel set during the Napoleonic Wars, exploring their impact on rural Mecklenburg. Reuter's use of Low German in his writing was significant in preserving and popularizing the dialect. It added authenticity to his portrayal of rural life and connected deeply with his audience. His works are characterized by their realistic depiction of rural life, combined with humor and a deep understanding of human nature. Reuter's stories often address social issues, reflecting the struggles and resilience of rural communities. Fritz Reuter is celebrated for his contributions to German literature and for promoting Low German. His works continue to be appreciated for their cultural and historical significance. Reuter is honored through numerous schools, streets, and institutions named after him, particularly in Northern Germany. Fritz Reuter remains a significant literary figure, known for his contributions to preserving Low German culture and for his engaging, realistic depictions of rural German life.

CONTENTS

CHAPTER I	9
CHAPTER II	17
CHAPTER III	30
CHAPTER IV	42
CHAPTER V	60
CHAPTER VI	76
CHAPTER VII	84
CHAPTER VIII	96
CHAPTER IX	108
CHAPTER X	118
CHAPTER XI	127
CHAPTER XII	139
CHAPTER XIII	156
FOOTNOTES	165

Well, well, it was not always so.--The father of the man who now rides to town with white reins for his horse, and who drinks his couple of bottles of champagne, had probably nothing better than small beer with which to quench his thirst, and had his reins tied together with his wife's garter. Ah, those were hard times in Mecklenburg when wheat was sold in barrels on the public road for sixteen pence a bushel, good measure too, to the labourers to feed their pigs with, and when, as in Rostock, a whole load of oats was given in exchange for a loaf of sugar.

Mecklenburg is a beautiful and a rich land, just the kind of country that delights a farmer, but at the time of which I am speaking there was great poverty and distress throughout the length and breadth of it, and the collector knocked at every door, and demanded that the rent should be paid, and whoever had anything to give, gave his last penny, and he who had nothing to give was sold up.

Let no one imagine from this that our country-people hobbled about the land like scare-crows during these hard times, or that one could read the "Vater-unser" through their sunken cheeks--Nay!--they were as true Mecklenburgers every bit then as now, only they had to manage differently. Now-a-days one says: "Butter costs a shilling a pound, which comes to so much a hundredweight, and if I sell so many hundredweights of it, I shall be able to buy a glass-coach and four horses to match from the sale of butter alone."--At that time one said: "What mother? Butter cost two-pence? Then let's eat it by itself.--What mother? The butcher offers fifteen shillings for the fat pig? Cut its throat, mother, and put it in our own salting-tub."--The country-people were all quite as strong and healthy then as now, and were quite as well off as regarded food in the third decade of this century as at the present day, it was the shoemakers' and tailors' bills that were the difficulty, and as for ready money, they learnt what that really was when they were called upon to pay their rent.

Yes, things are much improved of late years, and although the priests say a thousand times that the world is worse than it was, I maintain that it has grown better.

"Good morning, Mr. bailiff Wilbrandt!"--"Good morning, old friend, come and have some breakfast"--"Good morning, father Hellwig!"--"Don't bother me, I'm in a bad humour."--"Why, what's the matter?"--"A great deal's the matter. My rent has almost doubled itself, and Zirzow has done its part this year, and so here I am with £3000 that I don't know how to invest. The Rostock bank won't take in any more money, so what's to be done? Ah, Wilbrandt, it's a bad world!"--"Yes, it's a bad world," replied the bailiff; and I also said: "Very bad," without for a moment remembering the large sum of money I shall have to invest next term.--"Yes," continued Wilbrandt, "who the devil thought of mortgages in the old days?"--"True," said father Hellwig, "nobody thought of such things then. Look you, when I went to old Solomon in Stemhagen[1], and told him I wanted to borrow some money from him, he said to me: 'Hellwig,' he said, 'you have an honest face, it is marked with small-pox--but there's no harm in that--you shall have the money.' And then I had to spend one night in his house, and sleep in the same room as he did. Now I have a bad habit of smoking myself to sleep, and so I always take a freshly lit pipe to bed with me, and as Solomon was very nervous about fire, he kept continually calling to me: 'Hellwig, are you still smoking?' Ah, those were good old times!"--"Yes," said the bailiff, "and how we used to rejoice when we had paid off the last farthing of our small debts! The happiest part of my life passed away with my last debts. Those were good old times."--"No," said I, "they were bad old times. You managed to keep afloat in spite of hardships and difficulties, and therefore you are worthy of all honour and respect, but many other honest men couldn't do so, try as they might."--Then Mr. X Y Z, a land-owner in the neighbourhood, came up, and striking the table so hard with his walking-stick that all the bottles danced, said: "Those who didn't get the better of their difficulties weren't worth their salt."--"What," cried the bailiff, "have you got to say to that?"--Then father Hellwig rose, and looking at him with his honest old face, said: "You are a young man, and have inherited your estate from your ancestors. You hav'n't the faintest idea of the misery of those times.--You know all about it, old friend," he added, turning to me, "so tell us about what happened then."--"Yes," I answered, "I will tell the story of those old days."

.

CHAPTER I

On midsummer-day 1829, a man was seated in an arbour in a desolate garden, plunged in sad reverie. The land to which the garden belonged was a leasehold, situated on the river Peen, between Anclam and Demmin, and the man who was seated in the cool, shady arbour was the tenant farmer--that is to say; that is what he had been, for he was now bankrupt, and an auction was going on in his yard, and all his goods and chattels were being scattered to the four winds.

He was a tall, broad-shouldered man of forty-four years of age, with hair of a dusky blond colour. All that work can do for a man had been done for this man, and a better than he could nowhere be found. "Work," said his honest face: and "work" said his honest hands, which were now folded on his knee as if in prayer.

Yes, in prayer! No one in all Pomerania had so much need of a little talk with his God as this man. "Tis a hard blow for any one when he sees the household goods which he has brought together with the labour of his hands and the sweat of his brow scattered over the wide world. 'Tis a hard blow for a farmer when he is obliged to let the cattle he has reared with pain and trouble, pass into the hands of strangers, who know nothing of the struggles that have filled his life; but it was neither of these things that was lying so heavily on his soul just now, it was another grievous sorrow that made him fold his hands, and raise his eyes to heaven.

He had been a widower for one day only. His wife lay upon her last bed--his wife! For ten long years he had been engaged to her; for ten years he had toiled and laboured and done all that man could do to provide a fitting home for her. His deep faithful love for his promised wife filled his heart with tender music, such as the Whitsun bells ring out over the green fields and blossoming trees. Four years ago he had attained the end for which he had striven, had scraped together enough money to set up house. An acquaintance of his who had inherited two farms from his parents, let one of them to him at a high rent; a very high rent; he knew that, none better; but love gives a man courage, that kind of courage which conquers difficulties. All would have gone well with him, if his good little wife had not got up so early in the morning, and worked so hard, and if she had not come to have that burning red spot on each cheek. All would have gone well with him, if his landlord, instead of being a mere acquaintance, had been a friend--and he was not that, for it was because of him that the auction was going on in the farm-yard to-day.

Friend?--A man like that one who is sitting in the oak arbour can have no friends? He *had* true-hearted friends, but they could not help him, they had nothing to give or lend. Wherever he looked, it seemed to him as though he were surrounded by a high wall which hemmed him in and stifled him, and so he cried with all his strength to God to save him in his sore distress. A linnet and a chaffinch were singing in the oak-boughs above his head, their feathers shining in the sun, the flowers in the neglected garden scattered their fragrance all around, and the oak-trees cast their cool shadow over him. If two lovers had been sitting there, they would never have forgotten the place and how it looked all their lives long.

And had *he* not sat in that shady bower with a gentle hand clasped within his own? Had not the birds sung as cheerily, and was not the perfume of the flowers as sweet then as now? Had he not dreamt of sitting on that very seat in his old age, and while immersed in that dream of the future--who was it who had brought him a cool draught to refresh him after his hard day's work? Who was it who had shared the toil and care of his daily life, and had encouraged him by her sympathy?

Gone--all gone!--Everything he had was to be sold, and the gentle loving hand he had held in his own was stiff and cold. Then the man felt as if the birds no longer sang their glad songs for him, as if the flowers no longer grew for him in their sweetness and beauty, and as if the glorious sun no longer shone for him, although his poor overcharged heart still went on beating as strongly as before; and so he stretched out his hands beyond birds and flowers, and even the golden sun, to the divine Comforter, who better than any earthly joy can soothe the wounded heart.

Hawermann sat thus in silent prayer, his hands clasped, and his brave blue eyes, in which a wondrous light was shining as though from God's own sun, raised to heaven, when a little girl came up to him and laid a daisy on his knee. He drew the child,--she was his only one--closer to him, and rising, took her in his arms. His eyes were full of tears as he walked down the garden-path carrying his little girl and holding the daisy she had given him in his hand.

He came to a young tree that he himself had planted; the straw rope by which it was fastened to the pronged stick that supported it had become loose, and the young tree was leaning all on one side. He straightened it and fastened it again to its prop, scarcely conscious of what he was doing, for his thoughts were far away, but it was his nature to give help wherever it was wanted.

When a man is lost in thought, even though that thought may have led him up to the blue heavens, if any little bit of his daily work should happen to fall under his notice, he takes up the wonted task involuntarily, and does what may be required at the moment, and so he is wakened out of his reverie, and reminded of what is lying close at hand and ought to be done, and that it is so is a great gift of God.

Hawermann walked up and down the garden, his eyes saw what was round about him, and his thoughts returned to earth once more. Though the sky of his future life was heavy with black, stormy clouds, still there was one little scrap of blue that the clouds could not overcast, and that was the thought of his little girl whom he was carrying in his arms, and whose small childish hand was playing with his hair.

He left the garden and entered the farm-yard.--And what was going on there?--Indifferent strangers were pressing up to the table where the auctioneer was selling off the farmer's effects, each thinking only of the bargains he wished to make. One after another all of Hawermann's possessions were knocked down to the highest bidder. Those things that he had collected bit by bit with toil and trouble to furnish his house, were now being scattered abroad amid the jokes and laughter of all present. Even the old things were going--that cupboard had belonged to his old mother; that chest of drawers his wife had brought home with her when she was married; he had given her that little work-table when he was engaged to her.--His cows were tied in a long line and were lowing to be taken to the pasture-field. The brown heifer his wife had reared from a calf, and which had always been her pet, was standing amongst them. He went up to it, and passed his hand caressingly down its back. "Sir," said Niemann, the head-ploughman, "this is very sad."--"Yes, Niemann, it *is* sad, but it can't be helped," he answered, turnings away and mingling in the crowd round the auction-table.

As soon as the people saw that he wanted to get to the table they made room for him courteously and kindly. He asked the auctioneer if he might speak to him for a moment: "*Im*mediately, Mr. Hawermann," was the reply, "in one moment, I've just finished with the household things, then ...... a chest of drawers! six and two-pence! three-pence! six and four-pence! going! going!--six and four pence!--No one else bid anything?--Going! going! gone!"--"Whose is it?"--"Tailor Brandt's," was the answer.

Just at this moment some farmers rode into the yard, probably to look at the cattle which were now about to be sold. Foremost amongst them was a stout red-faced man, whose fat face was made even broader than it was by nature, by the insolent expression that it wore. Men of this species are often to be met with, but what distinguished this man from the rest of his type were the small cunning eyes that peeped out over his fat cheeks, and which seemed to say: It's all thanks to *us* that you are so well up in the world, *we* know how to manage. The owner of these eyes was also the owner of the farm of which Hawermann was tenant. He rode right in amongst the crowd, and when he saw his unhappy tenant standing among the other people, he was at once struck with terror lest he should not get his full rent, and the cunning little eyes that knew so well how to manage things for their own advantage said to the insolence that found its home on his mouth and in his expression: Up brother, now's the time to make yourself as big as possible, for it'll cost you nothing! Then forcing his horse closer to Hawermann, he called out in a loud voice so that every one might hear: "Ha ha! These are the clever Mecklenburgers, who think they can teach us how to farm properly! And what have they taught us? They've taught us to drink red wine and cheat at cards, but as for farming!--they can teach us better how to become bankrupt."

There was deep silence during this hard speech. Everyone looked first at the speaker, and then at the man whom he had addressed. Hawermann had started on hearing the voice and the words as though some one had plunged a knife into his heart, and now he stood gazing silently on the ground at his feet, not caring to defend himself, but a murmur arose among the people, and a cry of: "ss--ss--for shame! This man drank no red wine, he never cheated at cards--and his farming was most excellent!"--"Who's the great gaby that was talking such nonsense?" asked old Drenkhahn of Liepen, pressing closer with his heavy thorn-stick in his hand.--"It's the man whose labourers go about amongst us begging," cried lame Smidt.--"They hav'n't money to buy a coat for their backs," cried Brandt, the tailor from Jarmen, "and have to wear their Sunday clothes when they are working in the fields."--"Yes," laughed the smith, "it's the man who was so glad to see his labourers wearing such grand cloth coats when they were at work, and they only did it because they couldn't afford to buy smock-frocks, you know!"[2]

The auctioneer came up to the landlord, who was listening to all these remarks with perfect indifference, and asked him: "How *could* you say that, Mr. Pomuchelskopp, how *could* you?"--"Yes," said one of the men who had come with him, "these people are right, you should be ashamed of yourself for having aimed another blow at a man who is selling everything he has honestly, that he may meet and pay off all his debts."--"Ah," said the auctioneer, "if that were all. Mr. Hawermann's wife died yesterday, and is lying upstairs on her last bed, and so he is left alone in the world with a little girl, and *what* prospects?"--"I didn't know that," muttered Pomuchelskopp sullenly. The murmur of disapprobation now spread from the crowd to the landlord's companions, and in a few moments more, Mr. Pomuchelskopp was left alone, all the men who had accompanied him having ridden away to the other side of the yard.

The auctioneer now approached Hawermann and said: "You wanted to speak to me Mr. Hawermann?"--"Yes--yes," replied the farmer slowly, he seemed to be coming to himself again like a martyr when he has been removed from the rack. "I wished to ask you if you will also sell the few things that remain to me by law, at the auction. I mean the bed and the other things."--"With pleasure, but the furniture has sold badly, the people have no money, and if you really want to sell those things, it would be better to do so by private bargain."--"I haven't time for that, and I'm badly in want of the money."--"Well if you really wish it, I'll manage it for you," and then the auctioneer went about his business again.

"Hawermann," said farmer Grot, who was one of the people that had come on horseback, "you are so lonely here in your sorrow, do bring your little girl and come and pay me a visit, my wife will be so glad...."--"Thank you heartily for your kindness, but I can't accept your invitation, I have something to do here."--"You mean your dear wife's funeral, Hawermann," said farmer Hartmann, "when is it to be? We will all be glad to do her the last honours."--"Thank you, thank you, but that cannot be, it wouldn't be fitting, and I've just learnt that one oughtn't to stretch one's foot further than one's own roof will cover."--"Old friend, dear old neighbour and fellow-countryman," said Wienk, the farm-bailiff, laying his hand on his shoulder, "don't despair, things will get better."--"Despair! Wienk," said Hawermann earnestly, and pressing his child closer in his arms he looked calmly at the farm-bailiff with his honest blue eyes, and continued: "Is it despair when one looks one's future full in the face, and tries to find the best way of getting out of one's difficulties? I can't remain here, no one could stay in a place where his ship had run aground. I must live in another man's house. I must begin at the beginning again, and do as I did before. I must take service once more, and so earn my daily bread. And now good-bye all of you. You've been kind friends and neighbours to me. Good-bye--good-bye. Shake hands, Louie. Remember me to all at home. My wife...."--He was going to have said something more, but could not get out the words, so he turned quickly and hastened away.

"Niemann," he said to his head-ploughman whom he met at the other end of the yard, "tell the rest of my people that my wife's funeral will be at four o'clock to-morrow morning." Then he entered the house and went into his bed-room. Everything had been taken away, even his bed and the few small articles of furniture which had been left to him; nothing remained but the four bare walls. Except that there was an old chest in the corner near the window, on which the young wife of one of the labourers was seated, her eyes red with weeping, and in the middle of the room was a black coffin in which a pale, still, solemn figure was lying, and the young woman had a green branch in her hand, with which she fanned away the flies from the quiet face. "Stina," said Hawermann, "you may go now, I will remain here."--"Oh, Sir, let me stay."--"No, Stina, I shall remain here all night."--"Then, shall I take the little one home with me?"--"No, leave her, she'll go to sleep."--The young woman left the room. After a time the auctioneer brought Hawermann the money for his things, and then everyone left the yard, and all was as still and quiet without as within. He put the child down, and counted the money on the window sill: "so much for the carpenter for making the coffin; so much for the cross on the grave; so much for the burial fee; so much for Stina, and with what remains I can make my way to my sister's house."--It grew dark, the young woman brought in a candle, and placed it beside the coffin, and gazed long in the pale face of her dead mistress, then drying her eyes with her apron, she said: "Good night," and Hawermann was once more alone with his child.

He opened the window, and looked out into the night; it was dark for the time of year, no star was to be seen, the sky was covered with black clouds, and the light breeze that sighed in the distance was warm and fragrant. The quails were calling in the meadow, and a corncrake was sounding its rain signal, and the first drops of the coming shower were falling softly on the thirsty earth, which in its gratitude filled the air with that sweet smell, known and loved by farmers, the smell of the earth. How often had he been refreshed in spirit by such weather; how often had his cares been chased away, and his hope been renewed by it. Now he was free from those cares, but his joy was gone also--his *one* great joy had gone from him, and had taken with it all the smaller ones as well. He closed the window, and turning round saw his little daughter standing by the coffin, trying in vain to reach and stroke the quiet face within. He lifted the child higher so that she might do so, and the little girl stroked and patted her mother's face: "Mammy--oh!"--"Yes," said Hawermann, "Mammy's cold," and seating himself on the chest, he took the child on his knee, and wept bitterly; seeing this, the little one cried too, till she cried herself to sleep, so he held her gently in his arms, and drew his coat warmly round her. He sat there all night long, keeping a true lyke-wake by his wife and his dead happiness.

Next morning punctually at four o'clock the head-ploughman and the other men who worked on the farm arrived, the lid of the coffin was screwed down, and the procession moved off slowly to the little churchyard. His child and he were the only mourners. The coffin was lowered into the grave--a silent prayer--a handful of earth--and the form of her who had encouraged and comforted him for years, of her who had been his life and his joy, was hidden from his sight, and if ever he wished to see her, he must live over again in thought the happy old days when she was still at his side, until the time when the book of memory will be closed on earth, and then--yes, then, his dear one will reappear before him, beautiful and glorious.

He went and spoke to his work-people, shook hands with each of them, and thanked them for the last service they had rendered him, said good-bye to all, and then, after giving the head-ploughman the money to pay for the coffin, the cross, and the burial fee, he set out on his journey into the unknown future.

When he got to the last house in the hamlet, the labourer's young wife was standing at the door with a child in her arms, he went up to her, and said: "Stina, you nursed my poor wife faithfully in her last illness. Here Stina!" and he tried to slip a few shillings into her hand.--"Sir, Sir," cried the young woman. "Don't! you pain me. What have you not done for us when you were rich, and now that evil days have come to you, should we not do our part?--Ah, Sir, I have a favour to ask of you. Leave your little girl here with me. I will love and tend her as if she were my own. And is she not as good as mine? Did I not nurse her when her mother was too weak to do it herself? Let me have charge of the child!" Hawermann stood buried in thought. "Sir," continued the woman, "from what I hear you'll have to part with the child sooner or later, and--but see, here comes Joseph, he will tell you the same." The labourer came up, and as soon as he heard what they were talking about, said: "Yes, Sir, she shall be treated like a princess. We are strong, and well-to-do in the world, and the kindness you have shown to us, we will richly repay to her."--"Nay," said Hawermann, rousing himself, "that will never do, I can't consent to that. I may be wrong in taking the child with me when my future is so uncertain, but I've left so much behind me here, that I can't do without the last that remains to me. No, no, I can't," he exclaimed turning to go, "my child must remain with me. Goodbye, Stina--good-bye, Rassow."--"If you won't leave the child with us, Sir," said the labourer, "at least let me go with you, and carry her for you."--"No, no," replied Hawermann, "I don't find her at all too heavy." Then the young woman kissed and fondled his little daughter, and kissed her again and again, and after he had resumed his journey, both she and her husband stood for a long, long time looking after him. She, with tears in her eyes and thinking most of the child; he, gravely and thinking most of the man.--"Stina," he said, "we shall never have such another master."--"God knows that," said she, and then they both went away sorrowfully to their daily work.

CHAPTER II

About forty miles from the place where Hawermann had laid his wife in her quiet grave, was the farm of which Joseph Nüssler, his brother-in-law, was tenant. The offices were ill-built, had fallen a good deal out of repair, and the yard had altogether a very untidy appearance. There was a large manure-yard here, and a small one there, and carting and agricultural implements were all mixed up together in confused masses like people at a fair; the manure-cart said to the carriage: how did you get here, brother? and the plough asked the harrow to dance, but music was wanting, for there was dead silence in the yard. Every one was busy hay-making in the meadow, for the weather was lovely. No one was looking out of any of the small open windows in the long, low, thatched farm-house, for it was in the afternoon, and the cook had finished her kitchen-work, and the housemaid had done with her sweeping and dusting, and both of them had gone down to the meadow. Even the farmer's wife, who always kept such order in the house, had gone there too, rake in hand, for the hay ought to be in cocks before the evening-dews began to fall.

Still there was life in the house although it was so quiet. In the sitting-room, to the right of the entrance-hall, where the blue-painted cupboard stood--the bar as they called it--and the sofa covered with the black-glazed linen, which was rubbed up with boot-polish every Saturday till it shone again, and the oak chest with the yellow mounting, well, in this room sat two little girls of three years old with round flaxen heads, and round rosy cheeks, playing at making cheeses in a sand-box with their mother's thimble and two penny jars, which they filled with the damp sand, and pressed down as hard as they could, laughing gleefully whenever the lump kept its shape when turned out.

These children were Lina and Mina Nüssler, and with their rosy cheeks and yellow hair they looked for all the world like two little round apples, growing on one stalk. They were twins, and even people who knew them well, found it impossible to say which was Lina and which Mina, for their names were not written on their faces, and if their mother had not given them different coloured ribbons there would have been great mistakes made; even their father, Joseph Nüssler, could not distinguish the one from the other, he called Lina, Mina, and Mina, Lina. But now no such mistakes need be made, for their mother had tied up Lina's flaxen plaits with blue ribbon, and Mina's with red; but if any one had only taken the trouble to look closely at them he must have seen clearly that Joseph Nüssler was wrong, for Lina was half an hour older than Mina, and even when the difference in age is small, still birth-right always makes itself known, and Lina had quite the upper-hand of Mina, but she comforted her little sister whenever she was unhappy.

Besides these unimportant little twins there was yet another set of twins in the room, and they were an old, experienced and very important couple, who were peering down on the children from the oak chest, and shaking in the soft breeze that came in at the open window. These were the grandfather's peruke and the grandmother's best cap, which were hanging on a couple of cap-stands, all ready to play their part on the next day, which was Sunday.--"Look, Lina," said Mina, "there's grandfather's p'uke," she couldn't pronounce the letter "r" properly yet.--"You shouldn't say p'uke, you should say p'uke," said Lina who couldn't pronounce her "rs" a bit better, but being the eldest she had of course to put her little sister on the right way.

The little twins now got up, and standing in front of the chest looked at the old twins on the cap-stands, and Mina, who was still very thoughtless, stretched out her hand, and took her grandfather's peruke from the stand. Then putting it on her own head with a "just look at me" sort of expression, placed herself before the looking-glass, and arranged the wig exactly as her grandfather wore it on Sundays. Now Lina ought to have had more sense, but she began to laugh, and allowing herself to be carried away by the fun of the thing, took her grandmother's mob-cap from the other stand, and put it on in the same way as her grandmother did every Sunday. Then Mina laughed, and then they both laughed, and taking hands began to dance "Kringelkranz-Rosendanz," and then stopped and laughed, and after that they went on dancing again.

But Mina was really too thoughtless, she had kept her toy-jar in her hand, and now in the very midst of the fun she let it fall, and--crash--it was destroyed, and so was the fun. Mina began to cry bitterly over the broken jar, and Lina cried to keep her company, but after this had gone on for a short time Lina began to try to comfort her sister: "Never mind, Mina, the wheel-wright will mend it for you."--"Yes," sobbed Mina, but more quietly than before, "the wheel-wright must mend it."--And then the two sorrowful little creatures went out of doors, quite forgetting that they still had their grandfather's and grandmother's Sunday-finery on their heads.

Now many people would think that it was a silly fancy of Lina's that the wheel-wright could mend the broken jar, but who ever has known a real country wheel-wright is aware that such a man can do anything. When a wether is to be killed, the wheelwright is sent for. When a pane of glass is broken, the wheel-wright has to nail a board across the window that the rain and wind may not get it. When an old chair has lost a leg, he is the doctor who makes it stand steady again. When a bullock is to be blistered, he acts apothecary; in short, he puts everything right that has gone wrong, and so Lina was a very sensible girl when she proposed to take the jar to the wheel-wright.

Just as the children entered the yard a little man came in at the gate. And this little man had a red face, and a very imposing red nose which he always held cocked up in the air. He wore a square cap of no particular colour with a tassel in front, and a long-tailed, loose, grey linen-coat. He always kept his feet turned out in an exaggerated first position which made his short legs look as if they were fastened to his body in the wrong way. He had striped trousers and long boots with yellow tops. He was not stout, and yet he was by no means thin, in fact his figure was beginning to lose its youthful proportions.

The children walked on, and when they had got near enough for the farm-bailiff--for such was the calling of the little man--to see what they were wearing, he stood still, and raised his bushy yellow eye-brows till they were quite hidden under his pointed cap, treating them as if they were the most beautiful part of his face, and must therefore be put away in a safe place out of all danger: "Bless me!" cried he. "What's the matter?--What on earth have you been about?--Why you've got the whole of your old grandparent's Sunday-finery on your heads!"--The two little girls allowed themselves to be deprived of their borrowed plumes without remonstrance, and showing the broken jar, said that the wheel-wright was to mend it.--"What!" exclaimed Mr. farm-bailiff Bräsig--that was the way he liked to be addressed--"is it possible that there is such insummate folly in the world?--Lina, you are the eldest and ought to have been wiser; and Mina, don't cry any more, you are my little god-child, and so I'll give you a new jar at the summer fair. And now get away with you into the house."--He drove the little girls before him, and followed carrying the peruke in one hand and the cap in the other.

When he found the sitting-room empty, he said to himself: "Of course, every one's out at the hay.--Well I ought to be looking after my hay too, but the little round-heads have made such a mess of these two bits of grandeur, that they'd be sure to get into a scrape, if the old people were to see what they've been after; I must stay and repair the mischief that has been done."--With that he pulled out the pocket-comb that he always carried about with him to comb his back-hair over to the front of his head, and so cover the bald place that was beginning to show. He then set to work at the peruke, and soon got that into good order again. But how about the cap?--"What in the name of wonder have you done to this, Lina?--It's morally impossible to get it back to the proper *fassong*.--Ah--let me think.--What's the old lady like on Sunday afternoons? She has a good bunch of silk curls on each side of her face, then the front of the cap rises about three inches higher than the curls; so the thing must be drawn more to the front. She hasn't anything particular in the middle, for her bald head shows through, but it always goes into a great bunch at the back where it sticks out in a mass of frills. The child has crushed that part frightfully, it must be ironed out."--He put his clenched fist into the cap and pulled out the frills, but just as he thought he was getting them into good order, the string that was run through a caser at the back of the frilled mass gave way, and the whole erection flattened out.--"Faugh!" he cried, sending his eye-brows right up in the air. "It wasn't half strong enough to keep it firm. Only a bit of thread! And the ends won't knot together again! God bless my soul! whatever induced *me* to meddle with a cap?--But, wait a bit, I'll manage it yet."--He thrust his hand into his pocket, and drew out a quantity of string of different sizes, for like every farm-bailiff who was worth anything he always carried a good supply of such things about with him. He searched amongst his store for some thing that would suit the case in hand.--"Whip-cord is too thick--but this will do capitally," and then he began to draw a piece of good strong pack-thread through the caser. It was a work of time, and when he had got about half of it done, there was a knock at the door; he threw his work on the nearest chair, and called out: "Come in."

The door opened, and Hawermann entered with his little girl in his arms. Bräsig started up. "What in the," he began solemnly, then interrupting himself, he went on eagerly: "Charles Hawermann, where have you come from?"--"From a place, Bräsig, where I have nothing more to look for," said his friend. "Is my sister at home?"--"Everyone's out at the hay; but what do you mean?"--"That it's all up with me. All the goods that I possessed were sold by auction the day before yesterday, and yesterday morning"--here he turned away to the window--"I buried my wife."--"What? what?" cried the kind-hearted old farm-bailiff, "good God! your wife. Your dear little wife?" and the tears ran down his red face. "Dear old friend, tell me how it all happened."--"Ah, how it all happened?" repeated Hawermann, and seating himself, he told the whole story of his misfortunes as shortly as possible.

Meanwhile, Lina and Mina approached the strange child slowly and shyly, stopping every now and then, and saying nothing, and then they went a little nearer still. At last Lina summoned courage to touch the sleeve of the stranger's frock, and Mina showed her the bits of her jar: "Look, my jar is broken." But the little girl looked round the room uneasily, till at last she fixed her great eyes on her father.

"Yes," said Hawermann, concluding his short story, "things have gone badly with me, Bräsig; I still owe you £ 30, don't ask for it now, only give me time, and if God spares my life. I'll pay you back every farthing honestly."--"Charles Hawermann, Charles Hawermann," said Bräsig, wiping his eyes, and blowing his imposing nose, "you're--you're an ass! Yes," he continued, shoving his handkerchief into his pocket with an emphatic poke, and holding his nose even more in the air than usual, "you're every bit as great an ass as you used to be!"--And then, as if thinking that his friend's thoughts should be led into a new channel, he caught Lina and Mina by the waistband, and put them on Hawermann's knee, saying: "There, little round heads, that's your uncle."--Just as if Lina and Mina were playthings, and Hawermann were a little child who could be comforted in his grief by a new toy. He, himself, took Hawermann's little Louisa in his arms, and danced about the room with her, his tears rolling down his cheeks the while. After a short time he put the child down upon a chair, upon the very chair on which he had thrown his unfinished work, and right on the top of it too.

In the meanwhile the household had come back from the hay-field, and a woman's clear voice could be heard outside calling to the maids to make haste: "Quick get your hoop and pails, it'll soon be sunset, and this year the fold's[3] rather far off. We must just milk the cows in the evening.--Where's your wooden-platter, girl? Go and get it at once.--Now be as quick as you can, I must just go, and have a look at the children."--A tall stately woman of five-and-twenty came into the room. She seemed full of life and energy, her cheeks were rosy with health, work, and the summer air, her hair and eyes were bright, and her forehead, where her chip-hat had sheltered it from the sun, was white as snow. Anyone could see the likeness between her and Hawermann at first sight; still there was a difference, she was well-off, and her whole manner showed that she would work as hard from temperament, as he did from honour and necessity.

To see her brother and to spring to him were one and the same action: "Charles, brother Charles, my second father," she cried throwing her arms round his neck, but on looking closer at him, she pushed him away from her, saying: "What's the matter? You've had some misfortune!--What is it?"

Before he had time to answer his sister's questions, her husband, Joseph Nüssler, came in, and going up to Hawermann shook hands with him, and said, taking as long to get out his words as dry weather does to come: "Goodday, brother-in-law; won't you sit down?"--"Let him tell us what's wrong," interrupted his wife impatiently.--"Yes," said Joseph, "sit down and tell us what has happened.--Good-day, Bräsig; be seated, Bräsig."--Then Joseph Nüssler, or as he was generally called, young Joseph, sat down in his own peculiar corner beside the stove. He was a tall, thin man, who never could hold himself erect, and whose limbs bent in all sorts of odd places whenever he wanted to use them in the ordinary manner. He was nearly forty years old, his face was pale, and almost as long as his way of drawling out his words, his soft blond hair, which had no brightness about it, hung down equally long over his forehead and his coat collar. He had never attempted to divide or curl it. When he was a child his mother had combed it straight down over his brow, and so he had continued to do it, and whenever it had looked a little rough and unkempt, his mother used to say: "Never mind, Josy, the roughest colt often makes the finest horse."--Whether it was that his eyes had always been accustomed to peer through the long hair that overhung them, or whether it was merely his nature cannot be known with any certainty, but there was something shy in his expression, as if he never could look anything full in the face, or come to a decision on any subject, and even when his hand went out to the right, his mouth turned to the left. That, however, came from smoking, which was the only occupation he carried out with the slightest perseverance, and as he always kept his pipe in the left corner of his mouth, he, in course of time, had pressed it out a little, and had drawn it down to the left, so that the right side of his mouth looked as if he were continually saying "prunes and prism," while the left side looked as if he were in the habit of devouring children.

There he was now seated in his own particular corner by the stove, and smoking out of his own particular corner of his mouth, and while his lively wife wept in sympathy with her brother's sorrow, and kissed and fondled him and his little daughter alternately, he kept quite still, glancing every now and then from his wife and Hawermann at Bräsig, and muttering through a cloud of tobacco smoke: "It all depends upon what it is. It all depends upon circumstances.--What's to be done now in a case like this?"

Bräsig had quite a different disposition from young Joseph, for instead of sitting still like him, he walked rapidly up and down the room, then seated himself upon the table, and in his excitement and restlessness swung his short legs about like weaver's shuttles. When Mrs. Nüssler kissed and stroked her brother, he did the same; and when Mrs. Nüssler took the little child and rocked it in her arms, he took it from her and walked two or three times up and down the room with it, and then placed it on the chair again, and always right on the top of the grandmother's best cap.

"Bless me!" cried Mrs. Nüssler at last, "I quite forgot.--Bräsig, *you* ought to have thought of it. You must all want something to eat and drink!"--

She went to the blue cupboard, and brought out a splendid loaf of white household bread and some fresh butter, then she went out of the room and soon returned with sausages, ham and cheese, a couple of bottles of the strong beer that was brewed on purpose for old Mr. Nüssler, and a jug of milk for the children. When everything was neatly arranged on a white table cloth, she placed a seat for her brother, and lifting her little niece, chair and all, put her beside her father. Then she set to work and cut slices of bread, and poured out the beer, and saw that there was enough for everybody.

"I'll be ready to give you something presently," she said, stroking her little girls' flaxen heads fondly, "but I must see to your little cousin first.--Here's so chair for you, Bräsig--Come, Joseph."--"All right," said Joseph, blowing a last long cloud of smoke out of the left corner of his mouth, and then dragging his chair forward, half sitting on it all the time.--"Charles," said Bräsig, "I can recommend these sausages. Your sister, Mrs. Nüssler, makes them most capitally, and I've often told my housekeeper that she ought to ask for the receipt, for you see the old woman mixes up all sorts of queer things that oughtn't to go together at all; in short, the flavour is very extraordinary and not in the least what it ought to be, although each of the ingredients separately is excellent, and made of a pig properly fattened on pease."--"Mother, give Bräsig some more beer," said Joseph.--"No more, thank you, Mrs. Nüssler. May I ask for a little kümmel instead?--Charles, since the time that I was learning farming at old Knirkstädt with you, and that rascal Pomuchelskopp, I've always been accustomed to drink a tiny little glass of kümmel at breakfast and supper, and it agrees with me very well, I am thankful to say. But, Charles, whatever induced you to have any business transactions with such a rascal as Pomuchelskopp? I told you long ago that he was not to be trusted, he's a regular old Venetian, he's a cunning dog, in short, he's a--Jesuit."--"Ah, Bräsig," said Hawermann, "we won't talk about it. He might have treated me differently; but still it was my own fault, I oughtn't to have agreed to his terms.--I'm thinking of something else now. I wish I could get something to do!"--"Of course, you must get a situation as soon as possible.--The Count, my master, is looking out for a steward for his principal estate, but don't be angry with me for saying so Charles, I don't think that it would do for you.--You see, you'd have to go to the Count every morning with laquered boots, and a cloth coat, and you'd have to speak High-German, for he considers our provincial way of talking very rude and uncultivated. And then you'd have all the women bothering you, for they have a great say in all the arrangements. You might perhaps manage with the boots, and the coat, and the High-German--though you're rather out of practice--but you'd never get on with the women. The Countess is always poking about to see that all's going on rightly in the cattle-sheds and pigsties,--in short--it's, it's as bad as Sodom and Gomorrah."--"Bless me!" cried Mrs. Nüssler, "I remember now. The farm-bailiff at Pümpelhagen left at the midsummer-term, and that would just be the place for you, Charles."--"Mrs. Nüssler is right as usual," said Bräsig. "As for the *Counsellor* [4] at Pümpelhagen"--he always gave the squire of Pümpelhagen his professional title, and laid such an emphasis on the word counsellor that one might have thought that he and Mr. von Rambow had served their time in the army together, or at least had eaten their soup out of the same bowl with the same spoon--"As for the *Counsellor* at Pümpelhagen, he is very kind to all his people, gives a good salary, and is quite a gentleman of the old school. He knows all about you too. It's just the very thing for you, Charles, and I'll go with you to-morrow.--What do you say, young Joseph?" --"Ah!" said Mr. Nüssler meditatively, "it all depends upon circumstances."--"Good gracious!" exclaimed Mrs. Nüssler with a look of anxiety on her pretty face. "I'm forgetting everything to-day. If grandfather and grandmother ever find out that we've been having a supper-party here without their knowledge, they'll never forgive me as long as I live.--Sit a little closer children.--You might have reminded me, Joseph."--"What shall I do now?" asked Joseph, but she had already left the room.

A few minutes later she came back, accompanied by the two old people. There was an expression of anxious watchfulness and aimless attention in both faces, such as deaf people often have, and which is apt to degenerate into a look of inanity and distrust.--It is a very true saying that when a husband and wife have lived many years together, and have shared each other's thoughts and interests, they at last grow to be like one another in appearance, and even when the features are different the expression becomes the same. Old Mr. and Mrs. Nüssler looked thoroughly soured, and as if they had never had the least bit of happiness or enjoyment all their lives long, such things being too expensive for them; their clothes were thread-bare and dirty, as if they must always be save, saving, and even found water a luxury that cost too much money. There was nothing comfortable about their old age, not a single gleam of kindliness shone in their lack-lustre eyes, for they had never had but *one* joy, and that was their son Joseph, and his getting on in the world. They were now worn out, and everything was tiresome to them, even their one joy, their son Joseph, was tiresome, but they were still anxious and troubled about his getting on in the world, that was the only thing they cared for now. The old man had become a little childish, but his wife had still all her wits about her, and could spy and pry into every hole and corner, to see that everything was going on as she wished.

Hawermann rose and shook hands with the old people, while his sister stood close by looking at them anxiously, to see what they thought of the visitor. She had already explained to them in a few words, why her brother had come, and that may have been the reason that the old faces looked even sourer than usual, but still it might be because she had provided a better supper than she generally did. They seated themselves at table. The old woman caught sight of Hawermann's little girl: "Is that his child?" she asked.--Her daughter-in-law nodded.--"Is she going to remain here?" she asked.--Her daughter-in-law nodded again.--"O--h!" said the old woman, drawling out the word till it was long enough to cover all the harm she thought the cost of the child's keep would bring upon her Joseph. "Yes, these *are* hard times," she continued, as though she thought speaking of the times would best settle the question, "*very* hard times, and every man has enough to do to get on in the world himself."--Meanwhile the old man had done nothing but stare at the bottle of beer and at Bräsig's glass: "Is that my beer?" he asked.--"Yes," shouted Bräsig in his ear, "and most excellent beer it is that Mrs. Nüssler brews, it's a capital *rajeunissimang* for a weak stomach!"--"What extravagance! What extravagance!" grumbled the old man.--His wife eat her supper, but never took her eyes off the oak chest opposite.

Young Mrs. Nüssler, who must have studied the peculiarities of her mother-in-law with great care, looked to see what was the matter, and found to her horror and dismay that the cap was gone from its stand. Good gracious! what had become of it? She had plaited it up that very morning, and hung it on the stand.--"Where's my cap?" the old woman at last enquired.--"Never mind, mother," said her daughter-in-law bending towards her, "I'll get it directly."--"Is it done up yet?"--The young woman nodded, and thought, surely grandmother will be satisfied now, but the old woman glanced into every corner of the room to see what she could find out. Bräsig's countenance changed when he heard the cap spoken of, and he looked about him hastily to see where the "beastly thing" could have got to, but in another moment old Mrs. Nüssler pointed at little Louisa Hawermann, and said with a venomous smile, like a stale roll dipped in fly-poison: "It must be plaited all over again."--"What's the matter?" cried her daughter-in-law, and starting up as she spoke, she saw the ends of the cap ribbons hanging down below the hem of the child's frock; she lifted her niece off the chair, and was going to have picked up the cap, but the old woman was too quick for her. She seized her crumpled head-gear, and when she saw the flattened puffs, and Bräsig's bit of pack-thread hanging half in and half out of the caser, her wrath boiled over, and holding up her cap so that everyone might see it, exclaimed: "Good for nothing chit!" and was going to have struck the little girl over the head with her cap.

But Bräsig caught her by the arm and said: "The child had nothing to do with it," and then growled out in a half whisper: "the old cat!" At the same moment loud crying was to be heard behind the grandmother's chair, and Mina sobbed: "I'll never, never do it again," and Lina sobbed: "And I'll never do it again."--"Bless me!" cried young Mrs. Nüssler, "it was the little girls who did all the mischief.--Mother, it was our own children that did it."--But the old woman had been too long accustomed to turn everything to her own advantage, not to know how to make a judicious use of her deafness; she never heard what she did not want to hear; and she did not want to hear now. "Come," she shouted, and signed to her husband.--"Mother, mother," cried her daughter-in-law, "give me your cap, and I'll set it to rights."--"Who's at the fold?" asked the old woman as she left the room with old Joseph.--Young Joseph lighted his pipe again.--"Good gracious!" said Mrs. Nüssler, "she's quite right there, I ought to be at the fold. Ah well, grandmother won't be civil to me again for a month."--"Crusty," said Bräsig, "was an old dog, and Crusty had to give in at last."--"Don't cry any more, my pets," said the mother, wiping her little girl's eyes. "You didn't know what harm you were doing, you are such stupid little things. Now be good children, and go and play with your cousin, I must go to my work. Joseph, just keep an eye on the children, please," and then Mrs. Nüssler put on her chip-hat, and set off to the fold where the cows were milked.

"A mother-in-law's the very devil!" said Bräsig. "But you, young Joseph," he continued, turning to Mr. Nüssler, who was smoking as calmly as if what had happened was nothing to him, "ought to be ashamed of yourself for allowing your mother to bully your wife."--"But," said young Joseph, "how can I interfere? I am her son."--"You needn't actually *strike* her," said Bräsig, "because your parents are given you by God, but you might give her a little filial advice now and then, such as befits an obedient son, and so prevent the devil of dispeace getting into the house.--And as for you, Charles Hawermann, don't take a little tiff like this to heart, for your sister has a cheerful disposition, and an affectionate nature, so she'll soon be on good terms with the old skin-flints again, and they can't get on without her, she's the mainstay of the household.--But now," and he pulled an enormous watch out of his pocket, the kind of watch that is called a warming-pan, "it's seven o'clock, and I must go and look after my work-people."--"Wait," said Hawermann, "I'll go part of the way with you. Good-bye for the present, Joseph."--"Good-bye, brother-in-law," said young Joseph from his corner.

As soon as they were out of doors Hawermann asked: "I say, Bräsig, how could you speak of the old people in such a way before their son?"--"He's quite accustomed to it, Charles. No one has a good word for the two old misers, they've quarrelled with all the neighbours, and as for the servants, *they* take very good care to keep out of the old wretches' sight."--"My poor sister!" sighed Hawermann, "She used to be such a merry light-hearted girl, and now, shut up in a house with such people, and such a Nuss (slow) of a man."--"You're right enough there, Charles, he is an old Nuss, and Nüssler (slow-coach) is his name; but *he* never bullies your sister, and although he is such an ass that he can manage nothing himself, he has sense enough to see that your sister is quite able to keep everything straight."--"Poor girl!--She married that man for my sake, to make my way easier for me, she said; and for our old mother's sake, to give her a comfortable home with one of her children in her latter days."--"I know, I know, Charles.--I know it from my own experience. Don't you remember it was during the rye-harvest, and you said to me, Zachariah, you said, you must be in love, for you're leading in your rye quite wet. And I said; how so? On the Sunday before that we had had spruce-beer, and your sister was one of the party, or else I shouldn't have led in the rye in such weather. And then I told you that if I didn't change my mind your sister was the only one of my three sweethearts that I'd marry.--Then you laughed heartily, and said, she was too young.--What has being young to do with it? I asked.--And then you said that my other two sweethearts came first, and so they ought to have the preference. And then you laughed again, and didn't seem to believe that I was in earnest. A short time afterwards my lord the Count changed his mind, and said he wouldn't have a married bailiff. And then a little more time passed, and it was too late. Young Joseph made her an offer, and your mother begged her so hard to take him, that she consented.--Ah well, that marriage ought never to have been," and Bräsig looked down gravely. After a moment's silence he went on--"When I saw the twins I felt drawn to them, and thought that they might have been my own, and I almost wished that the old woman, old Joseph, and young Joseph were in their graves.--It was indeed a happy day for the old Jesuits when your sister brought her loving heart and cheerful nature into their house, if it had been any one else there would have been murder done long ago."

While they were talking they had left the village behind them, and were now beside the large garden. Suddenly Hawermann exclaimed: "Look there, the two old people are on the top of the hill yonder."--"Yes," said Bräsig with a derisive chuckle, "there they are, the hypocritical old Jesuits, standing in their hiding-place."--"Hiding-place?" asked Hawermann, astonished. "Up there on the hill?"--"Even so, Charles, the old creatures can trust no one, not even their own children, and when they want to say anything to each other that they can't explain by their usual signs, they always go to the very top of the hill where they can see that there are no eavesdroppers, and shout their secrets in one another's ears. Look at them cackling away, the old woman has laid another dragon's egg, and now they're both going to hatch it."--"How eagerly they're talking," said Hawermann. "Do you see how the old woman is gesticulating? What can it all be about?"--"I know what they are laying down the law about, for I know them well.--And Charles," he continued after a short silence, "it is better that you should understand the whole state of the case at once, and then you'll know how to act. They're talking about you, and your little girl."--"About me, and my little girl!" repeated Hawermann in astonishment.--"Yes, Charles--don't you see. If you had come with a great purse full of money, they would have received you with open arms, for money is the only thing for which they have the slightest respect; but as it is they regard you and the child in the light of beggarly poor relations who will take the very bread out of the mouth of their unfortunate son."--"Oh!" sighed Hawermann, "why didn't I leave the child with the Rassows?--Who is to take care of her?--Can you advise me what to do?--I can't leave her here in my sister's charge for my sister's sake."--"Of course you'd like to have her near you. Well, Charles, I'll tell you something. You must remain at the Nüsslers to-night. To-morrow we'll go and see the *Counsellor* at Pümpelhagen: if we succeed there we'll look out for a good place for the child in the neighbourhood; and if we don't succeed, we'll go to the town and board her for the present with Kurz, the shopkeeper. And now good-night, Charles! Don't be down-hearted, everything will look brighter soon."--And so he went away.

"Ah, if everybody was only like you," thought Hawermann as he was returning to his sister's house, "I should soon get the better of my difficulties.--And get the better of them I must and shall," he continued with a look of determination, his courage rising and dispelling his sadness, in like manner as the sun disperses the rain-clouds, "my sister shall not be made unhappy through me. I will work hard for my little girl." ....

Later in the evening, when the milk had been poured into the pans in the dairy, Hawermann and his sister went out into the garden together, and she talked to him about his affairs, and he to her about hers. "Don't be so sorry for me, Charles," she said, "I am quite used to my life. It's true that the old people are hard and disagreeable, but though they sometimes sulk with me for weeks at a time, I soon forget their crossness when I'm out of their sight, and as for Joseph, I must say this for him, he is never unkind, and has never said a hard word to me. If he were only a little more quick-sighted, and a better manager; but that's not to be expected of him. I've plenty to do with the house and dairy without having the farm on my hands too, and a woman can't manage that sort of thing properly, indeed Bräsig is the greatest possible help to me in that respect. He goes over the fields and sees what's being done about the place, and takes care that Joseph do'sn't get behindhand with the work."--"How are you getting on upon the whole? Does the farming pay well?" asked her brother.--"Not as well as it might. There isn't enough spent on the land, and the old people won't let us change the rotation of the crops, or try any new ways of farming.--We've always made the two ends meet as yet, and had the rent ready on the term-day; but now Joseph's two elder sisters, who are married to Kurz, the general merchant, and to Baldrian, the rector of the academy, are always dinning into the old people's and our ears that they want their dowries paid. The rector doesn't actually require it, but he is fond of money; Kurz would really be the better of his, for he is in trade, and of course wishes to extend his business. Now the old people want to make over nearly everything to Joseph at their death, and they won't part with a single farthing of what is in their possession just now, indeed grandmother has a hateful rhyme that she always repeats when she hears of a case of this kind:

'Wer seinen Kindern giebt das Brod
Und leidet endlich selber Noth,
Den schlag man mit der Keule todt.'

But it's wrong, very wrong of them, and they can't expect a blessing on it, for one child is as good as another, and so I told the old people at the very beginning. My goodness, what a rage they were in! *They* had made all the money, and what had *I* brought to my husband they'd like to know? I ought to go down on my knees, and thank God that they were going to make a rich man of Joseph.--But I had a good talk with Joseph, and now he has paid over nearly two hundred and twenty-five pounds to Kurz in instalments. His mother soon had an inkling as to what we were about, and was very curious to know all the ins and outs of the affair, but as Joseph isn't a good manager and can't do accounts well, I take care of the purse, and never give her the chance of peeping into it. No, no, grandmother, I'm not quite so stupid as that comes to!--That's the chief bone of contention between the old people and myself. They still want to keep Joseph under their thumb; but Joseph is nearly forty years old, and if he won't rule himself, *I* will rule him, for I am his wife and therefore the 'nearest' to him, as our parson's wife would say. Now, Charles, tell me, am I right or wrong?"--"You are quite right, Dorothea," said Hawermann.--Then they wished each other "good-night," and went to bed.

CHAPTER III

Bräsig arrived in good time next morning to go to Pümpelhagen with Hawermann. Mrs. Nüssler was sitting in the porch paying the farm-servants, and Joseph was sitting beside her smoking while she worked.--Neither of the old people had come down yet, for the grandmother had said to her daughter-in-law, she, at least, could not join them in the parlour, for she had nothing to put on her head; and the grandfather had said, they could all be quite happy without him.--"That's really kind of them," said Bräsig. "There's no fear of our dinner being spoilt now by their bad temper, for, Mrs. Nüssler, I'm going to spend the day with Charles.--Come, Charles, we must be off.--Goodbye little round-heads."

When they were out in the yard Bräsig stood still, and said: "Look, Charles, did you ever see anything more like the desert of S'ara? One heap of manure here and another there! And look, that's the drain old Joseph cut from the farm-yard to the village horse-pond. And as for the roofs," he continued, "they have enough straw to make new ones, but the old people think money expended on thatching sheer waste. I come here often, and for two reasons; firstly because of my stomach, and secondly because of my heart. I've always found that well cooked food is not only pleasant to the taste, but also produces a wholesome exhilaration when followed by one of the little rages I generally get into here. And I come here for the sake of your sister and the little round-heads. I know that I am of use to her, for young Joseph just rolls on smoothly like the wheel of the coach that runs every winter from here to Rostock. How I should like to have him as leader in a three horse team, harnessed into a farm cart, and then drive him with my whip!"--"Ah!" said Hawermann as they came to a field, "they've got very good wheat here."--"Yes, it's pretty fair, but what do you think they were going to have had there instead?--Rye!--And for what reason? Simply because old Joseph had sown rye in that field every year for twenty one years!"--"Does their farm extend to the other side of the hill?"--"No, Charles, it isn't quite such a fat morsel as all that, like bacon fried in butter and eaten with a spoon! No, no, the wheat on the top of the hill is mine."--"Ah, well, it's odd how soon one forgets.--Then your land comes down as far as this?"--"Yes, Charles; Warnitz is a long narrow estate, it extends from here on the one side as far as Haunerwiem on the other. Now stand still for a moment,

I can show you the whole lie of the country from this point. Where we are standing belongs to your brother-in-law, his land reaches from my wheat-field up there to the right, as far as that small clump of fir-trees to the left. You see, Rexow is quite a small farm, there are only a few more acres belonging to it on the other side of the village. To the right up there is Warnitz; and in front of us, where the fallow ground begins, is Pümpelhagen; and down there to the left, behind the little clump of firs, is Gürlitz."--"Then Warnitz is the largest?"--"No, Charles, you've mistaken me there. Pümpelhagen is the best estate in the neighbourhood, the wheat-land there produces forty-two loads, and that is eight more than Warnitz can show. It would be a blessing if all the other places were like it. The *Counsellor* is a good man, and understands farming, but you see his profession obliges him to live in Schwerin, so he can't attend to Pümpelhagen. He has had a good many bailiffs of one kind or another. He came into the estate when everything was very dear, and there are a considerable number of apothecaries[5] on it, so that he must often feel in want of money, and all the more so that his wife is extravagant, and likes to live in a constant whirl of gaiety. He is a worthy man and kind to his people, and although the von Rambows are of very old family--my master, the Count, often asks him to dinner, and he will not admit any but members of the nobility to the honour of his acquaintance--he goes about quite *doucimang*, and makes no fuss about his position."

Hawermann listened attentively to all that was said, for if he succeeded in getting the place of bailiff, these things would all be of importance to him, but his thoughts soon returned to the subject of his greatest present anxiety.--"Bräsig," he said, "who is the best person to take charge of my little girl?"--"I can't think of anyone. I'm afraid that we must take her to the town to Kurz. Mrs. Kurz is an excellent woman, and he, well he is a good hand at a bargain like all tradesmen.--Only think, he sold me a pair of trousers last year.--I wanted them for Sundays--they were a sort of chocolate colour: well listen: the first morning I put them on, I went through the clover-field, and when I came out of it, my trousers were as red as lobsters, as high as the knee--bright scarlet I assure you. And then he sent me some kümmel, it was Prussian made, wretched sweet stuff, and very bad. I returned it, and told him a bit of my mind. But he won't take the trousers back, and tells me he never wore them. Does the fellow imagine that *I* will wear red trousers?--Look, Charles, that's Gürlitz down there to the left."--"And that, I suppose, is Gürlitz church-steeple?" asked Hawermann.--"Yes!" said Bräsig, raising his eye-brows till they were hidden by the brim of his hat--he always wore a hat on Sunday--and opening his mouth as wide as he could, he stared at Hawermann as if he wanted to look him through and through. "Charles," he exclaimed, "you spoke of Gürlitz church-steeple, and as sure as your nose is in the middle of your face the parson at Gürlitz must take your child,"--"Parson Behrens?" asked Hawermann.--"Yes, the same Parson Behrens who taught you and me at old Knirkstädt."--"Ah, Bräsig, I was just wishing last night that such a thing were possible."--"Possible? He must do it. It would be the best thing in the world for him to have a little child toddling about his knees, and growing up under his care, for he has no children of his own, has let all the glebe land, and has nothing whatever to do but to read his books and study, till any other man would see green and yellow specks dancing before his eyes even with looking at him from a distance. It would be a capital thing for him, and Mrs. Behrens is so fond of children that the little ones in the village cling to her skirts whenever she goes there. She is also a most excellent worthy woman, and so cheerful that she and your sister get on capitally together."--

"If it could only be," cried Hawermann. "What do we not both owe that man Zachariah, don't you remember that when he was assistant to the clergyman at Knirkstädt, he held an evening class during the winter, and taught reading and writing, and how kind he always was to us stupid boys?"--"Yes, Charles, and how Samuel Pomuchelskopp used to get behind the stove and snore till he nearly took the roof off, while we were learning the three R's. Don't you remember when we got to the rule of three in our sums, and tried to get the fourth unknown quantity? Ah yes, in quickness I had the best of it, but in correctness, you had. You got on better than I did in o'thography, but in *style*, in writing letters, and in High German, I was before you. And in these points I'm much improved since then, for I've made them my study, and of course every one has his own *speshialitee*. Whenever I see the parson I feel bound to thank him for having educated me so well, but he always laughs and says he owes me far more for letting his glebe at such a good rent for him. He is on very friendly terms with me, and if you settle down here, I'll take you to call and then you'll see it for yourself."

Meanwhile they had reached Pümpelhagen, and Bräsig took Hawermann quite under his protection as they crossed the court-yard, and addressing the old butler, asked if his master was at home and able to see them.--He would announce the gentlemen, was the servant's reply, and say that Mr. Farm-bailiff Bräsig was there.--"Yes," said Bräsig.--"You see, Charles, that he knows me, and the *Counsellor* knows me also--and--did you notice?--announce! That's what the nobility always have done when any one calls on them, My lord the Count has three servants to announce his visitors; that is to say, one servant announces to another who it is that has called, and the valet tells his lordship. Sometimes queer mistakes are made, as with the huntsman the other day. The first footman announced to the second: 'The chief huntsman,' and the second added the word 'master,' and the third announced the arrival of a 'grandmaster of the huntsmen.' So the Count came forward very cordially to receive the strange gentleman who had come to see him, and--he found no one but old Tibäul the rat-catcher."

The butler now returned and showed the two friends into a good-sized room, tastefully, but not luxuriously furnished, and in the centre of the room was a large table covered with papers and accounts. A tall thin man was standing beside the table when they entered; he was a thoughtful-looking, gentle-mannered man, and the same simplicity was observable in his dress as in the furniture of his room. He appeared to be about fifty-two or three, and his hair was of an iron grey colour; he was perhaps shortsighted, for, as he went forward to receive his visitors, he picked up an eye-glass that was lying on the table, but without using it: "Ah, Mr. Bräsig," he said quietly, "what can I do for you?"--Uncle Bräsig now involved himself in such a labyrinth of words in his desire to speak grandly as befitted his company, that he would never have extricated himself if the squire had not come to the rescue. Looking more attentively at Hawermann, he said: "You want....? but," he interrupted himself, "I ought to know you.--Wait a moment. Were you not serving your apprenticeship twelve years ago on my brother's estate?"--"Yes, Sir, and my name is Hawermann."--"Of course it is. And to what do I owe the pleasure of seeing you here?"--"I heard that you were looking out for a farm-bailiff, and as I was in want of just such a place"--"But I thought you had a farm in Pomerania?" interrupted the squire.--Now was the time for Bräsig to speak if he was going to say anything of importance, so he exclaimed: "It's quite true, Mr. Counsellor von Rambow that he had one, *had* it, but has it no longer, and it's no use crying over spilt milk. Like many other farmers he met with inverses, and the hardness and wickedness of his landlord ruined him.--What do you think of that, Sir?"

At this moment there was a loud shout of laughter behind Bräsig's back, and when he turned round to see who it was he found himself face to face with a boy of ten or twelve years old. Mr. von Rambow also smiled, but fortunately it never occurred to Bräsig that their amusement could mean anything but satisfaction with a well delivered speech, so he went on seriously: "And then he came a regular cropper."--"I'm very sorry to hear it," said Mr. von Rambow. "Yes," he continued with a sigh, "these are very hard times for farmers, I only hope they'll change soon. But now to business--Alick, just run upstairs and see if breakfast is ready. It is quite true that I am looking out for a new bailiff, as I have been obliged to part with the last man, because of--well, his carelessness in keeping accounts--but," said he, as his son opened the door and announced that breakfast was ready, "you hav'n't had breakfast yet, we can finish our talk while

An Old Story of My Farming Days Vol. I | 33

we eat it." He went to the door, and standing there signed to his guests to precede him.--"Charles," whispered Bräsig, "didn't I tell you? Quite like one of ourselves?" But when Hawermann quietly obeyed the squire's sign and went out first, he raised his eyebrows up to his hair, and stretched out his hand as though to pull his friend back by his coat-tails. Then sticking out one of his short legs and making a low bow, he said, "Pardon me--I couldn't think of it--The *Counsellor* always has the *paw*."--His way of bowing was no mere form, for as he had a long body and short legs it was both deep and reverential.

Mr. von Rambow went on first to escape his guest's civilities, and Bräsig brought up the rear. The whole business was talked over in all its bearings during breakfast; Hawermann got the place of bailiff with a good salary to be raised in five or six years, and only one condition was made, and that was that he should enter on his duties at once. The new bailiff promised to do so, and the following day was fixed for taking stock of everything in and about the farm, so that both he and his employer might know how matters stood before the squire had to leave Pümpelhagen. Then Bräsig told the "sad life-story" of the old thorough-bred, which had come down to being odd horse about the farm, and which he "had had the honour of knowing from its birth," and told how it "had spavin, grease and a variety of other ailments, and so had been reduced to dragging a cart for its sins."--After that he and Hawermann took leave of Mr. von Rambow.

"Bräsig," said Hawermann, "a great load has been taken off my heart. Thank God, I shall soon be at work again, and that will help me to bear my sorrow.--Now for Gürlitz--Ah, if we are only as fortunate there."--"Yes, Charles, you may well say you are fortunate, for you are certainly wanting in the knowledge of life and fine tact that are necessary for any one to possess who has to deal with the nobility. How *could* you, how *could* you go out of the room before the *Counsellor*?"--"I only did as he desired me, Bräsig, and I was his guest, not his servant then. I wouldn't do so now, and believe me, he'll never ask me to do it again."--"Well, Charles, let me manage the whole business for you at the parsonage. I'll do it with the greatest *finesse*."--"Certainly Bräsig, it will be very kind of you to do it for me; if it were not for my dear little girl, I should never have the courage to ask such a favour. If you will take the task off my shoulders, I shall look upon it as the act of a true friend." When they passed Gürlitz church they heard from the singing that service was still going on, so they determined to wait in the parsonage till it was over, but on entering the sitting-room, a round active little woman of about forty years old came forward to receive them. Everything about her was round, arms and fingers, head, cheeks and lips; and her round eyes twinkled so merrily in her round smiling face that one would at once jump to the conclusion that she had never known sorrow, and her every action was so cheery and full of life that one could easily see that she had a warm heart in her breast. "How d'ye do, Mr. Bräsig, sit down, sit down. My pastor is still in church, but he would scold me if I allowed you to go away.--Sit down, Sir--who are you?--I should have liked to have gone to church to-day, but only think, the clergyman's seat broke down last Sunday; lots of people go to it, you see, and one can't say 'no,' and old Prüsshawer, the carpenter, who was to have mended it this week, is down with a fever."--Her words poured out smoothly like polished billiard-balls rolled by a happy child over the green cloth.

Bräsig now introduced Hawermann as Mrs. Nüssler's brother. "And so you are her brother Charles. *Do* sit down, my pastor will be delighted to see you.--Whenever Mrs. Nüssler comes here she tells us something about you, and always in your praise--Mr. Bräsig can vouch for that. Good gracious, Bräsig, what have *you* got to do with my hymn-book? Just put it down, will you. *You* never read such things, you are nothing but an old heathen. These are hymns for the dying, and what are hymns for the dying to you? *You* are going to live for ever. You're not a whit better than the wandering Jew!--One has to think of death sometimes, and as our seat is broken, and the old carpenter has a fever, I have been reading some meditations for the dying."--While saying this she quickly picked up her books and put them away, carefully going through the unnecessary ceremony of dusting a spotless shelf before laying them down on it.--Suddenly she went to the door leading to the kitchen, and stood there listening; then exclaiming: "I was sure I heard it. The soup's boiling over," hastened from the room.--"Well, Charles--wasn't I right? Isn't she a cheery, wholesome--natured woman?--I'll go and arrange it all for you," and he followed Mrs. Behrens to the kitchen.

Hawermann looked, round the room, and admired the cleanly, comfortable, home-like, and peaceful look of everything around him. Over the sofa was a picture of our Saviour, and encircling it, above and below, were portraits of Mr. and Mrs. Behrens' relations, some coloured, some black, some large, and some small. In the picture of our Lord, His hands were raised in blessing, so Mrs. Behrens had hung the portraits of her relatives beneath it that they might have the best of the blessing, for she always regarded herself as the "nearest." She had hung her own portrait, taken when she was a girl, and that of her husband in the least prominent place over against the window, but God's sun, which shone through the white window-curtains, and gilded the other pictures, lighted up these two first of all. There was a small book-case containing volumes of sacred and profane literature all mixed up together, but they looked very well indeed, for they were arranged more in accordance with the similarity of their bindings, than with that of their contents. Let no one imagine that Mrs. Behrens did not care for reading really good standard works, because she spoke the Provincial German of her neighbourhood. Whoever took the trouble to open one of the books, which had a mark in it, would see that she was quite able to appreciate good writing, and her cookery-book showed that she studied her own subjects as thoroughly as her husband did his, for the book was quite full of the notes and emendations she had written at the sides of the pages in the same way as Mr. Behrens made notes in his books. As for her husband's favourite dishes she "knew them," she said, "by heart, and had not to put in a mark to show where they were to be found."

And it was in this quiet home that Hawermann's little daughter was to spend her childhood, if God let him have his wish. The raised hands in the Saviour's picture would seem to bless his little girl, and the sunlight would shine upon her through these windows, and in those books she would read what great and good men had written, and by their help would gradually waken from childish dreams into the life and thoughts of womanhood.--

As he was sitting there full of alternating hopes and fears, Mrs. Behrens came back, her eyes red with weeping: "Don't say another word, Mr. Hawermann, don't say another word. Bräsig has told me all, and though Bräsig is a heathen, he is a good man, and a true friend to you and yours. And my pastor thinks the same as I do, I know that, for we have always been of one mind about everything. My goodness, what hard-hearted creatures the old Nüsslers are," she added, tapping her foot impatiently on the floor.--"The old woman," said Bräsig, "is a perfect harpy."--"You're right, Bräsig, that's just what she is. My pastor must try to touch the conscience of the two old people; I don't mean about the little girl, she will come here and live with us, or I know nothing of my pastor."--

Whilst Hawermann was expressing his deep gratitude to Mrs. Behrens her husband came in sight. She always talked of him as "*her*" pastor, because he belonged to her soul and body, and "*pastor*" because of his personal and official dignity. He had nothing on his head, for those high soft caps that our good protestant clergy now wear in common with the Russian popes were not the fashion at that time, in the country at least, and instead of wide bands, resembling the white porcelain plate on which the daughter of Herodias received the head of John the Baptist from her stepfather, he wore little narrow bands, which his dear wife Regina had sewed, starched and ironed for him in all Christian humility, and these little bits of lawn she rightly held to be the true insignia of his office, and not the gown, which was fastened to his collar with a small square piece of board. "For, my dear Mrs. Nüssler," she said, "the clerk has a gown exactly the same as that, but he dar'n't wear bands, and when I see my pastor in the pulpit with these signs of his office on, and watch them rising and falling as he speaks, I sometimes think that they look like angels' wings upon which one might go straight away up to heaven, except that the angels wear their wings behind, and my pastor's are in front."

The parson was not an angel by any means, and was the last man in the world to think himself one, but still his conduct was so upright, and his face so expressive of love and good-will, that anyone could see in a moment that he was a good man, and that his was a serious, thoughtful mode of life, and yet--when his wife had taken off his gown and bands--there was a bright sparkle in his eye that showed he did not at all disdain innocent mirth. He was a man who could give good counsel in worldly matters as well as in spiritual, and he was always ready to stretch out a helping hand to those in need of it.

He recognised Hawermann the moment he saw him, and welcomed him heartily: "How d'ye do, dear old friend, what an age it is since I saw you last. How are you getting on?--Good morning, Mr. Bräsig."--Just as Bräsig was about to explain the reason of his and Hawermann's visit, Mrs. Behrens, who had begun to take off her husband's clerical garments, called out: "Don't speak, Mr. Hawermann,--Bräsig be quiet, leave it all to me.--I'll tell you all about it," she continued, turning to her husband, "for the story is a sad one--yes, Mr. Hawermann, terribly sad--and so it will be better for me to speak. Come," and she carried her pastor off to his study, saying in apology for doing so as she left the room: "I am the nearest to him, you know."

When Mr. Behrens returned to the parlour with his wife, he went straight up to Hawermann, and taking his hand, said: "Yes, dear Hawermann, yes, we'll do it. We'll do all that lies in our power with very great pleasure. We have had no experience in the management of children, but we will learn.--Won't we, Regina?" He spoke lightly, for he saw how deeply Hawermann felt his kindness, and therefore wished to set him at ease.-- "Reverend Sir," he exclaimed at last, "you did much for me in the old days, but this ....."--Little Mrs. Behrens seized her duster, her unfailing recourse in great joy or sorrow, and rubbed now this, and now that article of furniture vigorously, indeed there is no saying whether she might not have dried Hawermann's tears with it, had he not turned away.--She then went to the door and called to Frederika: "Here, Rika, just run down to the weaver's wife, and ask her to send me her cradle, for," she added, addressing Bräsig, "she doesn't require it."--And Bräsig answered gravely: "But Mrs. Behrens, the child isn't quite a baby."--So the clergyman's wife went to the door again, and called to the servant: "Rika, Rika, not the cradle. Ask her to lend me a crib instead, and then go to the parish-clerk's daughter, and see if she can come this afternoon--Good gracious! I forgot it was Sunday!--But if thine ass falls into a pit, and so on--yes, ask her if she will come and help me to stuff a couple of little matrasses.--It isn't a bit heathenish of me to do this, Bräsig, for it's a work of necessity, as much so as when you have to save the Count's wheat on a Sunday afternoon.--And, my dear Mr. Hawermann, the little girl must come to us this very day, for Frank," turning to her husband, "the old Nüsslers will grudge the child her food, and Bräsig, bread that is grudged ....." she stopped for breath, and Bräsig put in: "Yes, Mrs. Behrens, bread that is grudged maketh fat, but the devil take that kind of fatness!"-- "You old heathen! How *dare* you swear so in a Christian parsonage," cried Mrs. Behrens. "But the short and the long of it is that the child must come here to-day."--"Yes, Mrs. Behrens," said Hawermann, "I'll bring her to you this afternoon. My poor sister will be sorry; but it's better for her and her household peace that it should be so, and for my little girl ....." He then thanked the clergyman and his wife gratefully and heartily, and when he had said good-bye, and he and Bräsig were out of doors, he drew a long breath of relief, and said: "Everything looked dark to me this morning, but now the sun has begun to shine again, and though I have a disagreeable bit of business before me, it is a happy day,"--"What is it that you have to do?" asked Bräsig.--"I must go to Rahnstädt to see old Moses. He has held a bill of mine for seventy-five pounds for the last eighteen months. He took no part in my bankruptcy, and I want to arrange matters with him."--"Yes, Charles, you ought to make everything straight with him as soon as you can, for old Moses is by no means the worst of his kind.--Now then, let's lay out our plan of operations for to-day. We must return to Rexow at once, dine there, and after dinner young Joseph must get the carriage ready for you to take your little girl to Gürlitz; from Gürlitz you should drive on to Rahnstädt, and then in the evening come over to Warnitz and spend the night with me, and early next morning you can be at Pümpelhagen with the *Counsellor*, who expects to see you in good time."--"That will do very well," said Hawermann.

After dinner Bräsig asked young Joseph, if he would allow the carriage to be got ready.--"Of course," cried Mrs. Nüssler.--"Yes, of course," said young Joseph, who immediately went out and ordered it himself.--"Charles," said his sister, "my dear brother, how willingly, how *very* willingly .... But you know why I can't. Bräsig will have told you.--Oh me! to have peace in the house. Don't imagine for one moment that Joseph and I are not of one mind, that he wouldn't do as much as I; but you see he doesn't understand how to manage it, and his words don't come easily to him. I'll always keep an eye on your child as if she were my own, although that won't be necessary at the parsonage."

The carriage drove up to the door.--"Why, hang it, young Joseph," cried Bräsig, "you've got out your state eq'ipage, the old yellow coach!"--"Yes, Sir," said Christian, who was seated on the box, "and I only hope we'll get safe home with the old thing, for it's rather shaky, and the wheels are so loose that they rattle as much as if one was riddling gravel through a sieve."--"Christian," said Bräsig, "you must first of all drive through the village pond, and then through the brook at Gürlitz, and lastly, into the pig's pond at Rahnstädt, that the wheels may draw properly."--"And then I'll be a real sailor," said Christian.

When Hawermann had taken leave of his friends, and had put his little girl in the carriage, young Joseph hastily forced his way through the group standing about the door; his wife exclaimed: "What's the matter?"--"There," he said, thrusting a pound of twist into little Louisa's hand--that was the only kind of tobacco he ever smoked--but on looking closer, Hawermann saw that it was a great lump of sausage which young Joseph had wrapped in tobacco-paper, having nothing else at hand in which to put it.

Christian drove through the pond and brook as he had been desired. The child was left at Gürlitz, and there is no need to tell how she was kissed and petted and made to feel at home with the kind people who had taken charge of her.--Hawermann drove on to Rahnstädt to see Moses.

Moses was a man of upwards of fifty. He had large expressive eyes, and thick black eye-brows, but his hair was very white. His drooping eye-lids and long dark lashes gave him a look of gentleness; he was of the average height, and his figure was comfortably rounded; his left shoulder was a little higher than his right, but that was caused by his way of standing. Whenever he stood up he used to put his left hand in his coat-pocket, and catch firm hold of the top of his trousers lest they should slip down, for he only wore them braced up at the right side. When his wife begged him to wear a strap at the left side also, he said: "Why should I? When I was young and poor and had no money I had only one strap to fasten my trousers, and yet I did my work and married my Flora, and now that I am old and rich and have my Flora why should I wear a second strap?" Then he patted Flora on the shoulder gently, thrust his hand deeper into his pocket, and went back to his work.

When Hawermann entered, he jumped up from his chair, and exclaimed: "There now, it *is* Hawermann!--Didn't I always tell you," he went on, turning to his son, "that Hawermann was a good man and an honest man?"--"Yes, Moses," said Hawermann, "I'm honest, but ...."--"Get up, David, let Mr. Hawermann sit down here beside me. Mr. Hawermann has something to say to me, and I have something to say to him.--Now, David, you told me

I ought to go to law.--And what did I say?--That I wouldn't go to law, for Mr. Hawermann was an honest man. I only went to law *once*, and that was when I had done business with a candidate for the ministry. When I sent the fellow a letter asking him for my money, he wrote and told me to read a verse in the Christian hymn-book.--What was it again, David?"--"It was an *infamous* verse," replied David:

> "'Mein Gewüssen beusst mich nicht,
> Moses kann mich nicht verklagen,
> Der mich frai und ledig spricht
> Würd aach maine Schulden tragen.
>
> "'Conscience doth not sting me
> Moses cannot touch me,
> He, who has set me free
> Bears all my debts for me.'"

"Yes," cried Moses, "that was it. And when I showed the letter in court every one laughed, and when I showed my bill, they shrugged their shoulders, and laughed again.--Aha, I said, you mean the paper is good, but the fellow is worth nothing.--They answered that I was right, that I might have him put in prison, but must pay for his keep while there--so that in gaining my cause I'd not only have to pay all the costs of the suit, but I'd also have to provide for the fellow who had swindled me as long as his term of imprisonment lasted.--If that's the way of it, I said, let him go free.--Mr. Hawermann, you will treat me better than the Prussian law-courts."--"That's all very well, Moses," said Hawermann, "but I can't pay you, at least not yet."--"But," said Moses, looking at him enquiringly, "you've got something left?"--"Not a farthing," answered Hawermann sadly.--"Good God! Not a farthing!" cried Moses starting to his feet; then addressing his son: "David, what are you about? What are you staring at? What did you hear? Go and fetch the book."--Then he began to walk up and down the room impatiently.--"Moses," entreated Hawermann, "only give me time, and you shall have every penny that I owe you, both principal and interest."--Moses stood still and listened attentively to what he said. "Hawermann," he cried at last, breaking into the patois of the district, for the Jews of the old time were just like the Christians, when they felt deeply they always used the dialect of the province in which they lived, "you're an honest man."--And when David returned with the book, his father said: "Why have you brought the book, David, take it away again." Then to Hawermann: "Well, well, I began with nothing, and you began with nothing. I have worked hard, you have also worked hard; I have been lucky, you have been unlucky; I understand my business, and you understand yours. What isn't to-day may be to-morrow, and to-morrow you may get a place, and if you do you will save up your wages and pay me, for you are an honest man."--"I've got a place already," said Hawermann much relieved, "and it's a good place too."--"Where?" asked Moses.--"With Mr. von Rambow of Pümpelhagen."--"I congratulate you, Hawermann. He is an excellent man. Though he finds the times hard, he's an excellent man, and though he doesn't do business with me, he's an excellent man.--Flora," he shouted, putting his head out at the door, "Mr. Hawermann is here, bring us two cups of coffee."--And when Hawermann wished to decline the coffee, he said: "You *must* have it. When I was a lad and used to travel about the country with a pack on my back, your mother often gave me a cup of hot coffee in the cold weather, and afterwards when you were farm-bailiff I never went to you in vain. We are both men. Drink it, Mr. Hawermann, drink it up."--

And so this business was settled too, and that night when Hawermann went to bed in Bräsig's house, his heart was much lighter and was full of courage, and as he lay awake thinking over the events of the past day, he could not help wondering whether his dear wife had been praying for him in her heavenly home, and whether she would be a guardian angel, ever at his side during the remainder of his life on earth.

Next morning he went up to Pümpelhagen, and when Mr. von Rambow and his little son left two days later, he had quite settled down to his new duties, and had got into the full swing of his work. There he remained for many years in peace and contentment, for in course of time he lived down his grief, and found his happiness in that of others.

CHAPTER IV

Wheat was again growing in the field by the mill, as when Hawermann came to Pümpelhagen eleven years before. Hawermann was on his way back from church, for it was Sunday, and he had that morning listened to Mr. Behrens' sermon and visited his little daughter. He was on foot, for the church was but a short distance from home, and the weather was as beautiful as midsummer could make it. As he went through the wheat-field his heart was full of joy at the thought of the visible blessing God had bestowed on that which had been sown in hope, and in ignorance of what the future might bring forth. He himself profited nothing by the blessing of the rich harvest, it all belonged to his master, but he had the pleasure of seeing it, and the sight made his heart overflow with joy and thankfulness. He whistled a merry air and then smiled at himself when he found what he was doing, for he very seldom felt inclined to show any outward signs of rejoicing. "Well," he said to himself, "I've gone my rounds here for eleven years now, and the worst is over. Let me go round once more, and other eyes shall see it."--He turned into the path leading through the garden, which lay on high ground to one side of a small plantation of oaks and beeches. The foot-path was well swept and weeded, for the Squire and his family were expected that afternoon. When Hawermann got to the edge of the wood, he turned round and looked back at the wheat-field, saying to himself with a smile: "Yes, it's a much heavier crop now than it was eleven years ago; but I must be just; the weather has been far better for farming this year than it was then. I wonder what the old gentleman will say to it.--There's still a good long time to pass before the harvest though, but we've got the rape as good as safe, that's one thing. I only hope and trust that it isn't sold already," and he sighed. Then thinking over the events of the past eleven years: "The old gentleman isn't a bit richer than he was when I came. Indeed, how could he, with five daughters and two sons-in-law to drain his purse, to say nothing of my lady, who seems to think that because money is round, it may be set rolling with impunity. And then the son, what a lot of money it takes to keep him in a Prussian cavalry regiment!--Yes, the times are better, far better than when I had my farm; but when a man once gets into difficulties it's hard work getting straight again, and he has grown so much older looking in the last year or two."--Hawermann was in no particular hurry to get home, as dinner was put off until Mr. von Rambow came, not that the Squire had given orders to that effect, but it was an understood thing: "Yes," he thought, as he seated himself in the shade, "he will be glad to see that the wheat is good, for it will help him on, and he is in need of money. Fortunately the times are better."

The times were really better, and for farmers the times may be likened to a long, long cord stretching over England and America and the whole earth, and uniting the different countries to each other. When this cord gets slack and entangled, things go ill with the farmers and the whole land, but when it is firm and steady again there is great rejoicing in every heart. The cord was drawn much tighter now in our little corner of the world, and young Joseph had turned his old clay-pipe, his leaden snuff-box, the blue painted cupboard, and the polished sofa out of the house, and the old yellow carriage was no longer in the coachhouse; instead of these he had now a silver-mounted meerschaum, and a "m'og'ny secletair," and a magnificent ottoman, and there was a new carriage in the coach-house, which Bräsig always called a "phantom," and he wasn't far wrong, for it was like a dream to see such a carriage there. And the same cord passing from the Count to Bräsig gave the latter, after his five and twenty years service, written permission to marry as soon as he liked, and the promise, also written, of a comfortable pension for his old age. When the cord was slack it had twisted itself all round little Mrs. Behrens, in like manner as boys tie up a cock-chafer, and when it was tightened she went to her pastor, and continually buzzed in his ear that he ought to get double the rent for his glebe lands now, to what he had done before. And when Moses, at the end of the preceding year, added up his sum total, and wrote under the long column of figures, a little one, and a five and two large noughts: "Take away the book, David," he said, "the balance is quite right."

But this cord, however straight and tight it may be drawn, is influenced by human action, though God takes care that the slackening and tightening are done properly, so that mankind is not either destroyed or allowed to tumble aimlessly about like peas in a bag that is violently shaken, but the *individual* has as little power over the cord as a cock-chafer has on the thread to which it is tied when children play with it; like it, he can only buzz about within the space allowed him. There is yet another cord which rules the world, and it comes down from heaven, and God himself holds the end of it; this cord was pulled a little tighter, and Zachariah Bräsig had gout, and it was pulled a little tighter still, and the two old Nüsslers lay upon their last bed; a little bit was broken off the end of it, an they were laid in the grave.

Zachariah Bräsig was very cross when he found he had gout, and in his ignorance declared that it was the new fashion of wearing brightly polished boots, and the cold damp spring they had been having which had given him gout, whereas he ought to have set it down to good eating and to his daily little glass kümmel. He was as troublesome as a gad-fly, and whenever Hawermann went to see him when the pain was bad, he used to find him studying the papers the Count had given him relating to marriage and a pension, and then he was always as cross as two sticks. "Don't you see," he would say, "what a horrible position the Count's paper puts me in. If I marry, my lord, the Count, will say that I am too young for the pension and if I ask for the pension, I acknowledge by so doing that I am too old to marry. Oh yes, the Count's not much better than a Jesuit. He speaks me fair, and gets the better of me. He writes down all sorts of scoundrelly padagraphs on a bit of paper which prevent a man, who for the last eight-and-twenty years has worn himself out in his service, enjoying his pension without blame; a man who was engaged to three women twenty years ago, and who, now that he is fifty cannot marry even *one* woman.--Oh, I laugh at my lord's padagraphs!"

One man's meat is another man's poison! Bräsig was angry because the cord had been pulled, but in young Joseph's home it had brought about a pleasant change. In the old days, Mrs. Nüssler had tried in vain to bring peace into the house, now it reigned there, and ruled the actions of the whole family. Mrs. Nüssler was careful to keep it there now that it had come; and the twins showed its gentle influence in their ways and thoughts, and young Joseph also felt the change and tried to do his duty as head of the family. It is true that he spoke as little as ever, and still disliked smoking any tobacco except twist, and it is true that he had not even yet grown out of tutelage, for after his parents' death Hawermann and Bräsig had undertaken the guardianship of all out-door affairs, had arranged about the work, had seen that the farm was properly stocked, and had got everything in order. As the old people had forgotten to take away with them the money they had hidden under pillows, in old stockings, and in odd corners, it was easy to make everything go on smoothly and well, and when at last the whole place was in good order, young Joseph said: "What am I to do now?" and left everything to go its own way. But the comfort and peace in which he now lived had made him much more cheerful, and his kindness of heart, which had never been allowed free play by his parents, was patent to all, and if it sometimes made him do foolish things, it mattered no more than did the schoolmaster's appearing at a funeral in a red waistcoat, for, as he said in excuse: "What does it signify, Reverend Sir, when one's heart is black?"

And what changes had time made at the Parsonage? The cord had been very little pulled there. When Mr. Behrens felt a light touch on his arm when he was busy writing his sermon, and looked round to see what it was, it was only his little wife standing beside him, duster in hand, and while she gave his chair an extra rub, she asked him whether he would like the perch to be fried or boiled, and if he had just got in his sermon to S. Peter's draught of fishes, or to the great fish-dinner mentioned in the Gospel, so many tiresome unchristian thoughts of fried fish served with horseradish and butter *would* disturb him, that he had hard work to keep his sermon and clerical dignity uninjured.--Once, a long time ago, I got a beautiful lily-root from my friend Jülke, the great gardener in Erfurt. Its leaves began to show in March, and the first thing I did every morning, was to go and see how much the leaves had grown during the night, and I watched it carefully to see when the flower-bud began to form. Long before there was any sign of the flower, when only green leaves were to be seen, I used to carry it from the cold window to the warm stove, and again from the dusty stove to the bright sunny window. And as with the plant, so with human life, there is to me great delight in watching and tending it as it grows.--The parson had also received a lily-root from the great Gardener, the Lord God of Heaven, and he and his little wife had loved it, and tended it, and now the flower was there--a human flower, which grew in the warm sun-light of loving hearts, and Mrs. Behrens went to look at her the first thing in the morning, buzzed round her at mid-day, rejoiced in her healthy appetite, and put another spoonful on her plate, for she said: food is necessary to life. In the evening under the lime-tree before the door, she drew the same shawl round herself and the little girl, that she might know the child was warm, and when it was time to go to bed she gave her a good-night kiss: "God bless you my darling, I'll call you to-morrow early, at five o'clock."

And the parson's first act was to go to her; he watched the tender green leaves opening, propped his lily carefully, and taught her how to grow straight and true, and when she had gone to bed, he said with the implicit faith of a little child: "Regina, our lily will soon blossom now."

So it came about without the dear old clergyman or his wife noticing it, and without the child noticing it, that she had grown to be the most important personage in the family. When she went dancing about the house in her simple frock, her little silk handkerchief round her neck, her cheeks rosy with health, and her hair hanging down her back unconfined by ribbon or comb, the whole household rejoiced in her happiness. When she sat quietly beside her foster-father learning her lessons, and looking up at him with her great eyes while he taught her something new and interesting, and then at last closed her books with a deep sigh, as though she were sorry that lessons were over for the day, and yet glad, for she had been hard at work for some time, and could not have properly understood anything more, Mrs. Behrens would leave her clippers at the door, and go about dusting the furniture in her stockings. She was afraid of disturbing the lessons: "For," she said, "teaching children is quite different from writing sermons, and if it's a deadly sin to speak to old people when they're busy, a child's mind--good gracious, the waving of a tulip-stalk would be enough to distract its attention!"

Hawermann's little daughter was always pretty, but she never looked so pretty as when running to meet her father, she took him by the hand and led him to the great lime-tree under which the good clergyman and his wife were sitting, and if Hawermann sometimes looked sad at the thought of how little he could do for his own child, there was a whole heaven of joy in her eyes because he was there, and she seemed to feel she could best repay the love and kindness her foster-parents showed her, through her love and gratitude to her father. She had just entered her thirteenth year, and as yet hardly understood the feelings and impulses of her own heart. She had never asked herself why her father was dear to her. With Mr. and Mrs. Behrens it was different. She had daily signs of their affection, and daily opportunities of doing little loving services for them in return. While with him--she only knew he was her father, and that he often said things to her that must have come from his heart, and often looked at her with a quiet sadness that could not fail to go to hers. If she had made out a debtor and creditor account, the clergyman and his wife deserved more at her hands, but still----! The Lord our God has so joined people together by the ties of nature that they cannot be divided.----

This day had been a happy one for both Hawermann and his child, and now he was sitting in the shady arbour overlooking the fields he had tilled and the neighbouring country. Spring was gone, and the summer sun was shining warmly and brightly through white fleecy clouds, a soft breeze slightly cooled the air, and the green ears of corn were waving in the sunshine as though the earth were fluttering her green silken banner in honour of her sovereign lady the sun. Her regimental music sung by thousands of birds was hushed now that the spring was gone, and only the cuckoo and corn-crake were to be heard; and instead of the songs that but a few weeks ago had sounded in every thicket, the wind came up over the fields laden with sweet odours, for the hay-harvest had begun. How pleasant it is to see a long stretch of country lying before one, divided into stripes of green and yellow, here and there interspersed with wooded hills; to see old earth decked out in the brilliant garments which the seasons have woven for her. But still life in such a place is not without its anxieties, and people are fearful lest by any misfortune they should not reap as abundant a harvest as they ought, from their little bits of land, and even these long lines of colour, and the hills and trees, seem in their eyes poor and barren.--I am quite aware that it is not so in reality, but they think so at the time.--With us it is quite different, our fields stretch out in one kind of corn as far as the woods, the rape-fields resembling a great sea in the golden sunlight. Large meadows and paddocks are to be seen full of cattle, and immense hay-fields in which long rows of mowers are at work in their white shirt-sleeves. Everything is for the best and works for a good end, and wherever the eye falls there is peace and fruitfulness.--I know quite well that it is not the case, but one thinks so at the time.--It all depends upon the way we look at a thing. One man sees nothing but riches and peace, while another slips away into the shade and lets the humming of the bees, and the soft fluttering of the butterflies around him sink into his heart.--Hawermann was filled with quiet thankfulness as gazing on this scene he went over again, in thought, the events of the past eleven years. Everything had gone well with him during that time, he had paid both Bräsig and Moses what he owed them, and he was on good terms with his employer. Indeed Mr. von Rambow had become almost confidential with him, for although he was not accustomed to talk over his private affairs with anyone, he had always found Hawermann so respectful, trustworthy and zealous in his service, that he had gradually got into the habit of consulting him about things that had more to do with himself individually than with the management of the estate. As yet however he had never spoken to him about his family worries, but now he was going to do so.

When Hawermann had been sitting in the arbour for a short time, he heard a couple of carriages drive up to the door. "Here they are already," he exclaimed, springing to his feet, and going towards the house to receive the squire and his family.

Mr. von Rambow, with his wife, his three daughters and his son, had come to spend six weeks or so at Pümpelhagen to enjoy a little country-air. "Well, Mr. Hawermann," he said, "I fear that we have come upon you sooner than you expected, but I got my business in Rostock finished much more quickly than I had thought possible.--How is all going on?--Is everything ready for the ladies?"--"Quite ready," said Hawermann, "but I'm afraid that you'll have to wait a little before dinner can be served."--"All the better," he answered. "The ladies will have time to dress, and you can show me the wheat-field.--Alick" turning to his son, a handsome young man in uniform, "you can afterwards take your mother and sisters for a turn in the garden, for," with an effort to smile, "you take no interest in agriculture."--"Dear father, I ....." the son began, but his father interrupted him, saying kindly: "Never mind, my boy.--Now, Mr. Hawermann, come and show me the wheat. It's in the field just below the garden, I think."

They walked away together. What a terrible change had taken place in Mr. von Rambow's appearance, he had grown so old, and it was not only the hand of time that had aged him, he seemed to have some anxiety which was wearing him out.--At the sight of his wheat-field he cheered up, and said: "What a splendid crop! I don't remember ever having seen such wheat at Pümpelhagen before."--Hawermann was much pleased, but like all of his class he did his best to hide it, and because his heart laughed within him, he just scratched his head, and said they must wait and see what sort of weather they had at the time of harvest, and that there was generally a frightful quantity of rust down there at the edge of the meadow.--"Anything that may happen to it now will be by no fault of ours," said Mr. von Rambow, "I am very much pleased with the look of this field.--Ah," he went on after a short pause, "why didn't we know each other twenty years ago, it would have been better for us both."--Hawermann became grave and sympathetic at once when he found his master was in trouble.--They had now reached the place where the Gürlitz estate marched with Pümpelhagen.--"That wheat doesn't look as well as ours," said the squire.--"Well," replied Hawermann, "the soil is every bit as good as ours, but it hasn't been well treated, it is the Gürlitz glebe."--"A propos," interrupted Mr. von Rambow, "do you know that Gürlitz is sold? It was sold a few days ago in Rostock for twenty-five thousand nine hundred and fifty pounds. Prices are rising, are they not, Hawermann? If Gürlitz is worth twenty-five thousand nine hundred and fifty pounds, Pümpelhagen would be cheap at thirty-six thousand," and he looked sharply at Hawermann as he spoke.--"Yes, Sir, it would," replied Hawermann. "But the sale of Gürlitz may bring you good luck in another way. You see it was arranged that the sale of the estate should break the lease of the glebe lands which belong to it, and as these lands march with your wheat-field, the best thing that you can do is to take a lease of them yourself."--"My dear Hawermann! *I* take the lease!" cried the squire, and then he turned away sadly, as if he could not bear to look at it any longer. "I have enough on my shoulders already," he added, "without undertaking anything new."--"You shall have no trouble whatever about it, only give me power to act for you, and I will arrange everything with Mr. Behrens."--"No, no, Hawermann, it's impossible. The expense, the payment of rent in advance, the large amount of stock required. I can't do it. I have so many calls on my purse as it is, that I hardly know where to turn."--Mr. von Rambow went back up the hill with so much difficulty, and stumbled so often over the stones on the road, that Hawermann sprang to him and offered him his arm. Just as they reached the garden the old man became so giddy that the bailiff took him into the arbour, and made him sit down and rest.--The squire soon recovered when brought out of the hot sun, but Hawermann looking at him could hardly imagine him to be the same man who had taken him into his service eleven years ago. At last he began to speak again, and it seemed a relief to him to unburden his mind.--"Dear Hawermann," he said, "I want you to do something for me. My brother's son, Frank--you used to know him--has left school, and will soon be of age, when he will have to take the management of his estate into his own hands. I am his guardian by my late brother's will, and have advised him to learn farming practically, and as he has agreed to do so, I have chosen you to be his teacher. You will find him an intelligent, good-hearted young fellow."--Hawermann answered that he would do his best, he had known the lad when he was quite a child, and had liked him.--"Ah!" sighed Mr. von Rambow, "why couldn't my own boy have done the same? Why was I weak enough to give way to my wife's entreaties against my better judgment? Nothing would satisfy her but he must go into the army.--And now it has come to this, he is deeply in debt, and I know he has not told me all, I see it in his manner. If he would only confess I should know where we stand, and I might be able to set him free from the money-lenders.--And what if I also were to fall into their hands," he concluded in a low, broken voice.--Hawermann was even more frightened by the expression of his master's face than by his words, and he answered with emotion: "It won't be so bad as that comes to, and then. Sir, you must remember that you have still to be paid for the fifteen hundred bushels of rape, and I'm certain there's all that."--"Ah," said Mr. von Rambow, "and I have already been paid for seventeen hundred bushels, and the money is all spent; but that isn't the worst of it. If that were all I shouldn't be so troubled," he exclaimed, as though he must speak and so lighten the burden of his anxiety. "The business I had to do at Rostock isn't settled yet, though I told you it was. I only said that for the sake of my family. I have undertaken to pay a debt of a thousand and fifty pounds for one of my sons-in-law, and I find that I cannot raise so large a sum in Rostock, though I had hoped to do so, and yet the money must be in the hands of the man who has just bought Gürlitz in three days' time.--Can you advise me what to do, old friend? You were once in the same position as I am now, and you succeeded in freeing yourself; don't be angry with me for referring to it. You are and have always been an honest man, and can understand how miserable it makes me not to know how to keep my honest name unstained."--Hawermann understood him perfectly, he had once been in the same distress for want of thirty pounds, as the squire was now for a thousand. "Have you spoken to the purchaser of Gürlitz?" he asked, after a long pause of deliberation.--"Yes," was the reply, "I told him frankly that I should find it difficult to pay so large a sum at once."--"And what was his answer?" said Hawermann, "perhaps that he was in want of it himself?"--"No, I don't think that was it, but I didn't like his looks at all, his manner was sly and smooth, and when I told him of my difficulty his proposals were so cunningly made to entangle me, that I at once broke off all negociations, and determined to do my utmost to raise the money in proper time. But I have failed as you know, and don't know where to turn, or what to do."--"I only know of one remedy," said Hawermann, "and that is to go to old Moses in Rahnstädt."--"To a Jew?" asked the squire. "No," he exclaimed, "I'll never do that.--I couldn't bear to fall into a usurer's hands.--No, rather than do that, I'd bear Mr. Pomuchelskopp's impertinence."--"*Whose* did you say?" cried Hawermann, starting as if a wasp had stung him.--"Why the new purchaser of Gürlitz of whom we have just been talking," said Mr. von Rambow, looking at his bailiff in astonishment. "He is a Pomeranian, and comes from a place nearer the river Peen; he is short and stout, and has a fat face."--"Yes," said Hawermann. "And so it is he who is going to be our neighbour here. It is he with whom you are going to have money-transactions.--No, no, Mr. von Rambow, I beg, I entreat you to have nothing to do with that man.--You can bear me witness that I have never said anything good or bad of the man who ruined me, but now that you are in danger, it becomes my duty to speak; that man was the cause of all my misfortunes," and springing to his feet he went on excitedly, his face as he spoke losing its usual calm expression, and an angry sparkle coming into his eyes. "Yes, that is the man who drove me out of house and home, who heaped one misery after another on me and my poor wife, so that she at last broke down and died.--Oh, Sir, whatever you do, beware of that man!"--The warning was too emphatic to be passed over unheeded.-- "But who can I get to help me?" he enquired.--"Moses," answered Hawermann, firmly and decidedly. The squire made a gesture of dissent, but Hawermann came a little nearer him, and went on still more emphatically than before: "Mr. von Rambow, Moses will help you, we will go to him after dinner, and I assure you on my own knowledge of the man that you will never repent going to him."

The squire rose and took Hawermann's arm. He found in him a support both physical and moral, for when a calm, even-tempered man loses his ordinary serene composure, he exerts a greater influence over others than people of a more impulsive nature ever can.

The conversation during dinner was slight and subject to long pauses. Each was busy with his own thoughts. Hawermann thought of his new and formidable neighbours, the squire of the money he wanted to raise, and the young lieutenant seemed as if he had lost himself in a long sum in addition which he could not manage to add up rightly, so that if my lady had not ridden her high horse a little, and spoken of the calls she intended to make on the grand people in the neighbourhood, and if the three girls had not chattered about the pleasures of a country-life, and about all the pretty things they had seen during their drive, it would have been a regular quaker's meeting.

After dinner Mr. von Rambow and his bailiff drove to Rahnstädt. The squire felt as he entered the door of Moses' house as if he were going to pick a guinea out of the mud with his hitherto clean hands. On the threshold he was greeted with a stuffy smell of tarry wool that had just left the back of the sheep on which it had grown, and which is a very different article from the same wool when it is woven into a carpet for a lady's boudoir. The entrance-hall and business-room were very untidy, for though Flora was a good woman she never could manage to keep the skins out of sight, for Moses said shortly that they were part of the trade, and David was continually adding new items to the list of things lying about, so that finally the house became a very paradise for rats, for these delightful little creatures take as kindly to the fusty smell of a wool-stapler's shop, as doves to oil of aniseed.

Mr. von Rambow did not feel more comfortable when he was in the business-room, for Moses was old-fashioned, and when business permitted always wore his worst coat on the Christian Sabbath, holding it an article of faith to make himself look as different as possible from Christians in their holiday-attire. When he came forward hastily to receive the squire, exclaiming: "Mr. von Rambow!--I am highly honoured!" and then turning to his son who was spending his Sunday-leisure from "wool-stapling" in the enjoyment of lying at full length on the sofa: "Why don't you move, David? Why are you lying there? Get up and let Mr. von Rambow sit down." And when he led the squire to the sofa, and signed to him to sit down in the place David had just quitted, poor Mr. von Rambow would willingly have left the guineas lying in the dirt--if only he had not been in such desperate need of them.

Hawermann at once set a chair for his master near the open window, and then began to explain the business that had brought them to Rahnstädt. As soon as Moses found what they had come for he sent David out of the room, for although he let his son manage the wool-stapling part of his trade as he liked, he did not consider him capable at five and twenty years old of taking even a subordinate place in the moneylending department. The moment the coast was clear--of David--he said again that it was a great honour to do business with Mr. von Rambow. "What have I always told you, Mr. Hawermann? Didn't I always say that Mr. von Rambow was a good man, a very good man.--And, Mr. von Rambow, what have I always said?--That Mr. Hawermann was an honest man, he worked and saved, and has paid me everything he owed me to the uttermost farthing."--But when he understood how large a sum was wanted he rather drew back, and wished to have nothing to do with it, and if he had not seen that Hawermann earnestly desired that he should undertake the business, he would have refused point blank. And who knows whether he would not have refused to have anything to do with the affair even then, if he had not heard that the money was wanted to complete the purchase of Gürlitz, and that failing his help the squire would have to come to an arrangement with Mr. Pomuchelskopp. When he heard that name Moses made a face of as much disgust, as if some one had offered him a bit of unclean meat on a plate, and then exclaimed: "With Pömüffelskopp!" that was the way he always pronounced the name. "Do you know what sort of man he is?" and as he spoke, he made a movement as though he were throwing a piece of unclean meat over his shoulder. "I advised my son David to have nothing to do with Pömüffelskopp--but young people!--David bought some wool from him. Very well, I said, you will see, I said. And what did we discover? He had mixed the lumpy wool of sheep that had died of disease with what was clean and good, and also the dirty skins of wethers that had been slaughtered by the butcher, to say nothing of two large stones that he had put in the centre. Two large stones!--Good, I said. I paid him in Prussian paper-money, making up the sum in small parcels containing about fifteen pounds each, and amongst them I slipped in a few notes that were either false, or which had passed out of currency, and lastly I added two old lottery-tickets--these are the two large stones, I said.--Oh, didn't he make noise enough about it? He came back with Slus'uhr the attorney--a man of like nature with himself--" with that he made as though he were throwing another bit of unclean meat over his shoulder.--"He looks for all the world like one of David's rats, his ears are put on his head in the same way--he must needs live, so he lives like the rats on refuse and garbage, and gnaws through the honest work of other people.--There was noise enough in all conscience now that the two were together. They said they'd go to law. What's the good of a law-suit? I asked. The wool and the money are on a par.--And do you know, gentlemen, I said something more. I said that though the attorney, Mr. Pömüffelskopp, and I are only *three* Jews, still we might be counted as *four*, for the two former were quite equal to three in their own person.--Oh dear, what a noise they made, they abused me to every one, but his worship the mayor said to me, Moses, he said, you do a large business, but have never yet gone to law with any one, leave them to do their worst. Mr. von Rambow, you shall have the money this very day at a reasonable percentage, for as you are a good man and deal kindly with your dependents, and have a good name in the country-side, you shall have nothing to do with that Pömüffelskopp."

Borrowing money is disagreeable work, and he who writes this book knows that it is so from his own experience, still there is a great difference between borrowing from a kind-hearted old friend, and applying to a man whose business it is to lend money.--The squire had a good many small debts on his estate, but there were no large mortgages on it, whenever he had wanted money before he had been able to get it from his lawyer, or from a tradesman, and this was the first time his old resources had failed him, and that he had been obliged to go to a Jewish moneylender. He had an intense dislike to the business he was about; the fear caused by the unwillingness Moses had at first shown to lend him the money, and then the sudden relief when he found he was to have it after all overpowered him so much, that he sank back in his chair pale and trembling. Hawermann asked for some water for him.--"Perhaps, Mr. von Rambow," asked Moses, "you'd like a mouthful of wine better."--"No, water, water," cried Hawermann, and Moses rushed to the door, and nearly knocked David down when he opened it, for David had been listening at the key-hole. "David," he exclaimed, "what are you standing there for? Why don't you go for some water?"

David brought the water, and the squire felt better as soon as he had drunk it. Moses counted the gold out on the table, and the squire, after picking them up, looked at his hands, and saw that they appeared every whit as white and clean as before. And after he was once more seated in the carriage, it seemed to him as he looked back at the money-lender's house, as if he had left the heavy load of care he had brought with him amongst the wool and sheep-skins in the warehouse. And Moses stood in the doorway and bowed, and bowed, and glanced from side to side to see whether his neighbours had observed that Mr. von Rambow was there.--Still he was not so much overwhelmed with the honour done him, as to be unable to look after his own affairs, he bent down his head, and drawing Hawermann aside, whispered: "You are an honest man, bailiff. When I concluded this piece of business I didn't notice how ill the squire was. You must promise me that the money will be paid off by the estate.--It is a question of life and death.--What have I to do with a sick man and a bond?"

Now that the squire's mind was at rest about his money-difficulties his health improved rapidly, and he began to look at everything in a more cheerful light, and when a few days later Hawermann again proposed that Mr. von Rambow should take a lease of the Gürlitz glebe, he consented at once, and gave Hawermann permission to make all the necessary arrangements with Mr. Behrens. Little Mrs. Behrens fluttered round her husband and Hawermann while they talked, and said that "the rent ought to be higher than before."--"Yes," answered Hawermann, "of course it ought. The rent must be raised, for the times are better than they were, but that matter will be easily settled, for it will be an advantageous arrangement for both sides."--"Regina," said the pastor, "it has just occurred to me that the flowers have never been watered this morning."--"Goodness gracious me," cried Mrs. Behrens as she hastened from the room, "I quite forgot the flowers."--"We'll get on quicker now," said the pastor. "I confess that I'd rather have an outsider for a tenant than the lord of the manor, for when the latter has the glebe-lands there are often little disagreeables and disputes that ought never to be between the parish-priest and his squire. Besides that, merely as a matter of personal feeling I'd far rather have Mr. von Rambow for a tenant than the new lord of the manor; you see I have known him for many years.--So you really think I ought to get a higher rent?"--"Most certainly, Sir, and I am commissioned to offer you half as much again as you used to get. If I *myself* were going to take a lease of it from you, I should offer you more, but ......"--"We understand each other, dear Hawermann," interrupted Mr. Behrens. "I agree to your terms."--So when Mrs. Behrens returned with little Louisa to say: "I needn't have gone after all, Louisa had done it for me," business was all arranged. The child threw her arms round her father's neck, exclaiming: "Oh father, father, what a good plan it is!"-- Why did she kiss her father, and what did it matter to her who got the lease of the glebe?--Well, well, if her father had the land he would have to look after it, and so she hoped to him oftener.

When Hawermann was walking down the path leading to the church he met Zachariah Bräsig coming towards him. Bräsig had quite recovered from the unphilosophical state of mind into which a fit of gout always threw him, and now that the pain was over could take things as calmly and philosophically as usual. "Good-day, Charles," he said. "I have been waiting for you for some time in your room, but as the time hung rather heavily on my hands I went at last to pay my respects to the *Counsellor*. He delighted to see me, and received me with the greatest possible kindness; but how dreadfully changed he is." True, Hawermann replied, his master had become terribly aged and feeble, and he feared that he would not long be spared to them.--"Yes," answered Bräsig, "but what is life after all, Charles? What is human life? Look you, Charles, it is as though it were a thing twirled round and round like an empty purse from which not a single farthing can fall, however long one may wait."--"Bräsig," said Hawermann, "I don't know what other people may think of it, but life and work always seem to me to be one and the same thing."--"Oh, ho! Charles, I have you now! You learnt that from parson Behrens. He has spoken to me now and then on the subject, and he always makes out that human life in this world is neither more nor less than a sort of seed-time, and that Christian faith is the sun and rain that makes the seed sprout and grow, and that only hereafter, in the other world, comes the harvest, for while he is on earth, man must labour and toil to the uttermost.--But, Charles, that is a wrong way of looking at it, it goes clean against Scripture.--The Bible tells us of the lilies of the field, how they toil not, neither do they spin, and yet our Heavenly Father feeds them. And if God feeds them, they are alive, and yet they do no work. And when I have that confounded gout, and can do nothing--absolutely nothing, except flap the beastly flies away from my face--can I be said to work? And yet I am alive, and suffer horrible torture into the bargain. And, Charles," he continued, pointing to a field on the right, "just look at those two lilies coming towards us. I mean the lieutenant and his youngest sister; now have you ever heard that lieutenants in a cavalry-regiment do any sort of hard work, or that young ladies of rank and position busy themselves with spinning? Yet there they come, alive and well, walking over the rape-stubble."--"Will you wait a few minutes, Zachariah?" said Hawermann. "They are coming straight towards us, and perhaps wish to speak to us."--"All right," said Bräsig. "But I say, just look at the young lady wading through the stubble with a long train to her gown, and thin shoes!--Nay, Charles, life and suffering are one and the same thing, and the suffering always begins at the small end, with the feet for instance; and that this is true, witness my confounded gout, and the young lady's thin shoes.--But what I wanted to say was this, that your happiest time here is past and gone, for when the *Counsellor* is dead, you may look out for squalls.--You will then see strange things come to pass with my lady, her unmarried daughters, and the lieutenant.--Charles," he continued, after a few minutes silent thought, "it would be well for you to be on good terms with the crown-prince."--"Oh, Bräsig, what are you saying?" interrupted Hawermann. "I shall keep to the straight road."--"Yes, Charles, I do so too, and so does everyone who is not a Jesuit; but look at the young lady, she is also going along the straight road, but it leads her through the stubble!--Charles ....."

The young people had now come too near to allow him to finish his sentence, so he only added in a sort of aside: "A Jesuit? No! But he's a regular vocative case!"--

"Thank you, Mr. Hawermann, for waiting for us," said Alick von Rambow, coming up to them. "My sister and I set out on our walk with two different ends in view: her object was to find corn-flowers, and mine was to find horses. She can't find any cornflowers, and I can't see any horses."-- "If you mean the common 'blue-bottle' by corn-flowers, Miss," said Bräsig. "But," he interrupted himself, "what a pity, that confounded rape-stubble has torn your pretty dress," and he stooped down as though he were about to try his hand at lady's maid's work.--"Oh, it doesn't matter," cried the young lady, starting back, "it's an old dress. But where shall I find the corn-flowers?"--"I'll show you. There are a good lot of them down there on the Gürlitz march; you'll find blue-bottles, red poppies, white gules, and thistles; in short, a whole plantation of weeds."--"That is a capital plan, Fidelia," said her brother, "while you go in search of corn-flowers with Mr. Bräsig, I will ask Mr. Hawermann to show me the young horses, for," turning to Hawermann, "you must know that my father was good enough to tell me this morning, that I might choose one of the best of the four-year-olds for my own use."--"I'll show them to you with great pleasure," answered Hawermann, "there are some really good horses amongst them."--So the two parties separated, and the last words Hawermann heard Bräsig say as he walked away with Miss Fidelia were, that he was delighted to make her acquaintance, for he had once had a dog that was called "Fidel," and that it had been a splendid ratter.

Hawermann and the lieutenant went together to the paddock, and as they walked they naturally talked about farming. The lieutenant was of a lively disposition, and Hawermann had known him from his childhood, but the bailiff found that he had learnt nothing about the subject on which he was talking, that his views were inpracticable, and his questions were so wide of the mark and displayed so much ignorance, that he could not help saying to himself: "He's good-natured, very good-natured, but he's very ignorant, and--good God!--when his father dies he will have the estate, and will have to make his living out of it!"

After they had reached the paddock, and had examined each of the young horses separately, the lieutenant said to Hawermann: "Well, what do you say? Which ought I to take?"--"The brown," replied the bailiff.--"I like the black better, don't you see the beautiful arch of his neck, and what a finely shaped head he has?"--"Mr. von Rambow," said Hawermann, "you don't ride on the head or neck of a horse, but on its back and legs. You want a hack, and you'll get three times as much work out of the brown as the black."--"The black looks as if he were partly English?"--"You're quite right there, he is descended from Wild-fire; but the brown is of the old Mecklenburg breed, and it is a pity that these horses should be allowed to die out, that one should not take pains to keep up what is good in our own country but should exchange it for English racers."--"That may be all quite true," said Alick, "but as all the officers in my regiment have black horses, I shall decide on taking the black."

As Hawermann could not see the force of this reasoning, he remained silent, and the conversation on the way back was not so easy as before; but when they had nearly reached the house--right in front of the door, and as if he had been preparing for this last step--the lieutenant stopped the bailiff, and said with a deep sigh, and as if lifting a heavy burden from his breast: "Hawermann, I have long wished to have a little private talk with you.--Hawermann, I'm in debt--you must help me.--I owe a hundred and thirty-five pounds, and I *must* have the money."--That was a bad proposal to make to Hawermann; but in really serious matters the bailiff used the influence of his age, he looked the young man of three and twenty full in the face, and said: "I can't help you in this, Mr. von Rambow."--"Hawermann, dear Hawermann, I'm desperately in want of the money."--"Then you ought to speak to your father."--"To my father? No, no! he has already paid so much for me, and now he is ill, it might do him harm."--"Still you should tell him. Such things as this ought never to be discussed with strangers, they should always be arranged between father and son."--"Strangers?" asked Alick, looking at him reproachfully. "Do you really look upon me as such a complete stranger, Hawermann!"--"No, Mr. von Rambow, no," exclaimed Hawermann, seizing his young master's hand, "you are no stranger to me. And I will do anything for you that I possibly can. This matter is in itself a mere nothing, and if I could not manage it alone, my friend Bräsig would make up the rest; but, dear Mr. von Rambow, your father is your natural helper, and it would be wrong to pass him over."--"I can't tell my father," said Alick, plucking the leaves off a willow-tree near him.--"You *must* tell him," cried Hawermann as emphatically as he could, "he feels that you are concealing some of your debts from him, and that pains him."--"Has he spoken to you about it?"--"Yes," replied Hawermann, "but only in connection with his own great need of money which you already know about."--"I know," said Alick, "and I also know the source from which my father received assistance.--Well, I can do what my father did before me," he added coldly and shortly as he entered the house.--"Mr. von Rambow," cried Hawermann, following him hastily, "don't do that, for Heaven's sake, you won't succeed, and you'll only be in a more unpleasant position than before."--Alick would not listen to him.

A couple of hours later, lieutenant von Rambow was standing amongst the wool-sacks and sheep-skins in the Jew's house, where David found his amusement amongst the articles of his trade, and he seemed to be making a despairing last appeal to Moses, who kept determined hold of his purse-strings. "Really and truly, my lord Baron, I can't do it. And why not? Can't I make by it? Can't I make a good deal by it?--Look you, my lord Baron, there is David--David, what are you doing? What are you looking at? Come here, David.--Look you, my lord Baron, here he is standing before you and me, I won't give him the least sign, but will go quietly into the next room, and then you can ask David." And with that he walked right shoulder first into the next room.

Poor Alick's affairs must have been in a bad way before he would have had anything to do with such a person as David, for if he in his grand new uniform looked fit to draw the king's carriage, David's outer man was so shabby and ill-conditioned that he was worthy of nothing better than dragging a scavenger's cart. But in this sort of business appearance is nothing, the chief thing is to know how to act in any emergency, and David was quite up to the mark there. He had three qualities that stood him in very good stead; firstly, he had the incomparably sly, sharp expression and features of the Jewish usurer, and as he stood before lieutenant von Rambow, chewing a bit of cinnamon stalk he had taken from his mother's store-closet, as a remedy against the close woolly smell of the warehouse, and gazing at him with his head bent a little sideways, and one hand in his pocket, he looked as impudent as if the ghosts of all the rats that had died in the house, during all the years that he had carried on the wool-trade there, had entered into him: secondly, he knew himself to be a far harder and more unyielding man of business than his father, for having had so much to do with wool, skins, &c., which are known to be difficult things to deal with, had taught him much: and thirdly, he was quite up to the most approved method of drawing on, or holding off, a customer, and this he had also learnt in the wool-trade.

Naturally Alick could make nothing of such a highly gifted individual, and very soon turned to go away with a heavy heart. David was so pleased with the way in which he had conducted the case in hand, that he began to compassionate the young man, and felt inclined to give him a little friendly counsel, so he advised him to apply to attorney Slus'uhr, "for he has the money, and he will arrange matters for you."

Lieutenant von Rambow had scarcely closed the door when Moses rushed in, and exclaimed: "David, have you any conscience?--I'll tell you something, you have none!--How could you send the lad to such a cut-throat?"--"I have only sent him to his own people," replied David maliciously. "He's a soldier, so he's a cut-throat too. And even supposing that the attorney *does* cut his throat, what's that to *you*? And if he cuts the attorney's throat, what's that to *me*?"--"David," said the old man, shaking his head, "I tell you again, you have no conscience."--"What is conscience?" growled David. "When you are doing business you send me away, and when you won't do business you call me."--"David," said his father, "you are too young," and with that he went into his room again.--"Am I too young?" muttered David between his teeth. "Am I always to be too young? Well, I know a place where I am not too young." Then he changed his coat, and set out in the same direction as he had sent the lieutenant, to the house of attorney Slus'uhr.

I do not know what he had to do there, but I know this, that young Mr. von Rambow had to write a good many letters that evening when he got back to Pümpelhagen, and that he sent a cheque in each of them, and that when they were all finished he gave a deep sigh as if he had got rid of a heavy burden. He did not know that although he had weathered the first storm, he had acted like the old woman who heated the yeast in her baking trough.

CHAPTER V

About ten o'clock in the morning, a few days later, the sun was peeping down on the garden of Gürlitz manor-house from behind a cloud. Her daughter, the earth, had been having a great washing-day, and she wanted to give her beloved child a little help with the drying of the clothes. There is nothing more delightful than to see old mother sun looking down sympathetically, her broad kindly old face showing between the white sheets of cloud, and to see her seizing her watering-can now and then to sprinkle the linen. At such times she is always in high spirits, and, in spite of her old age and experience, is as changeable in her humour as a young girl who is in love for the first time. One moment she is sad and tearful, and the next laughing and joyous.

The old lady laughed heartily as she looked down on the garden at Gürlitz. "Well," she cried, scattering her golden laughter over plants and bushes, "one sees queer things sometimes in this stupid old world! A neat white figure used to stand there, which by my help enabled those poor hungry children of men to know the exact time to eat their dinner, and now a fat, awkward looking fellow has taken its place, he has green-checked trousers on, and there is a pipe in his mouth. Nothing is done so foolishly anywhere else as in the world!" And with that she laughed merrily over the new squire, Mr. Pomuchelskopp, who was standing like a sun-dial, dressed in a yellow nankin-coat, and green-checked trousers, in the same place where the graceful heathen god Apollo used to be, except that while the god had a lyre in his hand, he was provided with a short pipe. The sun's face clouded over now and then when she saw her old friend, who, for so many years, had noted her doings faithfully, lying neglected among the rankgrass and nettles.--And then she began to laugh again.

Pomuchelskopp laughed too. There was no smile to be seen on his face, but when stretching himself up as high as his short stature would allow, he gazed around him, his heart rejoiced and cried: "It is all mine! All mine!" He did not see the sun-beams which gilded the earth, these made no impression on him; but the sun-beam within him, which was caused by nothing better than pounds, shillings, and pence, lighted up his heart, though it did not show in his face. Before an expression of amusement could be seen there something very humorous must take place, and matter to call it forth was not wanting.

His two youngest children, Tony and Phil, had come out into the garden, and Phil had made himself a rod of docken and nettle-stalks, with which he beat the statue of the fallen god, and that made father Pomuchelskopp laugh most heartily, and Tony ran into the kitchen and got a bit of charcoal, and was just going to give him a moustache, when his father stopped him, and said: "Tony, don't do that, you may spoil it, and perhaps we may sell it, Tony. But you may thrash it as much as you like."--And so they beat the statue with their stinging rods, and father Pomuchelskopp laughed till he shook in his green-checked trousers.

At this moment "madam" appeared, and she was Pomuchelskopp's sterner half. She was extremely tall, and as angular as king Pharaoh's seven lean kine, her forehead was always wrinkled into a frown, as if the cares of the whole world were laid upon her, or as if she were always suffering a sort of martyrdom, or as if all the crockery broken by all the maid-servants throughout the world belonged to her, and her mouth had such a bitter curve that one would have thought that, she was accustomed to drink vinegar, and eat sorrel. She wore every morning, in spite of the hot summer-weather, a black merino dress that she had bought once when she was in mourning, and that must therefore be worn out, and when she changed it she put on a cotton gown which she had had dyed olive green with elder-bark; and on such occasions as Pomuchelskopp wore a blue coat and brass buttons, she put on a cap with so many frills and furbelows that her weazened face peering out of it, looked for all the world like a half starved mouse in a bundle of tow; as for the rest of her dress, she wore petticoat on the top of petticoat, but still her poor shrunken legs looked like a couple of knitting-needles that had lost their way in a bag of odds and ends. At such times it was advisable that her servants should keep out of her way, for when she went about with velvet or silken streamers, her soul was weighed down with the constant fear, of unnecessary expense in housekeeping details.

She was a "mother" who pondered day and night how she might best make a waistcoat for Phil out of an old dress of Mally's. She loved her children according to the Scriptures, and so she chastened them, and Tony might count two slaps on the back for every stain on his coat, and two on the legs for every stain on his trousers. Yes, she was stern to her own flesh and blood, but still she was able to rejoice in due measure, as for instance to-day, when she came into the garden, and saw how her youngest olive-branches were amusing themselves, a smile then crossed her face like a pale gleam of sunshine in February when the earth is still frozen, and which seems to say: "Never fear, spring is coming at last."

She was the kind of wife of whom it might be said that she never in thought, word, or deed sinned against the letter of her duty, although Pomuchelskopp's conduct was rather trying, for in her opinion he was often guilty of too great levity; for instance, when he thought a joke a good one, he would laugh at it outright, and that was not seemly behaviour in the father of a family, and must necessarily end by impoverishing him, and bringing her and her children to beggary. She therefore did more than she was bound to do by her marriage-vows, she discouraged such outward signs of mirth, and gave him of her own vinegar to drink, and of her own sorrel to eat. She lectured him--that is to say when they were alone--as if he were her youngest son Phil, she treated him as if he were still a child; in short, she bullied him after her own fashion.--She never beat him--God forbid!--She contented herself with words. She understood how to bring him round to her way of thinking by the mode of her address: if he were behaving with undignified thoughtlessness, she called him coldly and hardly by the last syllable of his name, "Kopp," for she generally addressed him by the two middle syllables, "Muchel;" but when he was acting so as to meet with her entire satisfaction, for instance, when he sat crossly in the corner of the sofa, and slashed angrily at the flies, she called him by the beginning of his name in a loving tone, "Pöking."[6]

She did not call him "Pöking" to-day. "Kopp," she said, to show her disapproval of his undignified manner of testifying his amusement at what the boys were doing, "Kopp, why are you standing there smoking like a chimney? Let us go and call at the parsonage."--"My chick," involuntarily taking the pipe out of his mouth, "we can set off at once if you like. I shan't be a moment in changing my coat."--"Coat? Why! you don't suppose that *I* am going to put on my best black silk?--We are only going to call on *our* clergyman."--She laid as great an emphasis on the word "our," as if she had been speaking of her shepherd, or as if she thought that the parson was indebted to her for his daily bread.--"Just as you like, my Henny. I can put on my brown overcoat instead.--Phil, don't beat the statue any more, mama doesn't like it."--"Never mind the children, Kopp, you've got enough to do, to look after yourself. You'll go in your nankin-coat, it is clean and good."--"My chuck," said Pomuchelskopp, who, when he was of a different opinion from the wife of his bosom, always began with "Henny," and ended with "chuck," "always dress in good style, my dearest chuck. Even if we don't do it for the sake of the clergyman's family, let us do it for our own sake. And if Mally and Sally go with us, they ought to dress so as to make an imposing impression on the people at the parsonage."

This last reason was deemed a sufficient one, and gained Pomuchelskopp leave to put on his brown coat. He was made very happy by being allowed to have his own way, a piece of good fortune that did not often happen to him, so he felt proportionably grateful, and being desirous of pleasing his Henny in return for her kindness, he wished to make her partake in his joy. Let no one imagine however that Pomuchelskopp was so ill-bred as to give audible signs of merriment in his own house, no, he was always humble and quiet when there. He waved his hand towards the fields around him, and said; "Look, my chick, these all belongs to us!"--"Muchel," said madam shortly, "you are exaggerating, that is Pümpelhagen down there."--"You are right, Henny, that is Pümpelhagen.--But," he added, his little eyes twinkling avariciously as he looked down on Pümpelhagen, "who knows?--If I am spared, and if I sell my Pomeranian property well, and the times remain good, and the old *Counsellor* dies, and his son contracts debts ....."--"Yes, Muchel," interrupted his affectionate wife with the satirical curl of her lip, which the world had to accept as her only substitute for a smile, for it was the nearest approach to one that ever was seen on her face, "yes, that is just like old Strohpagel, when he said: if I were ten years younger, and were steadier on my legs, and hadn't my wife, you would all see what sort of fellow I really am!"--"Henny," said Pomuchelskopp, putting on an injured expression, "how can you say such a thing? How could I ever wish to get rid of you? I should never have been able to buy Gürlitz without the eight thousand five hundred pounds you inherited from your father. And what a splendid place Gürlitz is! All that land belongs to it," and he waved his hand as he spoke.--"Yes, Kopp," said his wife shortly, "except the glebe, which you have allowed to slip through your fingers."--"Dear me, chuck, will you never leave the subject of the glebe alone! What can I do?--You see I am a straightforward, honest man, so what chance have I with a couple of sly rogues like Hawermann and the parson? But we hav'n't done with each other yet, *Mounseer* Hawermann! We'll have some thing to say to each other before long, reverend Sir!"

Three neat little maidens were seated in Mrs. Behrens' tidy parlour in Gürlitz parsonage on the same morning. They were plying their needles and tongues busily, for they were trying a race both in sewing and in talking, and as they sat there they looked as sweet and rosy in contrast with the white linen, as freshly plucked strawberries on a white plate. And these three children were Louisa Hawermann, and the twins, Lina and Mina Nüssler.--"Children," said little Mrs. Behrens, on one of the many incursions from the kitchen into the parlour, "you can't think what a pleasure it is to me in my old age when I am laying the clean linen away in the chest, that I know exactly when I spun and hemmed each separate piece! How differently one treats it when one knows from experience how much trouble it has cost. Mina, Mina, that hem's all crooked. Goodness gracious me, Louisa, I believe you've been going on sewing without ever looking what you were about, don't you see that you haven't got a knot on your thread! Now I must go and see that the potatoes are boiling properly, for my pastor will soon be in," and then she hastened from the room, only popping her head in at the door again to say, "Mina and Lina, you are to remain to dinner," and so she kept flying about between kitchen and parlour in measured time like the pendulum of a clock and keeping everything in good order in both.

But how was it that Lina and Mina had joined Mrs. Behrens' sewing-class? This was how it happened--When the two little girls had grown so old that they could pronounce the letter "r," and no longer cared about playing with the sand-box, but ran after Mrs. Nüssler all day long, saying: "What shall we do now, mother?" Mrs. Nüssler told young Joseph that it was high time for the children to have some schooling: they must have a governess. Joseph had no objection, and his brother-in-law Baldrian the schoolmaster, was commissioned to engage one. When the governess had been six months at Rexow, Mrs. Nüssler said she was a discontented old woman who did nothing but nagg at the children all day long, and made her so uncomfortable that she scarcely felt at home in her own house. So that governess had to take her departure.--Kurz, the shop-keeper, chose the next, and one day, when no one in Rexow had any suspicion of what was going to happen, the door opened, and in marched an enormous woman, as tall as a grenadier, with strongly marked eye-brows, a yellow complexion, and spectacles on her nose, who introduced herself as the "new governess." She then began to speak French to the two little girls, and finding that they were innocent of all knowledge of that language, she addressed herself to young Joseph in the same tongue. Such a thing had never happened to young Joseph before, and it astonished him so much that he let his pipe go out, and as they were drinking coffee at the time, he said, in order to say something: "Mother, fill the new teacher's cup."--Well, in a very short time the new governess ruled the whole house, but at last Mrs. Nüssler who had borne it bravely as long as she could, said: "Stop, this will never do. If any one is to rule here, it is I, for I am the 'nearest,' as Mrs. Behrens would say," and so the grenadier had to march.--Uncle Bräsig now tried what he could do, "so that the little round-heads might learn something." He engaged what he called a "capital teacher," and "one who is always merry, and who is not to be beat in playing the piano-forty."--He was right. One evening in winter a red-faced, smiling little woman arrived at Rexow, and she had not been ten minutes in the house before she fell upon the newly bought second-hand piano, and beat it and thumped it as if she were threshing out corn. When she had gone to bed, young Joseph opened the piano, but as soon as he found out that three of the strings were broken, he shut it again, and said: "What's to be done now?"--There was great fun and laughter in the house in those days, for the governess played and frisked about with the little girls, till Mrs. Nüssler came to the conclusion that her eldest daughter Lina was on the whole a more sensible person than her teacher. She wanted to know what the children were taught, and therefore begged Madmoiselle to draw out a plan of lessons, and let her see it. Next day Lina brought her a large sheet of paper containing the plan, which was as follows: German, French, orthography, geography, religion, Scripture history, and the other kind of history, and Bible natural history, and at the end came music, music, music, music.--"Ah well," said she to Joseph, "she may teach music as much as she likes, if only the religion is all right. What do you think, Joseph?"--"Oh," said Joseph, "it all depends upon circumstances!"--Nothing more would have been said, if Mrs. Nüssler had not accidentally found out from Lina that the time that ought to have been devoted to Scripture history, was spent in playing at ball, and soon afterwards when she happened to be upstairs at the time of the religious lesson, she heard peals of laughter from the school-room, and on going there to see what sort of religion was being taught, she found--Mademoiselle playing at Tig with the children. Mrs. Nüssler would have nothing to say to a religious lesson of that kind, and so Mademoiselle "Jack in the box" had to beat a retreat like her forerunner the grenadier.

The worst of it was that it was in the middle of the quarter, and Mrs. Nüssler complained of the children being always in her way, to which Joseph merely said: "Oh, what can I do?" but at the same time he began to study the Rostock newspaper very attentively, and one day he put down the paper, and desired Christian to get the phaeton ready. His wife was rather uneasy because she had no idea what he was going to do, but as soon as she saw that his mouth was even more drawn down to the left than usual, which was his way of giving a friendly smile, she said to herself: "Let him be, he has got some kindly thought in his head."--Three days later Joseph returned, bringing with him a shadowy lady of a certain age, and the news spread like wild-fire: "Only think, young Joseph has engaged a governess by himself this time!"--Bräsig came on the following Sunday and looked her over, he was pretty well satisfied with her, "but," he said, "mark my words, young Joseph, she has got nerves."--Bräsig had not only a great knowledge of horses, he had also a knowledge of men, and he was right. Mademoiselle had nerves, many nerves. The twins had to go about the house on tip-toe. Mademoiselle took Mina's ball away from her because she had once thrown it against her window by mistake, and locked the piano to prevent Lina playing, "Our cat has nine kittens," the only air which Miss "Jack in the box" had taught her.--

In course of time Mademoiselle had fits of rigidity in addition to her nerves, and Mrs. Nüssler had to rush and administer all sorts of reviving drops to her, and Frida and Caroline had to sit up with her at night, for one would have been afraid to do it alone. "I should send her away if I were you," said Uncle Bräsig, but Mrs. Nüssler was too kind-hearted to do that, she sent for the doctor instead.--Dr. Strump came from Rahnstädt, and when he had looked at the clenched teeth of the patient, he said it was a very interesting case, and explained it by saying that he had lately been studying "The night-side of human nature."--Young Joseph and his wife thought no evil, except that they had been obliged to get up in the night several times, but something else was to come.--One day when the doctor was there Caroline rushed down-stairs: "Mistress, Mistress, the illness is at its height. The doctor has been waving his hands before Mamselle's face, and now she's prophesying, and she's telling the truth too. She told me that I had a sweetheart."--"Heaven preserve me!" said Bräsig who happened to be there. "The young woman ought to be in an asylum!"--And then he followed Mrs. Nüssler upstairs.--After a little he came down again, and asked: "What do you say *now*, young Joseph?"--Joseph sat silently thinking for some time, at last he said: "It's no use, Bräsig."--"Joseph," said Bräsig, striding up and down as he spoke, "I advised you to send her away before, but now I say, *don't* send her away. I asked her what sort of rain we shall have to-morrow, and she answered in her sun-and-bulist state, that we should have a regular plump. If there is a plump tomorrow, take your perometer down from the wall--perometers are of no more use, and yours has been standing at 'set fair' for the last two years--and then you can hang her in its place, and so make the fortune of the whole neighbourhood."--Young Joseph made no reply, and when he saw how frightfully it rained the next day, he still said nothing, but pondered over the marvellous circumstance for three days in silence. The news, meanwhile, spread throughout the countryside that young Joseph had engaged a prophetess, and that she had prophesied the heavy rain which had fallen on the previous Saturday, and also that Caroline Kräuger and Mr. Farm-bailiff Bräsig should be married before the year was out.--Naturally Dr. Strump was not behind-hand in publishing the details of the interesting case he was attending, and before long Mrs. Nüssler's quiet house became the meeting-place of all the neighbourhood, every one going there either from curiosity or to study the case from a scientific point of view; and as Mrs. Nüssler would have nothing to do with it, and young Joseph would have nothing to do with it, Zachariah Bräsig took the case in hand when the doctor was not there, and conducted the visitors up-stairs to Madmoiselle's apartment, and explained the nature of somnambulism to them. Christian, the coach-man, held watch by Madmoiselle's bed, because he was so brave that he did not fear the devil himself, and Caroline and Frida were too frightened to remain in the room, even in company, and indeed they did not consider it a proper occupation for them, for they thought a somnambulist must be a very wicked person.--Amongst the visitors was the young Baron von Mallerjahn of Gräunenmur, who came every day to enquire scientifically into the affair, and who at last used to go up to see Madmoiselle without waiting for Bräsig. Mrs. Nüssler was very angry when she found out that he did so, and told Joseph that he ought to be present at the interviews, but her husband answered that Christian was there, and so there was no need of him. At last however Christian came down, and said that the young Baron had turned him out of the room because he smelt too strongly of the stable, and that made Mrs. Nüssler cry with anger, and if Bräsig had not appeared at that moment she would herself have ordered the Baron out of the house, but Bräsig of course undertook to do it for her. He therefore went up-stairs, and said politely, but firmly: "My lord, will you be so good as to look at the other side of the door?"--The Baron seemed to understand what was meant, for he smiled rather constrainedly, and said that he was just then in magnetic rapport with Mademoiselle. "What do you mean by a 'monetary report?'" said Bräsig, "we want none of your money here, nor your reports either; that's the reason that Christian was told to sit here."--Now Bräsig was, without knowing it, in magnetic rapport himself, for whenever he saw Mrs. Nüssler shed tears, it put him in a rage, so he now ended by saying angrily: "And now, Sir, I must beg of you to go at once."--The Baron was naturally put out at being addressed in such an unceremonious manner, and asked haughtily, if Bräsig knew that he was extremely rude.--"If you call that rude," cried Bräsig, seizing the Baron by the arm, "I'll soon show you something else."--The noise they made wakened Mademoiselle from her sleep, she started up off the sofa, and, seizing the Baron by the other arm, declared that she would remain there no longer; no one understood her except him, and she would go with him.--"That's the best thing to do," said Bräsig. "One ought always to speed the parting guest. Two flies at one blow!" he concluded, showing them down-stairs.

The Baron's carriage drove up to the door, and the Baron himself looked nervous and uncomfortable, but Mademoiselle was determined. "Well, well, what's to be done now?" said young Joseph as he watched the departure from the window.--"Young Joseph," said Bräsig as the carriage drove out of the yard, "it all depends upon circumstances, and it's hard to say. And, Mrs. Nüssler, let them be, the Baron will soon find out now how to manage his monetary report."

For some time past Hawermann had been a great deal from home on his master's business, and when he returned for a few days he had too much to do about the farm to have time to attend to anything else. He had, it is true, gone to see his sister once or twice, and had comforted her by assuring her that the governess was ill, and would of course soon get well again, but once when he came home he found that the doings at Rexow were the talk of the whole neighbourhood. He was told that young Joseph's sleeping Mademoiselle had run away with the Baron von Mallerjahn, and that before she left she had infected Bräsig with the gift of prophecy, and Christian with that of sleeping, so that Bräsig now prophesied as he went about, and Christian could sleep standing.

Hawermann went to Mr. Behrens, asked him to tell him the rights of the story, and to accompany him to his sister's house. "With pleasure, Hawermann, I'll go with you gladly," said the clergyman, "but, to tell you the truth, I have not taken any notice of the affair on principle. I know that many of my brethren in Christ have tried the effect of exorcism when such cases have fallen under their notice, but in my opinion, in illnesses of this kind, the doctor is the proper person to consult, and sometimes," he added with a sly smile, "the police are of more use than any one else."

When they reached Rexow, they found Mrs. Nüssler, who was generally able to see the bright side of everything, looking sad and weary. "Oh, Mr. Behrens! My dear brother Charles!" she said. "That was a dreadful woman, and I have been in great distress about her, but indeed, all the governesses that I have tried have been dreadful people. That isn't the worst of it. I shall get over that in time. What makes me miserable is that my dear good little girls know nothing, and are learning nothing. I can't bear to think that the time may come when my children may have to sit silently amongst other young people of their own age and standing, because they are too ignorant to join in the conversation, and that perhaps they won't even be able to write a letter! Ah, reverend Sir, you who are so learned can't understand how bitterly one feels one's ignorance when one is in the company of people of one's own station who have been properly educated, but I can understand it, and so can you, Charles. Oh, Mr. Behrens, I'd rather send my little girls away to school, though it would break my heart to part with them, and Joseph and I would feel lost in the house without them, than that they should grow up stupid and ignorant. When Louisa comes here she can answer our questions sensibly, and she can read Joseph's newspapers. Mina can also read, but when she comes to a foreign word she has to spell it out. The other day Louisa read to us about 'Bordoe,' and that I suppose is the right way to call the town, but Mina said 'B-o-r-d Board, e-a-x oaks,' and what was the sense of calling it 'Boardoaks' when it is always pronounced 'Bordoe?'"

During this long address of Mrs. Nüssler's the clergyman rose, and walked thoughtfully up and down the room, at last he stood still and said: "I have a proposal to make to you, neighbour. Perhaps Louisa is farther advanced than your children, perhaps not. You need not part with your little girls, if you will send them to me, and let me teach them."--Whether Mrs. Nüssler had an undefined hope that her difficulties would be ended in this way, or whether it was an utter surprise to her, cannot be known, but this at any rate is certain, that the relief was like a sudden turning from darkness to light. She looked at the pastor with her frank blue eyes, and exclaimed: "Oh, Sir!" and springing from her chair she went on: "Joseph, Joseph, did you hear? Mr. Behrens says he will teach our little girls!"--Joseph had heard, and had also risen. He wanted to say something, but not being able to find the right words he just tried to seize the clergyman's hand, and when he had got hold of it, he pressed it, and drawing Mr. Behrens to the sofa, made him sit down by the little supper-table, and then when Mrs. Nüssler and Hawermann had told the good man how happy he had made them all, young Joseph said: "Mother, give the pastor a glass of beer."

So Mina and Lina became daily guests at Gürlitz parsonage. They were still as like each other as two peas, except that Lina as the eldest was a small half inch taller than Mina, and Mina was a good half inch rounder than Lina, and, if you looked *very* particularly, you could see that Mina's nose was rather more of a snub than Lina's.

And now we return to when the three little girls were having their sewing-lesson in Mrs. Behrens' parlour, on the day that the Pomuchelskopps came to pay their first visit at the parsonage, for as soon as the clergyman had finished his morning-lessons, his wife began her share of the children's education.

"Goodness gracious me!" cried Mrs. Behrens, running into the parlour. "Put away your sewing, children. Louisa, carry it all into my bed-room. Mina, pick up all the threads and scraps that have fallen on the carpet. Lina, put the chairs in order. The new squire is coming through the church-yard with his wife and daughters, and will be here in a minute--and my pastor hasn't come back from the christening at Warnitz!" As she spoke, she involuntarily caught up her duster, but put it down again immediately, for there was a knock at the door, and on her calling out "come in," Pomuchelskopp, his wife, and his two daughters, Amalia and Rosalia entered.

Pomuchelskopp tried to make a polite bow as he came in, but failed, owing to his style of figure being of the unbending order, and said: "We have done ourselves the honour of waiting upon Mr. and Mrs. Behrens--and--and--hope to have the pleasure of making their acquaintance, now--now--that we are such near neighbours."--Mrs. Pomuchelskopp stood behind her lord as stiff and straight as if she had swallowed the poker, and Mally and Sally in their bright silk dresses looked, in contrast with the three little girls in their washed out cotton-frocks, like gay butterflies beside common grubs.

Now although Mrs. Behrens was very confidential with her friends, her manner to strangers was rather formal, and in her husband's absence it was even more dignified than it would otherwise have been, so she drew herself up, and her lilac cap-ribbons rose and fell under her firm little chin with every word she spoke, as much as to say, "I am a person to be treated with respect."--"The honour," she said, "is on our side. I am sorry that my pastor is not at home.--Won't you sit down?"--And she signed to Mr. and Mrs. Pomuchelskopp to seat themselves on the sofa under the gallery of portraits, and the picture of our Saviour with His hands raised to bestow the blessing, which, like the rain and sunshine, falls alike on the just and the unjust.

While the elder people talked about indifferent subjects upon which there could be no diversity of opinion, Louisa went up to the two young ladies, and shook hands with them, and the twins followed her example.--Now Mally and Sally were eighteen and nineteen years old, but they were not at all pretty, for Sally's complexion was of an unwholesome greenish gray colour, and Mally was her father's own child. They had--alas--quite finished their education, and had been at the Whitsun and Trinity balls in Rostock, so that their interests were of course far removed from those of the little girls, and as they were not particularly good-natured, they rather snubbed the children. And the little girls either not wishing it to be remarked, or thinking it was all right and proper, would not allow themselves to be repulsed by cold answers, and Louisa said to Mally with great eyes of admiration: "Oh, what a pretty dress you have on!"--All ladies however highly educated are pleased with remarks of this kind, so Mally thawed a little, and answered with a smile: "It is only an old gown, my new one cost thirty shillings more with the trimming and making."--"Papa gave us our new dresses for the Trinity ball. Oh, how we did dance to be sure!" added Sally.--Louisa knew the proper services for Trinity Sunday, but she had never in all her life heard of a Trinity ball, and besides that, she had no very clear idea of what a ball was, for although Mrs. Behrens had often spoken of what she had done in the days of her youth, and had also confessed to having been at a ball, still when Louisa asked what a ball was, she answered with all the dignity of a clergyman's wife, that it was "a very silly kind of amusement," and alluded to the subject no more.--Lina and Mina knew even less about it than she did. Their mother had of course danced now and then when she was a girl, but only at dances got up on the spur of the moment; and as for young Joseph, he had certainly been at a ball once, but then he had stopped at the door of the dancing-room, for he was so overwhelmed with shyness when he got there, that he beat a speedy retreat without venturing further; and uncle Bräsig had described it to them in a totally incomprehensible manner, as a number of white dresses with red and green ribbons, clarionets and flutes, waltzes and quadrilles, and a great many glasses of punch. When uncle Bräsig told them this, he used to show them, with his own short legs, the difference between a glissade and a hop, and that made them laugh heartily, and was great fun, but what it all had to do with a "ball," a ball such as their last governess had taken away from Mina, they could not comprehend.

Mina therefore asked with great simplicity: "Do you play with a ball when you are dancing?"--This question showed what a stupid innocent little thing Mina was, but as she was the youngest and most inexperienced of the party, it was unkind of the Miss Pomuchelskopps to laugh at her as they did. "Well!" said Rosalia, "that is really too silly!"--"Dear me, how very countrified!" said Mally, drawing herself up, and putting on the high and mighty manner of a town-lady, and looking as if she wished it to be supposed that she had been accustomed to see Rostock cathedral out of her nursery-window from the time of her babyhood, and as if she and his worship, the mayor, had been old play-fellows.--Our poor little Mina blushed as red as a peony, for she felt that she must have said something very foolish indeed, and Louisa reddened with anger, for she could not bear to hear any one laughed at. She did not mind it so much for herself, but when one of her friends, any one whom she loved was treated so, it made her tingle all over.--"Why are you laughing?" she asked quickly. "What is there to laugh at in our not knowing what a ball is?"--"Look, look! What a rage she's in!" laughed Mally.--"Dear child ....." she could not finish her sentence, for Mr. Pomuchelskopp just then said excitedly: "I think it is very wrong, Mrs. Behrens. I am the squire of Gürlitz, and if your husband wanted to let the glebe....."--"My pastor has let it, and Mr. von Rambow is an old friend of ours, and his estate, which marches as well with our land as Gürlitz does, is also in this parish, and then Hawermann, his farm-bailiff ....."--"Is a cunning rascal," interrupted Pomuchelskopp.--"Who has cheated us once already," added his wife.--"What?" cried little Mrs. Behrens. "What?" She then stopped short, for she remembered that Louisa was present, and she was afraid of the child hearing and being hurt by what was said, so she contented herself with making signs to her visitors to change the subject. But it was too late. Louisa had heard, and was now standing before the surly looking man and his cold-hearted wife: "*What* did you call my father? *What* has he done?" And the gentle little creature who until that moment had lived in peace with all men, was filled with burning wrath against her father's slanderers, and her eyes flashed as she looked at them.--It is said that the beautiful green earth will one day burst out in fire and flame, and bury the work of men's hands and the temple of God in ashes.--It was much the same with the child, a temple of the living God that she had loved and revered was threatened with destruction, and her sorrow found relief in an agony of tears as her good foster-mother put her arm round her, and led her from the room.

Muchel looked at his Henny, and Henny at her Muchel; he had got into a nice scrape now. It was quite a different thing when one of his labourer's wives came to him weeping tears of blood, and told him a dismal tale of starvation and misery, he knew what to do to get rid of the woman, but now he could not think of anything to say or do, and as he looked about him awkwardly he caught sight of the raised hands in the Saviour's picture, and then he suddenly remembered one of the lessons he had learnt in his boyhood, that Christ had once said: "Suffer the little children to come unto Me, and forbid them not: for of such is the kingdom of Heaven."--He felt extremely uncomfortable. And even his brave strong-minded Henny was quite confounded; she had children of her own, and had often heard them cry when she punished them, but this was different; her Mally and Sally had often looked at her with angry eyes, and had stamped their feet at her with rage, but this was different. She soon recovered herself however, and said: "Don't look so idiotic, Kopp. What was that she said about her father? Is Hawermann her father?"--"Yes," wept Mina and Lina, "she is Louisa Hawermann," and then they left the room to join their tears with those of their school-fellow, for though they did not know how deeply their little cousin felt the blow she had just received, still their love and sympathy were so great that they longed to comfort her.--"I didn't know that," said Pomuchelskopp, using the same words that he had done eleven years before when told of the death of Hawermann's wife.--"A spoilt child!" said his Henny. "Come, Mally and Sally, we will go, I don't think that Mrs. Behrens intends to come back to us."--And so they departed like the year 1822, of which, to carry out the illustration, Henny might be called the 1, because she was always number 1 in her own estimation; Pomuchelskopp the 8, because of his round portliness, and the daughters the 2s, for they resembled, to my mind, the figure 2 that a goose makes when it is swimming in a pond.

Just as they left the house Mr. Behrens came back from Warnitz, accompanied by uncle Bräsig. He knew from the dress of the Pomuchelskopp family that they had come to pay a visit of ceremony, and hastened from the carriage that he might speak to them before they left. "Ah, how do you do! But," he added in astonishment, "where is my wife?"--"She went away and left us," said Mrs. Pomuchelskopp shortly.--"There must be some mistake," he said, "pray come in, and I will rejoin you in a few minutes." He went away to look for his wife.--Meanwhile Bräsig had approached his old acquaintance Pomuchelskopp. "Good morning, Samuel. How are you?" he said.--"Thank you, Mr. bailiff Bräsig, I am very well," was the answer.-- Bräsig raised his eye-brows, looked him full in the face, and whistled, and when Mrs. Pomuchelskopp curtsied to him before going away, she might have spared herself the trouble, for he had already turned his back upon them, and was entering the house. "Come, Kopp," said his wife crossly, and they went home.

Mr. Behrens found no one in the house; so he went into the garden, and shouted, and very soon the twins appeared, red-eyed, from behind the raspberry hedge. They pointed to the hornbeam arbour with anxious faces, as much as to say that he would find the cause of their sorrow there. He went to the arbour, and there he found his Regina sitting with Louisa on her knee, comforting her. As soon as she saw her pastor she put the child gently on the bench, and, drawing him away to a short distance, told him all that had happened.

Mr. Behrens listened silently, but when his wife repeated the cruel words that Mr. Pomuchelskopp had used in speaking of Hawermann, his face flushed with anger, and his eyes were full of a deep compassion, he then asked his wife to return to the house, for he would like to speak to the child alone.--His beautiful human flower had now been hurt for the first time, she had had her first blow from the pitiless world, a blow that her gentle heart would never forget as long as it continued to beat; she had now taken her place in the eternal battle of existence that will last as long as the human race. It must have come--it must have come to that at last, no one knew that better than he did, but he also knew that the great object of those who undertake the education of a human soul is to preserve it from such rude experiences until it has grown strong to bear, so that the blow may neither strike so deep, nor the wound take so long to heal--and this child knew nothing of the malice and uncharitableness of the world.--He entered the arbour.--Thou art still happy, Louisa, in spite of all that has come and gone, for it is well for him who in an hour like this has such a true-hearted friend by his side.

Mrs. Behrens found Bräsig in the parlour. Instead of sitting on the sofa, or on a chair like a reasonable mortal, he had perched himself on the edge of the table, and was working off the excitement caused by Pomuchelskopp's snub, by throwing his legs about like weaver's shuttles. "He had me there!" he muttered. "The Jesuit!"--When Mrs. Behrens came in, Bräsig got off the table, and exclaimed:[7] "What is it, when one has called a man by his Christian name for forty years, and when one on meeting that man addresses him as one has been accustomed to do, and meets with a frigid 'Mr. Bailiff Bräsig' in return?"--"Ah, Bräsig ....."--"That is what Pomuchelskopp has just done to me."--"Let the man alone! Just fancy what he did here," and then she told the whole story. Bräsig was angry, very angry, he rushed up and down the room puffing and blowing, and making use of such strong language that Mrs. Behrens would have bidden him be silent, if she had not been in as great a rage as himself; at last he threw himself into a corner of the sofa, and stared moodily at the opposite wall without uttering another word.

The clergyman soon afterwards joined them, and his wife looked at him enquiringly. "She is watering the flowers," he said with a reassuring smile, and then he began to pace the room thoughtfully. At length, turning to Bräsig, he said: "What are you thinking about, my friend?"--"The punishment of hell--I am thinking of the punishment of hell, reverend Sir."--"And why?" asked Mr. Behrens.--Instead of answering, Bräsig sprang to his feet, and said: "Is it true, Sir, as you once told me, that there are mountains that vomit fire?"--"Certainly," said the pastor.--"And is it a good or bad thing for man that they do so?"--"The people who live near these mountains regard it as a good thing, because it saves them from having such violent earthquakes."--"Ah, well," said Bräsig, apparently rather dissatisfied with the answer he had received. "But," he asked, "do the flames come out of a mountain such as that in the same way as out of one of our chimneys when it is on fire?"--"Something like it," replied the clergyman, who had not the faintest idea what Bräsig was aiming at.--"Then," said Bräsig with a stamp of his foot, "I wish that the devil would seize Samuel Pomuchelskopp, and put him on the top of a horrible fire-spouting mountain such as you have described, and roast him there for a little."--"Ugh!" cried little Mrs. Behrens. "Bräsig, you are nothing better than a heathen. How dare you express such a wish in a Christian parsonage?"--"Mrs. Behrens," said Bräsig, throwing himself once more into the corner of the sofa, "it would be a benefit to humanity, and it is just the sort of benefit that I should be the first to grant to Samuel Pomuchelskopp."--"Dear Bräsig," remonstrated the clergyman, "we must not forget that when those people spoke so offensively they did not intend to hurt our feelings."--"It's all the same to me," answered Bräsig, "whether they intended it or not. He enraged me intentionally, and what he said here unintentionally was a thousand times worse than that. Reverend Sir, it is quite necessary to get angry sometimes, and indeed a good farmer ought to be angry two or three times a day, it is part of his work, but of course I don't mean a regular passion, just enough vehemence to show the labourers that one is in earnest. I will give you an instance. I told the carters yesterday when I was top-dressing a field with marl, that I wished them to drive their carts in regular order. Then I took my station by the marl-pit, and saw that everything was done properly. Well, what do you think happened? That scoundrel, Christian Kohlhaas--he's as stupid as an ox--came up with his cart still full of marl! Why, you great ass, I said, what are you doing here with your full cart? And the silly fellow looked me full in the face, and said: he hadn't time to put the marl on the field before the other carts left, and so, as he had been desired to keep the line unbroken, he had just come away with his load.--Wasn't that enough to make me angry? I was rather angry, but, as I said before, one's rages are as different as their causes. An official outburst, such as I have described, does one good, especially after dinner, but this!--Pomuchelskopp and a farm-labourer are two very different people. This is horrible, most horrible, and you'll see, Mrs. Behrens, that I shall have another attack of that confounded gout."--"Bräsig," entreated the little lady, "will you do me a great favour? Don't tell Hawermann anything about what has happened to-day."--"What do you take me for, Mrs. Behrens?--But now I will go and comfort the child Louisa, and I will tell her that as true as the sun shines, Samuel Pomuchelskopp is an infamous wretch of a Jesuit."--"No, no," interrupted Mr. Behrens hastily, "don't do that. The child will get over it, and I hope that it has done her no harm."--"Well then, good-bye," said Bräsig, picking up his cap.--"Dear me, Bräsig, ar'n't you going to remain to dinner?"--"Thank you very much, Mrs. Behrens. There is a difference. I said that anger was good *after* dinner, not *before*, it does me harm then. I shall just go to work at the marl-pit at once; but take care, Christian, I advise you not to try that dodge again with the full cart!--Good-bye." And so he went away.

CHAPTER VI

Hawermann never heard of what had happened at the parsonage, but from that day his daughter was even more loving and tender to him than before, as if she had determined that her love should wipe away the scandalous words that had been spoken regarding him. Mrs. Nüssler of course heard all about it from her children, but she had not the heart to trouble her brother by telling him what would so sorely distress him; the clergyman and his wife were silent for the same reason, and also because they hoped that the circumstance would die out of their foster-child's memory, if it were never alluded to; Joseph Nüssler said nothing, and Bräsig held his tongue as far as Hawermann himself was concerned, but he indemnified himself for his silence, and for the sharp attack of gout which came on the day after the scene at the parsonage, by nearly raising the country-side against the Pomuchelskopps, who so little understood how to gain the love and good will of their neighbours, that they soon made themselves as disagreeable in the eyes of those who lived near them as my wife's[8] floors just before Whitsuntide--well-polished and shining as they are at other times.

Pomuchelskopp looked upon his surroundings as a great garden in which he might plant his self-esteem. Whether it gave him shade or flowers he did not care; as long as what was sowed there flourished and grew apace, it mattered not to him what form it took. He had come to Mecklenburg for two reasons: firstly, because he thought the purchase of Gürlitz a good bargain, and secondly, because he had an exalted idea of his future position as justice of the peace. "Henny," he said, "every one has the upper-hand of us here in Pomerania, and the Sheriff is all-powerful, but in Mecklenburg *I* shall be one of the law-givers. And besides that, I've always heard that if rich men of the middle-class only stick to the aristocracy through thick and thin, they receive a patent of nobility after a time. Only think, Chuck, Mrs. von Pomuchelskopp!--how would you like that? One mustn't crow too small in this world!"--That was a sin of which he never was guilty. He gave up his chief delight of making a great show with his money for fear of having to do it in the company of tenant-farmers and bailiffs, and he addressed old Bräsig coldly and distantly, and paid a visit of ceremony to Bräsig's master, the Count, instead of to his old acquaintance. He put on his blue coat with the brass buttons, and drove to Warnitz in his grand new carriage drawn by four brown horses, and when he got there he was as much out of place as a pig in a Jew's house. As soon as he reached home again he seated himself crossly in the sofa-corner, and flapped at the flies. His wife who was always loving to him when he was in a bad-humour, asked him: "What is the matter with you. Pöking?"--He growled out in reply: "What should be the matter with me? It isn't me, it's those confounded aristocrats who are friendly one moment, and turn a cold shoulder on one the next. He offered me a chair, and then asked me very politely how he could be of service to me--I didn't want his help, I'm better off than he is--but I couldn't think of anything to say at the moment, and the silence grew so frightful that there was nothing for it but to go away."--Notwithstanding this repulse Pomuchelskopp did not crow any lower; he hung on the skirts of the aristocracy as closely as the tail to the sheep, and though he had not a penny to give any of his own people when they were in distress, or to the poor artisans in the town who were often nearly starving, he always had plenty of money for any extravagant young sprig of the nobility who asked him for it; and though he prosecuted any poor man without mercy who ventured to cross one of his corn-fields, yet he gave Bräsig's master, the Count, leave to hunt over his land in harvest-time; and though he treated his clergyman scandalously with regard to the Easter-lamb, he allowed the Count's keepers to shoot a roe-deer at his very door without a word of remonstrance. Yes, Samuel Pomuchelskopp had high aims!

Hawermann kept out of his way, for he was of a quiet disposition and disliked quarrelling, he was contented with his lot, and had plenty to do. He felt like a storm-tossed mariner who had at last reached port, and he had nothing to trouble him but anxiety about his master's affairs.--A short time before he had received a letter with a black seal, and written in an unknown hand, in which the Squire informed him that he had had a slight stroke of paralysis, and had lost the use of his right hand, and that a still greater misfortune than even that had happened to him, his wife had died suddenly, and when apparently quite well. Then he went on to say that his nephew, Frank, might be expected at Pümpelhagen at the Michaelmas term to begin to learn farming, adding: "he wishes to put his own hand to the work, and to learn everything thoroughly, and I think he is right." These were the words the Squire had dictated to his secretary.--A few weeks later Hawermann got another letter in which Mr. von Rambow informed him that he had given up his government appointment in Schwerin, and intended to take up his abode at Pümpelhagen after Easter with his three unmarried daughters, he could not come before that, because he must spend the winter in Schwerin to be near his doctor. He then desired his bailiff to see that the manor-house was put in a thorough state of repair.--Of course, this change made a great difference to Hawermann, even though he had done nothing to make him fear his master's eye, and though he took great interest in all his concerns, yet he could not help thinking that the quiet simple tenour of his life would be changed, and besides--was not this the precursor of a still greater change?

Michaelmas came, and brought with it Frank von Rambow. He was by no means a handsome young man, but he was strong and healthy, and on looking closely at his grave face, one saw that his eyes had a very good-natured expression; the shade of melancholy which was often to be seen on his countenance was perhaps caused by his having lost both his parents in his childhood, and therefore feeling himself alone in the world. He was no genius, but he possessed sound good sense, and had made the most of his opportunities; he had passed through all the classes of the High School with credit, and had been thoroughly prepared for the University, but, above all, he had learnt what would be useful to him all his life long--to work! He might be likened to a young tree that had been grown in a nursery-garden in poor soil, whose stem had matured slowly, but was strong and good, whose top was firm and upright, and whose branches were spread out equally on every side, so that when the time came for it to be planted on other ground, it could stand by itself without artificial support, and the gardener said: "Let it be, it is straight and true to a line, it needs no stake to keep it steady."

Frank von Rambow, whom Hawermann remembered as a three years old child, was now twenty years of age, and had steady principles, views and opinions such as few other young men in the province were possessed of. He had two large estates, which had been completely freed from debt during his long minority. Of course, he could not remember the time when Hawermann was in his father's service, but he had been told how fond of him the bailiff had always been, and when a single-minded, good-hearted man knows that he sees before him one who has carried him in his arms when he was a little child, an involuntary feeling of trust and confidence in the man comes into his heart, and it seems to him as if the intervening years had passed away, and he were a child again, seeing the old sights and dreaming the old dreams.

And Hawermann returned the young man's trust and affection with all his heart. Carefully and patiently he taught his pupil the work he had come to learn, he showed him how to manage matters in byre and field, told him why he did this or that, and tried to make everything easy to him; but he found that his pupil would not have things made too easy for him, that he was determined to learn everything practically, and so he gave him his wish, and said of him what the gardener had said of the tree; "Let him be, he needs neither prop nor support."

A new inmate was soon to join this quiet couple, and bring life and excitement with him, and that was Fred Triddelfitz. As soon as Triddelfitz, the apothecary in Rahnstädt, who was brother-in-law of Mrs. Behrens, heard that Hawermann was teaching a young man farming, he took it into his head that his son Fred, a fine lad of seventeen, should also profit by Hawermann's lessons. "The higher branches of farming are all that I require," said Fred, "for I was twice at Möller's in the dog-days, and helped to lead in the corn there."

Little Mrs. Behrens refused to have anything to do with the arrangement, for she knew her nephew, and did not wish to trouble Hawermann with the charge of him, but her brother-in-law would not leave her in peace till she undertook the business. Hawermann would have gone through fire and water for the clergyman's family, but he could make no promise till he had consulted his master. He therefore wrote to Mr. von Rambow, and told him that young Triddelfitz was only in the third division of the High School, that his head was full of nonsense, but that he was a good-hearted lad all the same; still his principal merit was that he was nephew of the clergyman's wife to whom he, Hawermann, owed so much as the Squire already knew; besides that, the father offered fifteen pounds a year for his son's board. Would Mr. von Rambow allow Fred Triddelfitz to learn farming on his estate on these terms?--The Squire wrote to say that he would not hear of receiving money for the youth's board, that the fifteen pounds was to pay for the teaching he got, and that was Hawermann's business, not his. If Hawermann liked to do it, let him do it in God's name.--It was a great pleasure to Hawermann to be told this, he could now do something, however small, to show his gratitude to Mr. and Mrs. Behrens for the great service they had done him, and so he consented to receive Fred without the payment of any fee.

Fred Triddelfitz arrived. But how did he come? Being the only son of his mother--she had two daughters besides--he was so grandly got up for his new mode of life that he might have passed for a farmer's apprentice, a grain-merchant, a commercial-traveller, a farm-bailiff, a tenant-farmer or a country-gentleman, according to the part he was called upon to play, or as his own fancy dictated. He had kid-boots, and leather-boots, laced-boots, top-boots and high-lows; he had dressing-slippers, dancing-shoes, and shoes that came up well about his instep; he had buttoned leggings, leggings for riding in, and other kinds of leggings; he had evening-coats, linen smock-frocks, tweed-coats, and pilot-jackets, he had greatcoats, waistcoats, and water-proofs, and it would be impossible to mention the names of all the various kinds of trousers and breeches with which he was provided.--This outfit arrived at Pümpelhagen one beautiful morning in a number of huge boxes, together with a feather-bed and an enormous davenport; the carrier at the same time gave the pleasing intelligence that the young gentleman might be expected at any moment, for he was on the road, and his arrival had only been delayed by a slight difference between him and his father's old sorrel-horse which he was riding; the horse refused to go further than Gürlitz parsonage, because he had never before been required to do so. How the battle would end the carrier did not know, for he had left it still undecided, but the young gentleman was coming all the same.

The carrier's information was correct, the young gentleman came; but how did he come? He was dressed as grandly as if he had been the agent of two large estates, and had been asked by his master, the Count, to join his great hunting-party; he had on a green hunting-coat, white leather-breeches, boots with yellow tops, and spurs, and over all he wore a water-proof, not because it looked like rain, no, but because it was a new kind of dress, and he wanted to hear what people said about it. He was riding his father's sorrel-horse, and it was easy to see that they were not on the best of terms with each other. The sorrel had come to a stand in the middle of the large pond in front of the parsonage, and had refused to move to the great terror of little Mrs. Behrens, but at last after a struggle of about ten minutes, Fred got the mastery by the aid of his riding-whip and spurs, and now when he dismounted at Pümpelhagen his new water-proof was coated with mud. The sorrel stood quietly in front of the door of the home-farm at Pümpelhagen, stared straight before him, and asked himself: "Is *he* a fool, or am I one? I am seventeen years old, and so is he. I am of a reddish brown colour, and so is he. He got his own way to-day, but I'll have mine next time. If he ever attacks me with whip and spur again, I'll just lie down quietly in the pond."

When Fred Triddelfitz entered the room where Hawermann, young Mr. von Rambow, and the housekeeper Mary Möller were seated at dinner the bailiff was startled, for he had never seen his new pupil before. Fred, in his new green hunting-coat, looked exactly like an asparagus stalk that had run to seed, he was so small and thin in the waist that any one could easily have cut him in two with his own riding-whip. It was quite true as the sorrel-horse had said, that he had red hair, his cheek bones were high, his face freckled, and his manner self-confident and bored. Hawermann could not help saying to himself: "Heaven preserve me! Am I to teach this young fellow? It's all up with me now!"--He was roused from his disagreeable reflections by a great shout of laughter from Frank von Rambow in which Mary Möller joined, secretly and holding her table-napkin up to her face to hide that she did so.--Fred, wishing to talk down their laughter, had just begun: "Good morning. Sir, I hope I see you well," when he caught sight of his old school-fellow at Parchen, Frank von Rambow, who was in convulsions of laughter; he looked at him rather sheepishly at first, but after a moment joined heartily in the laugh against himself, and even grave old Hawermann laughed till the tears rolled down his cheeks.--"Why," cried Frank, "whatever induced you to get yourself up so grandly?"--"One should do everything in style!" said Fred, whereupon Mary Möller once more disappeared behind her table-napkin.--"Come, Triddelfitz," said Hawermann, "sit down and have some dinner."--Fred did so, and anyone would have said that the rascal was in luck, he had begun his country life at the best time of the year for food, when geese were in season, and as it was Sunday, a finely browned roast goose was on the table, so that his first experience of a farmer's life might well be a pleasing one to him. He did not spare the goose in any way, and Hawermann thought that, if he sat on horseback as he did at table, if he paid as much attention to the labourers as he did to the goose, if he understood foddering a horse as well as feeding himself, and if he swept everything under his charge as clean as his plate, he might expect him to be a great acquisition to the place.

"Now, Triddelfitz," said Hawermann as soon as dinner was over, "go to your room and change your clothes, and don't forget to wrap up your grand riding-costume carefully for fear the moths should get at it, for you won't want it again during the first two years that you are here. We don't ride here, for all our work can be done on foot, and I do any riding that may be necessary myself, when it is convenient."--Fred soon returned to the parlour wearing good strong leather boots, breeches, and a sort of pilot-jacket made of grass-green cloth.--"That's better," said Hawermann, "now come with me and I will show you what we are doing."--They went out.--Next morning Fred went with seven of the young men and women who worked on the farm, along the Rahnstädt road to open any drains that were blocked up and so let the water run off wherever it had collected in pools--what made this occupation especially unpleasant was that it was a November day, and that a small persistent rain was falling.--"Hang it all!" said Fred Triddelfitz, "I never thought that it would be as bad as this."

One Sunday afternoon, about a fortnight or so after his arrival, Bräsig rode up to the farm. Fred had by this time grown so far accustomed to his position with Hawermann, to his monotonous employment, and to the everlasting rain, that he was able partly to understand his duties as a farming apprentice, and with his customary good nature had begun to pay all sorts of little attentions to everyone about him. So when he saw Bräsig ride up to the door, he ran out to meet him and take his horse; but Bräsig shrieked out: "Keep away from me. Don't touch me. Keep ten feet away from me.--Let Charles Hawermann come out and speak to me."--Hawermann came: "Why don't you dismount, Bräsig?" he asked.--"Don't help me down, Charles--

just fetch me a soft chair, so that I may dismount gently and gradually, and then put a sheep-skin mat or something soft beside the chair for me to step upon, for I've got that confounded gout again."--Everything was done as he wished. Foot-stools were laid from the chair to the door, and then he slid slowly and carefully from his saddle, and limped into the parlour. "Why didn't you let me know you were ill, Bräsig, and I'd have gone to see you with pleasure?"--"It wouldn't have been of any use, Charles, I had to crawl out of the hole myself. But I came to tell you that I've given up all hope."--"Of what?"--"Of marrying. I intend to accept the pension that the Count promised me."--"I think that I should do the same in your place, Bräsig."--"Your advice is very good no doubt, Charles, but it is hard for a man of my age to give up the darling wish of a life-time, and go to a water-cure place, for it's there Dr. Strump wants to send me. I don't have Dr. Strump to attend me because I believe that he knows how to cure me, but because he suffers from that wretched gout himself, and when he's sitting beside me talking learnedly about the benefit to be derived from taking Polchicum and Colchicum, I feel comforted by the thought that such a clever man has gout as badly as myself."--"Then you are going to a water-cure establishment?"--"Yes, but not till spring. I've arranged all my plans. I'll just manage as well as I can this winter; in spring I'll try the water-cure, and at the midsummer term I'll retire on my pension, and go to live at the old mill-house at Haunerwiem. I thought at first that I'd go to Rahnstädt, but I shouldn't have a free house there, and I'd have found a leg of mutton now and then too expensive a luxury to be indulged in."--"You're quite right, Bräsig. It's much better for you to remain in the country and near us; indeed I don't know what I should do if I hadn't a sight of your honest old face every few days."--"Oh, you wouldn't miss me much, you have so many people about you, especially these two lads. And that reminds me, there was another thing I wanted to say to you. Old Bröker in Kniep, and Schimmel in Radboom want you to teach their sons fanning. I should consent to take them if I were you, and by adding a room or two to the old farm-house you'd be able to set up quite an aquademy of agriculture."--"You're joking, Bräsig! I've enough to do with the two pupils I have already."--"Do you think so? I hope they are well."--"Yes. You know them both, and I want you to tell me what you think of them."--"I can't give any opinion as yet, I must first see their way of going on. The first thing to teach a young farmer is what a colt is always taught, to lead with the right foot. Look, there's your young nobleman, call him here that I may have a better sight of him."--Hawermann laughed, but agreed to Bräsig's proposal and called Frank von Rambow. "Hm!" said Bräsig, "he walks steadily and not too hurriedly, and doesn't put off time with looking about him, but goes straight to the point. He'll do, Charles. Now for the other!"--"Mr. von Rambow," asked Hawermann when the young man had come up to the window, "where is Triddelfitz?"--"In his room," was the answer.--"Hm!" said Bräsig. "Is he resting?"--"I don't know."--"Tell him to come down," said Hawermann, "and you'd better come back soon yourself, for coffee will be ready immediately."--"Charles," said Bräsig, "you'll see that the apothecary's son is sound asleep this afternoon."--"Never mind if he is, Bräsig, he was up very early this morning giving out the feeds of corn for the horses."--"He oughtn't to do it, Charles, young people get into the habit of sleeping in the afternoon only too easily. Ah, there he is. Send him past the window that I may get a good side view of him!"--"Triddelfitz," cried Hawermann, putting his head out at the window, "go to the stable and tell Joseph Boldten to have a pair of horses ready to drive Mr. Bailiff Bräsig home later in the afternoon."--"Bon," said Fred Triddelfitz, and then he set off at a good swinging pace along the causeway.--"Bless my soul!" exclaimed Bräsig. "What a high action the fellow has! Look at him, did you ever see such loose joints, soft muscles, and thin flanks! You'll have to feed him up for a long time, Charles, before he has what can be called a body. *How* he's getting over the ground! He's a quick dog that, a regular greyhound, and you'll soon have your hands full with him I wager."--"Ah, Bräsig, he's so young. He'll soon quiet down."--"Quiet? Sleeps after dinner? Says 'bong' when you send him a message? And, look there--yes--he's coming back without ever having been at the stables at all!"--"Didn't you say, Sir, that Joseph Boldten was to drive?"--"Yes," cried Bräsig sharply, "Joseph Boldten is to drive, and is not to forget what he is told.--Don't you see now that I was right, Charles?"--"Oh, Bräsig," said Hawermann, who felt rather cross with Fred for his stupidity, "let him be. We're not all alike. He'll do well enough if he only pays a little more attention to what he is told."

Hawermann seldom lost his temper, when he felt inclined to be cross he struggled against the feeling until he conquered it. In spite of the other ills of life which often filled his heart, such as care and anxiety, he always refused Captain Cross-patch admittance, and if ever he succeeded in making good his entrance, whispering ill-natured remarks and lies in his ear, he showed him the door at once and bid him begone, so that it was not long before he got rid of the intruder on this occasion also, and was able to enjoy a confidential chat with Bräsig which lasted till his friend went home.

CHAPTER VII

The winter passed without the occurrence of any event of particular interest. Hawermann was accustomed to the monotony of his life, and was perfectly contented with it as far as he himself was concerned; but the young people sometimes found it dull and lonely, especially Frank von Rambow, for Fred Triddelfitz had his aunt at the parsonage, and his dear mother a little further off at Rahnstädt, to say nothing of the housekeeper, Mary Möller, who was close at hand, and who comforted him in his loneliness with many a savoury morsel of spiced goose, or sausage, so that there was soon a secret understanding between them. Sometimes they treated each other like mother and son, for Mary Möller was seven years older than Fred, she was *quite* four and twenty; sometimes a more tender sentiment was infused into their intercourse, for Mary Möller was *only* four and twenty, and Fred had always studied novels more diligently than Latin grammar when he was at school; indeed he had been a regular subscriber to the circulating-library, and was therefore quite up to the most approved method of conducting an affair of the kind. Besides that, his father's last words to him when he left home were: Learn everything practically, a piece of advice which Hawermann was also continually dinning into his ears, so he thought a love-affair might be as useful to him as any other branch of knowledge, and--do not misunderstand me, no harm was done--so it was, in providing him with an abundant supply of spiced goose and sausages.

Hawermann therefore had not to find amusement for Fred, but Frank was different, as he knew no one. Hawermann took him to call on Mr. and Mrs. Behrens, and when Christmas came he offered to take him to the parsonage, as Fred was in Rahnstädt with his mother. Frank accepted the invitation. It was splendid weather for sledging, so they drove down to the parsonage, where they found little Mrs. Behrens standing sentry by the parlour door to prevent them going in: "No, Hawermann, no! You mustn't go in there. Mr. von Rambow, may I ask you to go to my pastor's study."--And the moment they entered the study Louisa sprang to her father, kissed him, and told him in a whisper what presents she had prepared, and where she had hidden them, what she was going to do, and who was to act the part of Julklapp[9], so that she had only time for a passing bow to Mr. von Rambow. The clergyman however shook the young man warmly by the hand, and told him how glad he was to see him in his house on this festival day. "But," he added, "we must do as we are bid this evening, my wife is commander-in-chief to-day, and her love of rule is never so strongly developed as on Christmas-eve"--He was right there, for Mrs. Behrens popped her head in at the door every moment to say: "Be patient for one minute. Pray sit still, the bell is just going to ring," and then she rushed through the study with a blue paper parcel hidden under her apron, and next moment she might be heard laughing in the parlour.

At last the bell rang, the door flew open, and--ah!--there was the fir-tree standing on the round table in the centre of the room, and under it were arranged as many plates of apples, nuts, and gingerbread-nuts as there were people in the house, and two extra ones, one for Hawermann, and the other for his pupil. Mrs. Behrens bustled round the table, seized Hawermann and Mr. von Rambow by the hand, and, leading them up to the table, said: "This is your plate, and that is yours. Louisa and my pastor will be able to find their own for themselves," then turning round, she called out: "Come in," and the pastor's man, George, and her own two maids, Rika and Dolly, appeared in the door-way, ready to take their part in the rejoicings of the evening, "Come in, that's your plate with the half-crown stuck in the apple, and those with the red shawls are for the two maids, and the one with the red waistcoat is for George. And Louie ...," she got no further in her speech, for Louisa rushed at her with a cherry-coloured woollen dress in her hand, seized her round the neck, and stopped her mouth with kisses: "Mother, how good of you!" And now I must needs confess with sorrow that little Mrs. Behrens so far forgot herself as to tell a fib, not in words, but by nodding and winking at her pastor; so Louisa sprang to her foster-father, and exclaimed: "It was you who gave it me!" but Mr. Behrens shook his head, and replied that he was innocent of the charge. Then she threw her arms round her own father's neck, saying: "It was you, it was you." But the good old bailiff confessed with a sad smile that he had had nothing to do with it, and there were tears in his eyes, when after having stroked her hair fondly, he took her by the hand and led her to Mrs. Behrens, saying: "This is the person you have to thank, Louie," but the clergyman's wife was too busy at that moment at least to listen to thanks, for she called her husband to come and try on his new dressing-gown to see how it fitted him, and asked whether it was not lucky that she had fixed upon a new dressing-gown for his present, instead of the pair of trousers she had at first thought of. And as the dressing-gown fitted beautifully and was very becoming, she went back a few steps, and looked at her husband in the same way as a child, who has put her new doll in the sofa-corner that she may examine it from a little distance. When she turned round she saw a blue paper parcel lying on her plate, which Mr. Behrens had placed there unnoticed by her. She seized upon it, and while untying the string, wondered audibly what it could contain, and said she felt certain some one had been playing her a practical joke; at last the paper was removed, and there was a beautiful piece of black silk, enough to make a dress!--Every one was happy: Hawermann had found a new pipe on his plate, which he filled and began to smoke; the pastor had placed himself in the sofa-corner in his new dressing-gown, and rejoiced in seeing the happy faces around him; Mrs. Behrens and Louisa found it impossible to sit still, but were continually moving about the room, and holding the materials for their new dresses under their chins to see how they would look when made up, and stroking them to show how smoothly they would lie. Frank on the other hand withdrew a little into the background oppressed by the sad feeling that he had never known a happy home-like Christmas-eve. He rested his head on his hand as he thought that when kind friends and relations had asked him to spend his Christmas-holidays with them, he had there most of all missed the presence of the originals of the two portraits over which he had placed garlands of *immortelles*. He felt that he belonged to no one in this house either, but he must not destroy the pleasure of others by showing his sadness, and with a great effort he forced himself to look up and smile, and as he did so he found Louisa's large beautiful eyes fixed on him full of sorrowful sympathy as if she had been able to read his very heart.

"Julklapp!" cried Rika in her loud voice, and a parcel flew in at the door addressed to "Mrs. Behrens." It was a pretty ruche, and no one knew who had given it. And "Julklapp!" was shouted again. It was a beautifully worked cushion for Mr. Behrens' arm-chair this time, and of course nobody had had anything to do with it--Oh, what fibs were told at the parsonage that evening!--And "Julklapp!" A letter was thrown into the room which told of another letter that was to be found upstairs in the garret, and that told of another in the cellar, and that one of another, and again another ..... in short, if Mrs. Behrens wished to get a very pretty embroidered collar which was intended for her, she would have to run all over the house, and would at last find it close at hand in the cupboard where her husband kept his boots.--And "Julklapp!" It was a tremendous package this time, with Mr. Behrens' name upon it, but when the outer covering was taken off it was addressed to Mrs. Behrens, and then to George, and then to Rika, and last of all to Louisa, and when the last paper was taken off a small worktable was displayed, such as Hawermann had given his wife years ago.--No one knew that, however, but himself.--And "Julklapp!" Books for Louisa.--And "Julklapp!" A worsted-work footstool for Hawermann.--Rika acted her part to perfection.--But now it was all over and she came in to collect the bits of paper and string that were scattered over the floor; but the door opened again suddenly and unexpectedly, and "Julklapp!" cried a clear sweet voice, and when they looked at the packet they saw that it was addressed to "The honourable Francis von Rambow." Immediately afterwards Louisa slipped softly into the parlour from the study, her face beaming with happiness.

Frank was overwhelmed with confusion, but when he opened the parcel, he found a letter from his youngest cousin Fidelia, which informed him that she and her two unmarried sisters had each sent him a Christmas present. Alberta gave him a sofa-cushion, though he never lay on the sofa; Bertha--a saddle-cloth, though he had no horse, and Fidelia--a cigar-case, though he never smoked.--But what of that? They were all things that might have been useful, and it is the giver, not the gift that one thinks of at Christmas.--He no longer felt himself so much alone in the world, and when he saw how much Louisa rejoiced for him, he quite recovered himself and laughed and joked about his presents, and whether Louisa would or not, she had to receive his thanks for them, for he had recognised her voice when she threw in the parcel.

Rika then came back, and said: "They are all here now, ma'am."--"Then we'll go to them," answered Mrs. Behrens.--"No, dear Regina," said her husband, "let them come in here."--"But," she remonstrated, "they'll bring in so much snow on their boots."--"Never mind that," said the clergyman, then turning to the maid, "you won't object to get up a little earlier than usual to-morrow morning to put the room in order again, will you, Rika?"--No, Rika would do that with pleasure, and so the door was thrown open and in streamed, one after the other, all the little children in the village, flaxen heads, black heads and all! There they stood rubbing their noses, staring with great eyes at the apples and ginger-bread-nuts, and opening their mouths widely, looked as if they wished to show the good things on the table the way in which they ought to go.--"Now," said Mrs. Behrens, "let all our god-children stand in the first row. You know, Hawermann," she added, "that we, that is, my pastor and I stand nearest to our god-children after their own parents,"--More than half of the children came forward, for Mr. and Mrs. Behrens had stood sponsor for the greater number of the little boys and girls in the village. An impostor took his place amongst the rest, Joseph Rührdanz by name; he had noticed on the preceding year that the god-children got more presents than the others; but Stina Wasmuth saw what he was about, and pushed him away, saying: "You are not a god-son, boy!" so he slunk back unable to carry out his deception.

Mr. Behrens came forward with a pile of books under his arm, and he gave a hymn-book to each god-child whom he was preparing for confirmation, and to the others he gave copy-books, and slates, and primers and catechisms as they were most wanted, and each of the little ones said: "Thank you, god-father," but those who got the hymn-books said: "Thank you very much, reverend Sir," for they were older than the others.--Now it was Mrs. Behrens' turn. "Come," She said, "I'll take the nuts; Louisa there's the ginger-bread for you, and Mr. von Rambow, please take the basket of apples, and let us go down each row.--Arrange yourselves in line, children, and have your dishes ready."--There was so much pushing and shoving that this was a work of time, for everyone wished to be in the first row,--at last they were all ready with their dishes in their hands. The little girls held their aprons up at the corners, but the boys were provided with anything and everything that would hold their cakes and fruit; one had a tin measure; another a flour bowl; another his father's hat, and another with quiet self-possession held up a great five bushel sack in the firm persuasion that it would be filled to the very top.--Now the division of the spoil began.--"Look! here, here, here--stop!" cried Mrs. Behrens as she reached a mischievous looking little lad, "this boy is to have no apples, Mr. von Rambow, for he helped himself in the garden last summer."--"Oh, ma'am!"--"Boy, didn't I myself chase you out of the big apple-tree near the wall with a pitch-fork?"--"Oh, Mrs. Behrens!"--"No, no, the boy who steals apples, gets none given him at Christmas."--The division went on quietly again till they came to Joseph Rührdanz, when the clergyman's wife stopped, and said: "Wasn't it you who fought with Christian Casbom last week at the parsonage gate, till Rika had to go out and separate you?"--"Yes, ma'am. He said to me ...."--"Hush!--Louisa, Joseph is to have no gingerbread."--"But, ma'am, we've made it all up again."--"Ah then, Louisa, you may give him the gingerbread."--At last the fruit and cakes were all distributed, and the children went away with their share, each merely saying; "Good-night, good-night," for it was not the fashion amongst them to say thank you.--No sooner were they gone than a different set of people came in coughing and scraping. They were the old spinning women, and the old brush-binders and wooden-shoemakers &c., in fact everyone in the village who was too old and frail to work any more. Mr. Behrens said a few kindly words of help and counsel, which were well received, and his wife gave them each a tea-cake which they were also glad to get, and as they went away, they prayed that the "blessing of God" might rest on their pastor and his family.

At last, George, the clergyman's man-servant, and Hawermann brought the sledge to the door, and then the two guests said good-bye. Hawermann's first action before driving away was silently to take off the sledge-bells, for the great bells in the church-tower were ringing out their message to the whole world, while the sledge-bells only kept up a merry tinkle for the high road. They drove through the village at a foot's pace, and as they passed along they heard a sweet Christmas Carol rising from many a labourer's hut and ascending to the quiet heavens where God had placed the lights of His great Christmas tree, under which the earth was stretched like a table covered with the pure white cloth of snow that winter had spread over it, and which spring, summer and autumn were in turn to deck with flowers and fruit in due season.

They drove slowly out of the village, and when they came to the turn of the road, Frank caught sight of Pomuchelkopp's manor house with its brilliantly lighted windows: "They are keeping Christmas there too," he said.--Yes, presents were given and received there, but Christmas was not kept.

Pomuchelskopp had bought everything in Rostock, nothing in Rahnstädt. "One should always do things in style!" he said, and then he told how much he had paid for Mally's and Sally's new dresses, and when Sally heard that Mally's had cost six shillings more than hers, she was jealous of her sister, and Mally thought herself much better than Sally. Then Phil and Tony quarrelled about a sugar doll, and when Pomuchelskopp decided the dispute in favour of his pet son Phil, Tony lost his temper and struck at Phil's head with his toy whip, but instead of striking his brother, he hit the large mirror so hard that it was broken in pieces; so Henny called order, and taking the tawse out of the cupboard, punished Tony first, because of his naughtiness, and then Phil, and lastly the other boys to keep them company. She did not call her husband, Pöking, once during the whole evening, no, not even when he gave her a new winter-bonnet trimmed with ostrich feathers, she only said, as she took it: "Do you want to make a guy of me, Kopp?"

When Frank went to bed that night he confessed to himself that he had never spent such a pleasant Christmas in his life before, and when he asked himself the reason, the sweet face of Louisa Hawermann appeared before his mind's eye, and he said to himself: "An innocent happy child like that makes a merry Christmas."

Something very unusual happened between Christmas and New-year's-day. Joseph Nüssler drove up to the farm at Pümpelhagen in the phaëton and wearing an enormous blue cloak with seven capes.--He could not get out of the carriage, he said, for he had been away from home for a good hour and a half, and had only called to say that the clergyman, and his family and Bräsig were coming to a party at his house on Sylvester's day, and that he wanted his brother-in-law to join them with his two young people, and he, for his part, would as host provide a good bowl of punch for the evening's entertainment. As soon as he had finished this long speech, he shut up completely, and when Hawermann had accepted his invitation, and

Christian had begun to turn the carriage, he merely muttered something like: "Good-bye then, brother-in-law," from beneath the seven capes, so Christian turned his head round and called out: "The mistress told me to say that she expected you to come to coffee."

Frank wrote and told Fred, who was still in Rahnstädt with his mother, of the invitation, at the same time telling him that as his holiday was over he had better go straight to Rexow on the last day of the year, and then he could return to Pümpelhagen with Hawermann and him in the evening.

A regular thaw had set in before Sylvester's day, and when Hawermann and Frank arrived at the muddy farm-yard at Rexow, they saw Joseph Nüssler standing in the doorway with bent knees. He was dressed in the black coat and trousers that his wife had given him at Christmas, and as he had put on the red cap which Mina had crocheted for his Christmas present, he looked in the distance exactly like a stuffed dignitary of the church. Bräsig, however, pushed him out into the yard, saying: "Show yourself, Joseph. Do *les honours* properly, so that Charles' young nobleman may see that you know something of life."

As soon as Joseph had got over his labours of receiving the company, and Mr. and Mrs. Behrens had arrived and had spoken to the twins, Mrs. Nüssler took her brother aside and told him how the farm had been paying that year; Mr. Behrens entered into conversation with Mr. von Rambow; his wife talked to the little girl about their Christmas presents; Joseph seated himself in his old corner by the stove and said nothing, and Bräsig went about from one group to another, his feet and legs incased in seal-skin boots that came up as high as his waist, as though Christmas were come again and he were going to act Ruklas[10] to frighten the children.--The sun shone in at the window and gilded the steam that curled from the coffee-pot, and the thin cloud of smoke from the clergyman's pipe, reminding one of the light fleecy clouds which float upon the summer sky, but a black wintry storm-cloud rose from behind the stove, for Joseph was sitting there smoking as though for a wager.--Fortunately for those present, his wife had taken the precaution of emptying his tobacco-pouch of the twist he kept there, and of putting a very mild kind of tobacco in its place, but he had been so long accustomed to the hard work of smoking the coarse native tobacco he was in the habit of using, that he thought the same exertion was necessary with the mild foreign tobacco he had now in his pipe. Outside the house black clouds were gathering on the horizon, but no one in the cosy parlour was troubled by thoughts of a coming storm.

Mrs. Nüssler's parlour-maid now came in, and telling her mistress that a carter had just brought a box from the apothecary in Rahnstädt, asked where it was to be put.--"Good heavens!" cried Mrs. Behrens, "it will be Fred's clothes. My dear pastor, you will see that my brother-in-law has been so foolish as to let the boy ride again, and on that wild sorrel horse too that no one else has ever ridden!"--"You needn't be anxious, Mrs. Behrens," said Hawermann with a half laugh he could not suppress, "the sorrel isn't so bad as you think."--"Oh, but Hawermann, when he was riding to Pümpelhagen before, I saw how the horse stood still and refused to move."--"Ah," said Bräsig "the mere obstinacy shown by the beast is nothing, the danger is, that when the young rascal conquers, the horse generally starts forward suddenly, and then the rider is apt to lose his balance and tumble off."-- But little Mrs. Behrens was not to be comforted by what Bräsig told her, she opened the window and asked the carter whether Fred was riding, and whether the horse was wild.--"As quiet as a lamb," was the answer, "and if he lets the horse alone, it'll let him alone. He isn't far off now."--That was a pleasant piece of news, and Mrs. Behrens seated herself on the sofa again with a sigh of relief, saying: "Ah me, I always tremble for my sister's sake when I see that boy. He's continually getting into some stupid scrape or other."--"You may depend upon that," said Bräsig.

They were both right. In the short time, between Christmas and New-year's-day, he had got into no end of scrapes, and all of them in his grand new clothes too, for in spite of the bad weather he wore his green hunting-coat, white leather breeches, and top-boots regularly every day, and sometimes even during the night; that is to say, that on one occasion when he had remained till a late hour at a supper-party composed of merry young farming apprentices as great dandies as himself, he was found lying on the top of his bed with his boots and spurs on by the servant when she took him his hot water in the morning.--Some people might be inclined to laugh and shrug their shoulders, but the fact of the matter is, that at this party, Fred had happened to meet his old friend Augustus Prebberow, who had been going about in top-boots for a year and a half longer than himself, and that the joy of seeing his old friend again, and the highly intellectual conversation in which he had taken part, had rather overcome him. Augustus Prebberow had taken the opportunity of giving him a great deal of good advice as to how he ought to behave to his "governor"--that was what he called Hawermann, and what was the best way of managing his governor, and then he had gone on to give him examples from his own experience, of the proper way to treat the bondager-lads, how to make them go head over heels, climb a greased pole, &c. &c. As soon as they had exhausted that branch of farming they had turned the conversation to horses. Fred had then told the whole of his experience with the sorrel. He had taken care to explain that the sorrel was a good horse, but that as his father, the apothecary, who had had him since he was a foal, loved him as the apple of his eye, he had never cared to cure him of his tricks, and now the horse had grown obstinate in his own opinion, and thought he knew better than anyone else; but that he, Fred, was determined to teach him better manners. His chief fault was that he absolutely refused to go a step further when he had taken it into his stupid old head that he had done enough, and that then neither working the bit, nor tche-tcheing, neither whip nor spur made the slightest impression on him.--"And you really allow that?" Augustus had asked. "Well, then I'll tell you what to do next time. Take a large jug of water with you, and ride on quietly till he comes to a stand-still and refuses to move--listen--pull at the bit, give him the spur, and fling the jug of water between his ears--all at the same time you understand--so that the crockery should break on his head and the water run into his eyes."

When Fred set out for Rexow he remembered this piece of advice, and determined to try whether it would really succeed. So off he set, the reins in his left hand, the whip under his left arm, and a large jug quite full of water in his right hand. Of course his progress was only at a foot's pace, for if he had gone fast he would have spilt the water, and as the sorrel was too old to care about going quickly everything went well till they reached the farm-yard at Rexow. Fred then wished to turn his gallant steed down the drive leading to the front-door, so he gave the sorrel a touch of the spurs in his ribs, and immediately the horse stopt as though rooted to the spot; whether it was only his way, or whether he was a sly dog and remembered what had happened at the parsonage-pond is more than I can tell. Now was the time for Fred to try his stratagem. He jerked the bit, used his spurs energetically, and dashed the jug of cold water between the horse's ears. "Ugh!" grunted the sorrel with a shake of the head, to show that he had no intention of moving on, but was quite contented to remain where he was, and then he sank down gently and quietly to the ground where he stretched himself out at full length. Fred was obliged to follow his example, for though he had sufficient presence of mind to free himself from the stirrups, still he could not help falling beside his horse.

The company assembled in Mrs. Nüssler's parlour had seen the whole dispute between Fred and the sorrel, and little Mrs. Behrens trembled for her sister's darling when she saw Fred raise himself in his stirrups, and fling the great kitchen-jug at his opponent, but when she saw the sorrel's gentle reproof, and her nephew lying on the soft but slightly cool "bed of honour" which Heaven had covered with a coating of mud, made by the rain and thaw, and which Joseph Nüssler had also aided to soften with his farm-carts, she could not help joining in the hearty fit of laughter with which the rest of the party had greeted Fred's down-fall. She then said to her husband: "It will do him a great deal of good!"--"Yes," said Bräsig, "and a cold in the head will do him no harm either. What business had he to treat the poor old beast so shockingly."

Fred approached like the half-moon, one side shining and brilliant, the other dark, and gloomy. "What a mess you've made of your clothes, my dear boy," cried his Aunt from the open window. "Don't come into the parlour in that state. Fortunately your box has arrived, so you can easily change your things."

This was done, and then Fred made his appearance in his grandest clothes: a blue cut-away coat and black cloth-trousers, and went about the room with all the airs and graces of a young squire, though inwardly he was fretting and fuming over Bräsig's pointed jests and Mrs. Behrens' remarks. Frank on the contrary was in high spirits, he talked and joked with the three little girls, got the twins to let him see their Christmas presents, and laughed, heartily when Lina and Mina showed him two great flannel-bags which uncle Bräsig had given them "to keep their extremities warm, and so prevent them having gout before their time." He had never before been in the society of girls younger than himself, and was so pleased with the innocent confidences made to him by these three little maids, that when supper-time came he seated himself beside the children, and when Mrs. Nüssler asked him to take his proper place near the head of the table, he begged to be allowed to remain where he was.

It was a merry supper-party, every one except Fred and Joseph took part in the conversation. Fred was cross and uncomfortable, and was angry with himself for not being able to talk and laugh like Frank. Joseph was also silent, it is true, but then he was always ready to laugh, and if Bräsig so much as opened his mouth, he prepared to join in the burst of laughter which was sure to follow. When the punch was placed on the table, Lina, as the steadiest of the two sisters, was chosen to dispense it to the company, and her father recovering speech for the time being, and determining to do his duty as host, said, or rather murmured: "Give Bräsig some punch, Lina."--The punch helped Fred also to find his tongue, though it did not improve his temper. He was displeased with Frank's way of behaving, and thought that though the little girls were quite children, they ought on this occasion to be treated like grown-up young ladies, and have a higher sort of conversation addressed to them, he therefore took up the same theme which he had found answer at the Rahnstädt ball when he was dancing the cotillion with the mayor's daughter, a lady of five and twenty. "Miss Hawermann," he began. The child looked at him in astonishment, and when he once more said: "Miss Hawermann," she burst out laughing, and said: "I'm not Miss, I'm only Louisa Hawermann!" And Frank could not help joining in her merriment.--Disagreeable as this was, Fred was too well aware that his behaviour was correct, to be much put out by the reception it met with, he therefore proceeded to describe the ball he had been at in Rahnstädt, and to repeat what he had said to the mayor's daughter, and what she had said to him, and as he did so he addressed the twins as well as Louisa, taking care to call them "Miss Nüssler" and "Miss Mina Nüssler." As every one at table was talking and laughing, he raised his voice higher and higher, till at last there was dead silence all round him, and every eye was fixed on him in astonishment. Joseph, who sat beside him, drew back a little, and stared at him in blank amazement, that any one man could pour forth such a stream of words. Bräsig peered round the corner at him from behind Joseph, and winked at Hawermann as much as to say: "Didn't I tell you, Charles, that he was a regular greyhound?"--Hawermann kept his eyes fixed on his plate, and looked angry. Mrs. Nüssler was anxious and ill at ease, feeling that as hostess it would hardly do for her to desire her guest to be quiet, and to choose a different style of conversation. The pastor shook his head gravely, while little Mrs. Behrens gave more decided tokens of disapprobation by burying her chin in her breast till her cap-ribbons were almost lost to view, and by flouncing up and down on her chair as if it were too hot for her; but when Fred began to describe the schottish, and told how the gentleman puts his arm round the lady's waist, she started up exclaiming: "Don't any of you speak! I'm his Aunt, and am therefore the nearest to him. Come here Fred."--And when Fred rose slowly, and approached her with an air of high-bred nonchalance, she seized him by the lappel of his coat, and pulling him towards the door, said: "Come, my dear boy, come away with me," and so left the room with him. They could all hear the murmur of Mrs. Behrens' voice as she lectured her nephew, her words flowed on uninterruptedly in spite of his protestations until she had finished what she wanted to say, when she reopened the door, and leading Fred into the room, pointed to his chair, and said: "Sit down there, and speak like a reasonable mortal."

Fred did as he was bid, that is to say, he obeyed the first command; the second was too hard for him. How was it possible to talk sensibly after having begun by talking sentimentally, and so make a flat ending to a well begun conversation.--Frank and the three children gradually resumed their former merry talk, while the older people spoke about graver subjects, and so the conversational coach rolled on smoothly, except when Bräsig drove it against a stone with a sudden jerk. Mrs. Behrens managed to act the part of moral policeman towards the offender while taking her full share in the conversation of the elders, and Fred sat silently fuming, and pouring punch, like oil, on the flames of his wrath, internally stigmatising Frank as a "sneak," and the little girls as "silly baggages," who understood nothing of the ways of polite society.

But notwithstanding the contempt he felt for the society of such mere children, he was seized with a certain feeling of jealousy, when he saw, as he imagined, that Frank liked talking to Louisa Hawermann best of all, he made up his mind to put an end to that state of things, and to try what he, Fred Triddelfitz could do, that is to say, when his aunt was not there.

Meanwhile it had grown very late without anyone having noticed how quickly time was flying, when suddenly a terrible form was seen standing in the parlour; it was dressed in warm patch-work garments, and blew a loud blast on the cow-horn it held in its hand, and then began to ring still more discordantly. It was Augustus Stowsand, a half-witted fellow who lived on the estate, and whom Joseph Nüssler, having no other use for him, had made night-watchman. The serving men and maids peeped in at the open door to see how he got on, and giggled, and pushed each other forward, and drew each other back. Everyone began to wish everyone else a happy new year, and then as soon as quiet was restored, the pastor made a little speech which began jestingly, and ended seriously. He reminded his auditors that every year they were nearer death than before, and that every year they might have the comfort of making new ties of friendship and love, and of drawing the old ones tighter. And when he looked round the room on the conclusion of his address, his little wife threw her arms about him; Mr. and Mrs. Nüssler drew closer to each other, Hawermann and Bräsig clasped hands; the twins embraced, and Frank stood by Louisa Hawermann's side. Fred was nowhere to be seen, his bad temper had conveyed him out of the room.--Thus ended the year 1839.

CHAPTER VIII

Bräsig set out on his journey to the water-cure establishment[11] at Easter, and at the same time Mr. von Rambow and the three daughters arrived at Pümpelhagen.--"I fear that there's no chance of his ever getting better," said Hawermann to himself when he saw the squire, and Frank was of the same opinion, and as they sat together on the evening of the family's arrival, they talked sadly of what was surely coming, and the next day when Frank had, as was natural, gone to live with his uncle and cousins at the manor-house, Hawermann felt the old farm-house dull and empty without him, for he had grown to love his pupil.

The neighbours all came to call on the squire during the first week after his coming home. Pomuchelskopp amongst the number. He was dressed in his blue coat with the brass buttons, and drove up to the door in his grand new carriage which looked, even more imposing than before, because of the coat-of-arms on the pannels. He had paid half a sovereign to a man in Vienna for the arms, which were a cod's head on an azure field, but the stupid labourers who knew nothing about cod-fish, and who perhaps saw a certain resemblance between the coat of arms and their master, always spoke of it as a "fool's head on a blue ground." Pomuchelskopp had given up all thought of being on visiting terms with Bräsig's master the count, and there were no other members of the aristocracy in the neighbourhood, so he rejoiced in Mr. von Rambow's coming to Pümpelhagen; but he met with a disappointment. He told the old butler, Daniel Sadenwater, in a tone of heart-felt anxiety of his distress where he heard of Mr. von Rambow's illness, and how he could not resist coming to enquire after him personally, adding that he had known the squire well in Rostock. Daniel listened with stolid gravity, and then went to tell his master who it was that had called, he returned in a few minutes, as stolidly grave as before, and said that the squire regretted that he did not feel well enough to admit visitors. Pomuchelskopp was very much put out by this, and spent the rest of the afternoon sulking in his favourite sofa corner, and his wife, who was always loving and tender to him at such times, called him "Pöking," which must have gone a long way towards making up for his disappointment.

Mr. von Rambow required no other society than he had at home. His two elder daughters had no other thought from morning to-night than how best to nurse and take care of him, and the youngest, who was the pet and darling of the whole family, and who was perhaps a little spoilt, and rather too young and girlish for her age, did her utmost to cheer and amuse him. Frank had constituted himself his uncle's secretary, and besides that took care to smooth down all the small worries that necessarily arise in a household so conducted as that at Pümpelhagen, especially when there is illness in the family; but Hawermann above all was of service to the squire, who could not do without him, and who consulted him about many things which did not properly fall under his jurisdiction. So it happened that Hawermann had no time to go down to the parsonage, and if Louisa wanted to see him she had either to join him in the fields, or to come up to the farm-house when he was in at dinner. Miss Fidelia von Rambow sometimes met her at such times, and as was natural took a fancy to her, for young maids and old maids like each other's society, and women who have not yet left early youth very far behind them, are refreshed and attracted by the youthfulness of girls who are standing on the brink of womanhood, and thus it was that the child and the young lady soon became fast friends. I cannot answer the question whether it is good for a young girl to be on intimate terms with a woman much older than herself with the customary "yes," for it depends very much on the character of the elder lady whether such a friendship does good or harm, but in this case Louisa was not hurt by it. Miss Fidelia was good and true, and was unusually free from the small vanities of good society, and although her mother used to be distressed at it, as tending to unfit her for taking her proper place in society, her father rather encouraged her in her inartificial ways. Unfortunately, however, it was his fault that she was somewhat gushing, and that she would never grow any older than she was, for she had always had to laugh and coax away his cares and troubles, and so had, unconsciously, retained ways and manners only suited to a very young girl. The business of the day engaged her attention too much to allow of Louisa taking part in her vagaries or copying her ways, and her companionship had a salutary effect, for Louisa was of a thoughtful disposition, and had sufficient good sense only to learn those pretty gracious little ways which were in keeping with her own character. There was give and take on both sides.

If Louisa did not know the ways of good society, Miss Fidelia knew as little about the ways of the world in which she was now living, and Louisa was often of great use to her in that respect. A disagreeable thing happened to the young lady about this time. Her father had sent for a beautiful new chess from Schwerin for a birthday-present for her; Alberta gave her a summer-hat, and Bertha, a shawl. When the things arrived the two elder sisters at once began to dress their darling in her new clothes, and then standing round her, looked at her from head to foot, and admired her in her finery, and Bertha exclaimed: "What a little *fée* she is!"--Now Caroline Kegel, the housemaid, happening to be in the room at the time, and having nothing particular to do, went downstairs to the kitchen, and said: "Girls, only fancy. Miss Bertha says that our little Missy looks like a 'little quey'!"[12]--Of course this was too good a joke to be allowed to die out, and before long Miss Fidelia was known by no other name than the "little quey." This went on for some time, but at last it reached the young lady's ears, and then there was great displeasure shown, and after due enquiry Caroline Kegel was dismissed from the house in an agony of tears.--Louisa coming to call met Caroline walking down the steps roaring and crying, and on going into the house found Miss Fidelia crying in her room. One word led to another, and as soon as Louisa understood what was the matter, she felt very sorry for both of them, and laying her hand on the young lady's shoulder, said: "The servants meant no harm."--"Yes," cried Fidelia, "they did, they did. They are rude coarse creatures."--"No, no, don't say that," Louisa entreated. "Our servants are not rude, they have as tender hearts as the higher classes. As my father says, they only require to be known to be valued, and it is difficult to do that, for their language separates them from their masters."--"That's got nothing to do with it," cried Fidelia, "'little quey' is a rude coarse expression."--"It was a misunderstanding," said Louisa, "the country-people had never heard the word '*fée*' before, and as they have a word which sounds something like it, 'quey,' they thought that was what your sister meant, and naturally it struck them as being very odd. They never intended to hurt your feelings.--You are loved by all your servants."--This last piece of information, which Louisa did not mean as flattery, but merely as a statement of fact, went a long way to destroy the impression that the nick-name "little quey" had made on the young lady, and when she went on warmly and impressively to describe what Mr. Behrens, who knew the people in their joys and sorrows, had told of their loyalty and depth of feeling, Fidelia was quite appeased, and regained her natural good-humour. She said that she was determined to try to know and understand the people about her, so that she might not misjudge them for the future, and then she took Caroline Kegel into favour again.

Fidelia questioned Frank on the subject, and he praised the peasantry of Pümpelhagen highly. The squire also bore witness to the good character of his people, and went on to say that the forefathers of his vassals had lived under his ancestors from time immemorial. The first Mr. von Rambow of whom anything was known had two serving-men, one of whom was called

"Äsel" and the other "Egel"--so the story goes at least. In course of time the descendants of these two men grew and multiplied, and many mistakes were made amongst the "Äsels" and "Egels." One Egel often got a bushel of rye that was intended for another Egel, and one Äsel a good beating which another Äsel should by rights have had. These mistakes increased in number during the rule of one of his ancestors who--he confessed it with shame--was troubled with a short memory, and came to such a pass that the Mrs. von Rambow of that day, who was much cleverer than her husband, could stand it no longer.--A good plan occurred to her, and as her will was law in the house she had power to carry it out. One Sunday morning she called together all the householders in the village, and asked each of them his Christian name and surname. These she wrote down--for she knew how to write, and then taking the first letter of the Christian name, she added it to the surname, and so rechristened the whole village: for instance: "Korl Egel," became "Kegel;" "Pagel Egel," "Pegel;" "Florian Egel," "Flegel;" and "Vulrad Äsel," "Väsel;" "Peiter Äsel," "Päsel," and "David Äsel," "Däsel," &c. &c. &c. "And," the squire went on, "it is a very remarkable fact that according to tradition the forefather of the line of 'Egel' had flaxen hair, while the first of the 'Äsels' had black hair, and this is still a characteristic of their descendants. Besides that, they have kept up their family talents as well as their family looks: old documents tell us that the original Egel was very skilful in making trowels, spoons, rakes and sabots, while the first Äsel had a wonderfully fine voice for singing, and so it is to this very day, and that is why my ancestors and I have always been particular in choosing an Äsel as night-watchman, and an Egel as wheel-wright. And so Fidelia," he said in conclusion, "you will find that the night-watchman is David Däsel, and the wheel-wright, Fritz Flegel."

Miss Fidelia was delighted with this story, and having a great deal of time on her hands, the whim seized her to visit all the labourers' cottages, and when there she hindered the women at their work with her idle chatter, and distributed her cast off finery amongst the children. Indeed, if Louisa had not interposed, she would, on one occasion, have presented Päsel's Molly, a child of eleven, with an old veil and a hat trimmed with ostrich-feathers, and another time, she wanted to give Däsel's Chrissy, whose work it was to take the geese down to the pond, a beautiful pair of pale blue satin-shoes.

The village fathers shook their heads gravely over this state of matters, but the mothers were better pleased with it, "for," they said, "if she's a little weak-minded, still she's good and kind," and instead of calling her "little quey" as they had done at first, they had now no other name for her but "nice homely little quey."

Parson Behrens shook his head also when he heard of this kind of beneficence. He said that the Pümpelhagen peasantry were the best in his parish because they had always been under the rule of the same family, and had always been treated justly and kindly, while the Gürlitz villagers had been spoilt by a constant change of masters. He was well aware that nothing is so hurtful to the character as receiving lavish and undeserved benefits, and therefore determined to speak to the young lady. He did so on the first opportunity, and explained to her that the Pümpelhagen vassals were so well off that unless any of them were thrown out of work by age or ill-health, or had lost their cattle by an epidemic, they were quite able to support themselves, and added that indiscriminate alms-giving only taught people to rely upon outside help instead of on their own exertions; he showed her that the common people, as well as those in a better worldly position, should be allowed to go their own way independently, and that no outsider ought--even in kindness--to meddle in their private affairs.

I am happy to say that Miss Fidelia took the hint, and for the future limited her charity to those who could not help themselves, that is, to the sick and aged, and these looked upon her, not as a "little quey," but as a sweet little fée. Louisa helped her in this good work, and Frank, who sometimes accompanied them, saw to his surprise that the merry little maiden could at times look very grave and thoughtful, and that her great eyes rested on sick old women with the same comprehending and sympathetic compassion as they had done on him last Christmas-eve. He was glad to see that it was so, but he did not know why.

Spring was gone, and summer had come, when one Sunday morning Hawermann received a letter from Bräsig dated from Warnitz, in which his friend requested him to remain at home that day, for he had returned and intended to call on him that afternoon. When Bräsig arrived, he sprang from his saddle with so much force that one might have thought he wanted to go through the road with both legs. "Oho!" cried Hawermann, "how brisk you are! You're all right now, ar'n't you?"--"As right as a trivet, Charles. I've renewed my youth."--"Well, how have you been getting on, old boy?" asked Hawermann, when they were seated on the sofa and their pipes were lighted.--"Listen, Charles. Cold, damp, watery, clammy--that's about what it comes to. It's just turning a human being into a frog, and before a man's nature is so changed, he has such a hard time of it, that he begins to wish that he had come into the world a frog: still, it isn't a bad thing! You begin the day with the common packing, as they call it. They wrap you up in cold, damp sheets, and then in woollen blankets, in which they fasten you up so tight that you can't move any part of your body except your toes. In this condition they take you to a bath-room, and a man goes before you ringing a bell to warn the ladies to keep out of your way. Then they place you, just as God made you, in a bath, and dash three pails of water over your bald head--if you happen to have one, and after that they allow you to go away. Well, do you think that that's the end of it? Nay, Charles, there's more to follow: but it's a good thing all the same. Now you've got to go for a walk in a place where you've nothing earthly to do. I've been accustomed all my life to walk a great deal, but then it was doing something, ploughing or harrowing, spreading manure or cutting corn, and there I'd no occupation whatever. While walking you are expected to drink ever so many tumblers of water, ever so many. Some of the people were exactly like sieves, they were always at it, and they used to gasp out 'What splendid water it is!' Don't believe them, Charles, it is nothing but talk. Water applied externally is bad enough in all conscience, but internally it's still more horrible. Then comes the sitz-bath. Do you know what a bath at four degrees below zero is like? It's very much what you would feel if you were in hell, and the devil had tied you down to a glowing iron chair, under which he kept up a roaring fire; still it's a good thing! Then you've to walk again till dinner-time. And now comes dinner. Ah, Charles, you have no idea what a human being goes through at a water-cure place! You've got to drink no end of water. Charles, I've seen ladies, small and thin as real angels, drink each of them three caraffes as large as laundry-pails at a sitting--and then the potatoes! Good gracious, as many potatoes were eaten in a day as would have served to plant an acre of ground! These water-doctors are much to be pitied, their patients must eat them out of house and home. In the afternoon the water-drinking goes on as merrily as before, and you may now talk to the ladies if you like; but in the morning you may not approach them, for they are not then dressed for society. Before dinner some of them are to be seen running about with wet stockings, as if they had been walking through a field of clover, others have wet bandages tied round their heads, and all of them let their hair hang down over their shoulders, and wear a Fenus' girdle round their waists, which last, however, is not visible. But in the afternoon, as I said, you may talk to them as much as you like, but will most likely get short answers unless you speak to them about their health, and ask them how often they have been packed, and what effect it had on them, for that is the sort of conversation that is most approved of at a water-cure establishment. After amusing yourself in this way for a little you must have a touche (douche), that is a great rush of ice-cold water--and that's a good thing too. Above all, Charles, you must know that what every one most dislikes, and whatever is most intensely disagreeable is found to be wholesome and good for the constitution."--"Then you ought to be quite cured of your gout," said Hawermann, "for of all things in the world cold water was what you always disliked the most."--"It's easy to see from that speech that you've never been at the water-cure, Charles. Listen--this is how the doctor explained the whole thing to me. That confounded gout is the chief of all diseases--in other words, it is the source of them all, and it proceeds from the gouty humour which is in the bones, and which simply tears one to pieces with the pain, and this gouty substance comes from the poisonous matter one has swallowed as food--for example kümmel or tobacco--or as medicine at the apothecary's. Now you must understand that any one who has gout must, if he wishes to be cured, be packed in damp sheets, till the water has drawn all the tobacco he has ever smoked, and all the kümmel he has ever drunk out of his constitution. First the poisonous matter goes, then the gouty matter, and last of all the gout itself."--"And has it been so with you?"--"No."--"Why didn't you remain longer then? I should have stayed on, and have got rid of it once for all if I had been you."--"You don't know what you are talking about, Charles. No one could stand it, and no one has ever done it all at once.... But now let me go on with my description of our daily life.--After the touche you are expected to walk again, and by the time that is finished it has begun to grow dusk. You may remain out later if you like, and many people do so, both gentlemen and ladies, or you may go into the house and amuse yourself by reading. I always spent the evening in studying the water-books written by an author named Franck, who is, I understand, at the head of his profession. These books explain the plan on which the water-doctors proceed, and give reasons for all they do; but it's very difficult to understand. I could never get further than the two first pages, and these were quite enough for me, for when I'd read them I felt as light-headed and giddy as if I had been standing on my head for half an hour. You imagine, no doubt, Charles, that the water in your well is water? He does not think so! Listen, fresh air is divided into three parts: oxygen, nitrogen, and black carbon; and water is divided into two parts: carbon and hydrogen. Now the whole water-cure the'ry is founded on water and air. And listen, Charles, just think of the wisdom of nature: when a human being goes out into the fresh air he inhales both black carbon and nitrogen through his windpipe, and as his constitution can't stand the combination of these two dreadful things, the art of curing by water, steps in, and drives them out of his throat. And the way that it does so is this: the oxygen grapples with the carbon, and the hydrogen drives the nitrogen out of your body. Do you understand me, Charles?"--"No," said Hawermann laughing heartily, "you can hardly expect me to do that."--"Never laugh at things you don't understand, Charles. Listen--I have smelt the nitrogen myself, but as for the black carbon, what becomes of it? That is a difficult question, and I didn't get on far enough with the water-science to be able to answer it. Perhaps you think that parson Behrens could explain the matter to me, but no, when I asked him yesterday he said that he knew nothing about it. And now, Charles, you'll see that I've still got the black carbon in me, and that I shall have that beastly gout again."--"But, Zachariah, why didn't you remain a little longer and get thoroughly cured?"--"Because," and Bräsig cast down his eyes, and looked uncomfortable, "I couldn't. Something happened to me. Charles," he continued, raising his eyes to his friend's face, "you've known me from my childhood, tell me, did you ever see me disrespectful to a woman?"--"No, Bräsig, I can bear witness that I never did."--"Well, then, just think what happened. A week ago last Friday the gout was very troublesome in my great toe--you know it always begins by attacking the small end of the human wedge--and the water-doctor said: 'Mr. Bailiff,' he said, 'you must have an extra packing. Dr. Strump's colchicum is the cause of this, and we must get rid of it.' Well, it was done; he packed me himself, and so tight that I had hardly room to breathe, telling me for my comfort that water was more necessary for me than air, and then he wanted to shut the window. 'No,' I said, 'I understand the the'ry well enough to know that I must have fresh air, so please leave the window open.' He did as I asked, and went away.[13] I lay quite still in my compress thinking no evil, when suddenly I heard a great humming and buzzing in my ears, and when I could look up, I saw a swarm of bees streaming in at my window, preceded by their queen. I knew her well, Charles, for as you know I am a bee-keeper. One spring the school-master at Zittelwitz and I got fifty-seven in a field. I now saw that the queen was going to settle on the blanket which the doctor had drawn over my head. What was to be done? I couldn't move. I blew at her, and blew and blew till my breath was all gone. It was horrible! The queen settled right on the bald part of my head--for I had taken off my wig as usual to save it--and now the whole swarm flew at my face. That was enough for me. Quickly I rolled out of bed, freed myself from the blanket, wriggled out of the wet sheets, and reached the door, for the devil was at my heels. I got out at the door, and striking out at my assailants blindly and madly, shrieked for help. God be praised and thanked for the existence of the water-doctor--his name is Ehrfurcht--he came to my rescue, and, taking me to another room, fetched me my clothes, and so after a few hours rest I was able to go down to the dining-room--*salong* as they call it--but I still had half a bushel of bee-stings in my body. I began to speak to the gentlemen, and they did nothing but laugh. Why did they laugh, Charles? You don't know, nor do I. I turned to one of the ladies, and spoke to her in a friendly way about the weather; she blushed. What was there in the weather to make her red? I can't tell, nor can you, Charles. I spoke to the lady who sings, and asked her very politely to let us hear the beautiful song which she sings every evening. What did she do, Charles? She turned her back upon me! I now busied myself with my own thoughts, but the water-doctor came up to me, and said courteously: 'Don't be angry with me, Mr. Bailiff, but you've made yourself very remarkable this afternoon.'--'How?' I asked.--'Miss von Hinkefuss was crossing the passage when you ran out of your room, and she has told every one else in strict confidence.'--'And so,' I said, 'you give me no sympathy, the gentlemen laugh at me, and the ladies turn their pretty backs upon me. No, I didn't come here for that! If Miss von Hinkefuss had met *me*, if half a bushel of bee-stings had been planted in *her* body, I should have asked her every morning with the utmost propriety how she was. But let her alone! There is no market where people can buy kind-heartedness! Come away, doctor, and pull the stings out of my body.'--He said he couldn't do it.--'What!' I asked, 'can't you pull bee-stings out of a man's skin?'--'No,' he said, 'that is to say, I *can* do it, but I dare not, for that is an operation such as surgeons perform, and I have no diploma for surgery from the Mecklenburg government.'--'What?' I asked, 'you are allowed to draw gout out of my bones, but it is illegal for you to draw a bee-sting out of my skin? You dare not meddle with the outer skin which you can see, and yet you presume to attack my internal maladies which you can't see? *Thank* you!'--Well, Charles, from that moment I lost all faith in the water-doctor, and without faith they can do nothing as they themselves tell you when it comes to the point. So I went away quietly and got old Metz, the surgeon at Rahnstädt, to draw out the stings. That was the end of the water-cure; still it's a good thing; one gets new ideas in a place like that, and even if one's gout is not cured, one gains some notion of what a human being can suffer. And now, Charles, this is a water-book I have brought you, you can study it in the winter-evenings."--Hawermann thanked him, and the conversation was changed to farming, and then to the two apprentices.--"Well," asked Bräsig, "how's your pupil, Mr. von Rambow, getting on?"--"Very well, indeed, Bräsig, he's getting to understand the work, I'm only sorry I can't have him more with me. He does what he has to do without loss of time, and more than that, I know from Daniel Sadenwater that he spends many a night by my old master's sick-bed, even though he must often be very tired. He's like the man mentioned in the Bible whose hand always finds something to do, and whose heart is full of love."--"Well, Charles, your greyhound?"--"Oh, he isn't so bad, he has a lot of maggots in his head, but there's no harm in him. He does what he is told, though he's sometimes a little forgetful--but so were we at his age."--"The best thing about your lads is that they are strong. I was at Christian Klockmann's, and he has a son of fourteen who isn't at all well. He complains of feeling tired all day long, and is always half asleep. He won't eat at proper times, and when out in the fields always wants something to eat."--"Oh, no," said Hawermann, "my boys are not like that."--"And so Mr. Frank watches by the old gentleman at night," said

Bräsig, "that's pretty hard work for him. Then the *Counsellor* must be really ill. Remember me to him, Charles. And now good-by, I must be going, for my lord, the Count, wants to see me about particular business." And Bräsig rode away.

The squire had grown very weak in the last few days, he had had another slight stroke, but fortunately it had not affected his speech, and that evening Frank asked Hawermann to go up to the manor-house, for his uncle wanted to speak to him.

The bailiff found Fidelia in the sick-room trying to amuse her father by telling him this or that little incident in her lively girlish way.--Alas, poor thing, she little knew that her father would soon be beyond the reach of her voice. The squire desired her to leave him alone with Hawermann, and as soon as she was gone, he looked at the bailiff sorrowfully, and said: "Hawermann, dear Hawermann, when our greatest joys cease to affect us, it shows that the end is at hand."--Hawermann looked at him earnestly and could not hide from himself that the worst would soon come, for he had often seen death before, so he bent his eyes sadly on the ground, and asked: "Wasn't the doctor here to-day?"--"Ah, Hawermann, the *doctor*. What good can he do? I'd rather have Mr. Behrens with me now.--But first of all I want to speak to you on business of importance. Sit down there beside me."--When the bailiff was seated the Squire went on quickly and brokenly as if he felt that his time was as short as his breath. "My will is in Schwerin. I have thought of everything, but--when my illness came on so suddenly--and my wife's death too--I am afraid that my affairs are not in such good order as they ought to be."--After a few minutes rest he went on. "My son will have the estate, and my two married daughters have received their share, but the three unmarried ones--poor children!--I have been able to do very little for them. Alick must help them--and alas, he will have enough to do to provide for himself. He writes that he wishes to remain in the army for a few years longer--it would be quite right for him to do so, if he would only live economically--he could then save some of his farming profits--to pay his debts.--But the Jew, Hawermann, the Jew! Will he wait do you think? Did you speak?"--"No, Sir; but Moses will wait; I am quite sure that he will wait. And even if he does not, a great deal of money can be raised on the estate, far more than would have been possible a few years ago."--"Yes, yes. Land has increased in value very much. But still--Alick knows nothing about farming--I have made Frank send him numbers of agricultural books--he ought to study them--they would be of great service to him, would they not, Hawermann?"--"Ah," said Hawermann to himself, "my old master would never have trusted to mere book knowledge when he was well, he was far too practical and wise to have done such a thing; but there is no use troubling him now if the thought comforts him." So the bailiff only said that he thought so too.--"And, dear old friend, you will remain with him," entreated the Squire, "give me your hand, and promise that you will remain with him."--"Yes," said Hawermann, his eyes full of tears, "I will not leave Pümpelhagen as long as I can be of use to you or yours."--"I knew it," said his master, sinking back upon his pillow exhausted; "but--Fidelia must write--I must see him again--see him with you."--His strength was going fast, and his breathing had become heavy and gasping.

Hawermann rose softly and rang the bell, and when Daniel Sadenwater came, he drew him into the ante-room: "Sadenwater, our master is much worse, I don't think it can last long now, you had better call the young ladies and their cousin; but don't say anything too certainly."--A sad look came over the old servant's calm face, stirring it as the evening breeze passing over the quiet waters of a lake. He looked in at the half open door of the sick-room sorrowfully, and murmured as though he wished to excuse himself to himself: "Oh God! And I have served him for thirty years ...." And then he turned and went away.

Frank and the young ladies came in.--The poor girls had no idea how quickly the stone was rolling down hill now, they had always felt so certain that their father would get better, that the doctor would cure him, or if it were beyond his power, that God would do so. They had hitherto taken it in turn to watch by their father, and why were they all sent for at once, and here were Frank, Hawermann and Daniel too?--"Oh God! what is ..... what is .....?" asked Fidelia turning anxiously to the old bailiff.--Hawermann took her hand and pressed it: "Your father," he could not have said "the Squire" at such a moment, "is much worse; he is very ill, and wishes to see your brother .... Mr. von Rambow; if you will write him a line and tell him, the coachman can post the letter on his way to fetch the doctor. Your brother may be here in three days time."--"It can hardly last three hours," said Sadenwater who joined Hawermann in the ante-room.

The three daughters sat or stood round their father's bed weeping silently, for they saw that they would soon lose him who had been their comfort and support all their lives, and their heart beats quicker and quicker as they tried to think of something that would keep him a little longer amongst them, while his heart beat more faintly and slowly every minute.

Frank sat in the ante-room and listened to every sound, and now and then joined his cousins in the sick-room for a few minutes. He had never before seen a human life ebbing away, and his thoughts turned to his own father, whom he had always pictured to himself as resembling his uncle, and he felt as if he were losing his father for the second time. He sorrowed for his cousin Alick who was absent, and who could not possibly arrive in time.--Hawermann stood by the open window and looked out into the night. It was just such a sweet calm night as that one long ago when his heart was full of grief. His wife had passed away then--and now his friend was going. Who would be the next?--Would it be his turn, or ...? Only God could answer that question, for all things are in His hands.--And Daniel Sadenwater sat by the stove with a basket on his knee containing the silver forks and spoons he had burnished every evening for thirty years. On a chair beside him were a piece of chamois-leather and a blue checked pocket-handkerchief, and he alternately rubbed up the silver with the one, and dried his eyes with the other; but when he came to the fork which had his master's name upon it, and which he had cleaned every evening for thirty years there was such a mist before his eyes that he could not see whether it was bright or dull, so he put the basket down by his side, and sat staring at the fork while the tears ran down his cheeks and his heart was full of the unspoken question: "Who will use it now?"

During all this time of restless sorrow, the pendulum of the old clock on the wall kept up its measured beat as though time were sitting by the bed rocking her tired child gently and surely to sleep--his last sleep. At length it came, and the Squire's eyes were for ever closed, the dark curtain separating here from hereafter had fallen softly, and on this side of it the three daughters wept aloud for him who was gone from amongst them, and wrung their hands as they mourned the sorrow that had come. Fidelia threw herself on her father's body with a passionate burst of crying that ended in a fit of hysterics, and Frank, full of compassion, took her in his arms and carried her out of the room. The two elder sisters followed, their hearts filled with a new sorrow, fear for their darling. Hawermann on being left alone with Daniel Sadenwater, quietly closed his master's eyes, and then went away with a heavy heart, while Daniel, still holding the fork in his hand, seated himself at the foot of the bed, and turned his calm face on his master's which was even calmer than his own.

CHAPTER IX

Three days later Alick arrived, too late to see his father, but not too late to pay him the last honours. The postilion blew the usual cheery blast on his horn as they drove into the court-yard, and three pale women dressed in black at once appeared in the doorway of the manor-house.--What is our grief to the rest of the world?--The young Squire soon got to understand his real situation, for the full weight of all the disagreeables of his position, whether caused by his own fault or not fell upon him at once: the visitation of God, his own ignorance and folly, the poverty of his sisters and his powerlessness to help them, and the memory of his father's love and kindness which had never failed in good or evil days. These things all weighed upon him. It was his nature to feel a sort of nervous irritation when things went ill with him, even when matters were not so grave as they now were. He sighed and bemoaned himself, and asked again and again why this or that was the case, and when he heard from Frank that his father's last words had been spoken in private to Hawermann, he called the old bailiff aside and questioned him as to what had passed between them. Hawermann told him the whole truth, making him understand that his father's last trouble had been uneasiness about his future, and whether he would be able by good management of his estate to keep himself and his sisters.

Yes, of course he would do that! He swore to himself that he would do it when a short time afterwards he was alone in the garden; he would double his profits, he would live quietly, would do without society, and would not join in the extravagant amusements of his brother officers. He could do that easily, quite easily, but he could not leave the army as Hawermann proposed, and go somewhere to learn farming thoroughly; no, *that* was impossible, he was too old for that, and then too it would be derogatory to his position as an officer, and besides that, it was unnecessary. When he came to live at home he would soon get into the way of it all, and meanwhile he would live economically, would pay his debts, and would study the agricultural works his old father had had so much at heart.

Thus it is that people deceive themselves, often even at the gravest and most important time in their lives.

The funeral took place on the following day. No invitations were given, but the Squire had been so much loved and respected that a number of the neighbours attended of their own free will. Bräsig's master, the Count, came amongst others, and showed by his manner that he thought it a great honour to be allowed to be present. Bräsig was there also, he stood near the coffin, and when everyone else cast down their eyes, he raised his, and when Hawermann passed near him, he caught him by the coat and whispered: "Ah, Charles, what is human life?" He said no more, but Joseph Nüssler who was standing beside him, muttered: "What can anyone do now?"-- Round about them were the villagers, all the Pegels and Degels, and Päsels and Däsels were there, and when Mr. Behrens came in with the youngest daughter by his side, and standing by the coffin gave a short address which touched the hearts even of the strangers present, many tears were shed by old eyes for the kind master who was gone. They were tears of gratitude to the old Squire, and of fear lest the young Squire might not resemble his father.

When the address was finished the procession moved off to the churchyard. The coffin was placed in a carriage, and Daniel Sadenwater took his seat beside it, and sat there as stiff and motionless, even to the calm serenity of his face, as if he had all his life been a monument at the head of his master's grave. Then came the carriage containing the young Squire and his three sisters, then the Count's carriage, then the clergyman and Frank who tried to persuade Hawermann to go with them, but he refused, saying that he wished to accompany the labourers, then several more carriages, then Joseph Nüssler, and lastly Hawermann on foot with Bräsig and the villagers.

When they got to Gürlitz, Bräsig stooped towards Hawermann and whispered: "I have it now, Charles."--"What have you got, Zachariah?"-- "The pension from my lord the Count. When I left you after my last visit, I rode straight to him and got it all right, padagraph by padagraph, thirty-seven pounds ten a year, ten-thousand peats, and rooms in the mill-house at Haunerwiem rent free, and besides that, I am to have a small garden for vegetables, and a bit of potato-ground."--"I'm glad to hear it, Zachariah. You'll be able to spend your old age there very comfortably."--"Yes, indeed, Charles, especially when I add to that the interest of the money I have saved. But why are we stopping?"--"They are going to take the coffin out of the carriage," said Hawermann. He then turned to the villagers, and said: "Kegel, Päsel! You'd better go now, my lads, and help to carry the coffin." He went forward with the men to make the necessary arrangements. Bräsig followed him.

Meanwhile the mourners had all got out of the carriage, and when Alick and his three sisters were standing on the road little Mrs. Behrens and Louisa Hawermann, who were both dressed in black joined them, and Mrs. Behrens with heart-felt compassion pressed the hands of the two elder ladies who had hitherto always held themselves aloof from her, because they were so much impressed with the dignity of their social position--but death and sorrow make all men equal, the great and mighty of the earth bow beneath the hand of God, for they feel that they are nothing in comparison with Him, and at such times the lowly come forward to meet them, for they know that the sympathy which they show comes from God.--To-day David Däsel had had the pleasure of shaking hands with the ladies, and they had had the comfort of seeing in his honest face and tearful eyes how truly he grieved for them.--Louisa threw her arms round her friend, Miss Fidelia, and not knowing how to express her sympathy with her, contented herself with saying: "There!" with a deep sigh, as she thrust a bunch of red and white roses into her hand, and while doing so she looked at her friend as much as to say that she intended the flowers, which were her greatest treasures to be a sign of her loving sympathy.

All eyes were turned on the child of fourteen--but was she still a child?--Are those only buds, or are the leaves really showing when the birch-tree shimmers green after a warm shower of rain in May? And as for the human soul, it puts forth its leaves when first under the influence of some strong feeling, in like manner as the birch after rain. "Who is that?" Alick asked his cousin who was staring at the child.--"Who is that young girl, Frank?" he asked again, touching his cousin's arm.--"That young girl?" asked Frank as if he could hardly take away his eyes from her, "that child, you mean? She is Mr. Hawermann's daughter."--The bailiff was also watching her, and as he did so he remembered his thoughts on the night of the Squire's death. "No," he said to himself, "surely the Lord won't do that."--Nonsense!--She was not ill. Oh God, if she had inherited her mother's constitution, his poor wife had had just such beautiful rosy cheeks.--"I say, just look!" said Bräsig rousing him out of his reverie.--"It *is* him! Just look, Charles, here's Samuel Pomuchelskopp! And he has got on a black swallow-tail coat!"

He was right.--Pomuchelskopp advanced and made as low a bow to the ladies as his short stature would permit, then turning to the lieutenant: "Pardon me--neighbourly friendship--*extreme* sympathy with you on this melancholy occasion--*greatest* respect for the late Mr. von Rambow--hope that there may be friendship between Pümpelhagen and Gürlitz"--In short he said whatever occurred to him on the spur of the moment, and when the young Squire had thanked him for his attention, he felt as happy as if he had bestowed all possible sympathy. He then passed the whole procession under review, and when he found that the Count was the only other landed proprietor there, he edged himself amongst the people so that he should at least come immediately behind him, and as they proceeded to the churchyard he took care to put his feet down on the foot-prints of his aristocratic acquaintance, and this, though a matter of complete indifference to the Count, was a great pleasure to him.

The funeral was over.--The mourners assembled for a short time at the parsonage. Little Mrs. Behrens was torn in two by conflicting feelings, for on the one hand she would have liked to have joined the three Miss von Rambows on the sofa, and to have comforted them; and on the other hand she wanted to move about the room, and offer the cake and wine to her guests, but as Louisa had undertaken the latter, and her pastor the former duty, she sat as despondingly in her large arm-chair as if old Mr. Metz the surgeon had been sewing the two halves together again, and she was still suffering from the pain of the operation.

Louisa had done her part, and the guests were all going away one after the other; Joseph Nüssler, who was one of the last, made a half bow to the lieutenant, and then going up to Mrs. Behrens pressed her hand as emphatically as if it had been her father who had just died, and said sorrowfully: "Ah yes, it all depends upon circumstances!"--The parson had also done his part as well as he could, but it is much easier to satisfy the hungry stomach with food and wine than to feed the hungry heart with hope and courage. He gently led the Miss von Rambows from thoughts of the past to thoughts of the future, and helped them to lay out a plan for their new life. He advised them as to what was best and wisest for them to do, and as to where they should live, so that when they went away with their brother they had gained courage to face what was before them and consult how they could best arrange their future lives so as to make the two ends meet.

But other people were also trying to shape the future after their own fashion. There were not only flowers of mourning and sorrow growing on the Counsellor's grave, but thistles, nettles and weeds of all kinds were to be found there sown by the lost happiness of Pümpelhagen, and surrounding all was a thick border of usurer's daisies.[14] He who would reap that harvest must have no fear of being stung by the nettles. He who has to deal with nettles must grasp them firmly, and the man dressed in green-checked trousers, who is now standing in Gürlitz garden and looking down upon Pümpelhagen will seize them boldly, but he must wait till the right moment comes. The usurer's daisies must have time to grow and bear seed.

"*That* stone is well out of my way now," he thought with a smile of satisfaction, "and it was the cornerstone.--Who is there now?--The lieutenant?--We'll soon manage him, we'll give him plenty of money on mortgages, renew his bills, and in short gradually lead him on, and then we'll have it all our own way. Or, let me see? Mally is a pretty girl; or Sally; she would do as well. Mr. von Zwippelwitz said the other day when I was lending him money to buy the sorrel-colt, that Sally's eyes were like--what was it he said? fire wheels, or torches?--but it doesn't much matter, Sally will remember.--I know how to deal with people of this kind now, and there's no fear of my being taken in.--He'd only do it if his affairs were in a desperate condition; safe is safe.--Always keep a tight hold of the purse strings!--If he ever does it there'll be no end of a fuss made; but he'll never consent till he's at the last gasp.--And what else?--Hawermann.--The cunning scoundrel!--What?--This very morning.--He made no sign that he had ever seen me before!--Did he really think that I should have bowed first?--A fellow like that!--Why he is in service!--Wait a bit, once let me have the upper hand of the lieutenant and you shall see my friend!--And then Bräsig.--The rascal!--Does he mean to put another stumbling-block in my way?--Ha, ha! It's a great joke, the old fool doesn't know that it was I who had him turned out of Warnitz, that the attorney, acting under my directions, gave the Count a hint that the farming at Warnitz was disgracefully bad.--So there Bräsig, you are well out of my way now at Haunerwiem.--And the parson!--Yes, Mr. Behrens.--I was asked to go into his house to-day, and we were so civil to each other.--Oh! *I* know your civility!--There are the glebe-lands right before me.--What?--Deny me your glebe, and then offer me civility!--Ah! Just wait a little, and I'll get the better of you all, for I have the power to do so.--I have *money*."--And with that he slapped his breeches pocket with his fat hand in the joy of his heart till the gold seals on his watch-chain danced like a tailor on a meal-tub, but suddenly he became quiet, for a hard hand tapped him on the shoulder and Henny said: "Muchel, you are wanted"--"Who is it, my chuck?" asked Pomuchelskopp very gently, for his wife's presence always subdued him.--"Attorney Slus'uhr, and David the son of old Moses."--"Capital, capital!" said Pomuchelskopp throwing his arm round his Henny's waist, so that he looked exactly like a cucumber hanging to a hop-pole. "Just look at Pümpelhagen; what a fine place it is! Isn't it a shame that it's in such hands?--That both these men should have come to-day is almost like the leading of Providence, isn't it, my chuck?"--"Ah, it's a toss up, Kopp!--You'd better try something more likely; but come and speak to those people. Plans such as you were talking about are too long in coming to pass to please me."--"Never be in too great a hurry, too great a hurry, chuck," said Pomuchelskopp as he followed his wife to the house.

Slus'uhr and David were standing in Pomuchelskopp's room, and David was going through a sort of martyrdom. When he set out that day he had unfortunately put his large signet-ring on his finger, and fastened his gold watch-chain across his waist-coat, and, in spite of his unwonted grandeur, when he entered the room he placed himself modestly with his back to the window, but Philipp Pomuchelskopp caught sight of the ring, and Tony of the shining chain, so they fell upon David's jewelry like a couple of ravens, and pulled at the ring and tugged at the chain, and while Tony danced upon David's splay feet, Phil who had one knee on a chair kicked his shins which were his weak point. His flat feet might be likened to arable land in March, on which the devil had sown a goodly crop of corns; and his shins had to be tenderly treated because they alone supported the weight of his body, as nature had not endowed him with calves to help them in this necessary duty.--The attorney was standing in the other window in front of Sally's chair. That young lady was busy making a sofa cushion for her father in tent-stitch. Her work represented a picture of country life. There was a long barn, and beside it a plum-tree on which were hanging blue plums as large as your fist; in front of the barn several hens and a cock with brilliant plumage were scratching the ground, beyond the fowls was a pond on which were swimming ducks and geese that were white and beautiful as swans, and in the foreground was an immense pig, fat and ready for the butcher.--Old Moses was right, the attorney was the very image of a rat, his ears were set on his head in the same way as a rat's, and he was small and thin like all the rats in Rahnstädt which had not been fattened in David's warehouse. His complexion was yellow-grey, his eyes were yellow-grey, and his hair and moustache were yellow-grey, but Mally and Sally Pomuchelskopp declared that he was very interesting--Bräsig called it, interested--he could talk so pleasantly.--It was natural that the attorney should like talking of his own cleverness better than of the folly of other people, for no business man ever likes to point out a good thing to other people till he has got all that he can out of it. And how could the attorney help it, if his cleverness was so great that it could not be hidden? Was it his fault if his cleverness grew so much that there was no room in his soul to contain both it and that stupid little virtue honesty, so that the latter had to be cast out neck and crop?--We men cannot judge such matters fairly--rats are rats--and as David himself said when rats were mentioned: They are too much for me.

 This afternoon, he was telling with great glee how he had promised to provide a silly fool with a rich wife, and how he had fleeced him every time he sent him to pay his court to some impossible person till at last the stupid idiot had lost almost everything he possessed.--"How very interesting," tittered Sally as Pomuchelskopp came into the room, saying: "Ah, here you are!--Glad to see you Mr. Slus'uhr.--How d'ye do, David!"--Sally was still in fits of laughter, but as father Pomuchelskopp signed towards the door with his head, she collected her plums, fowls, ducks, geese and pig, and then saying: "Come away, Tony and Phil, father's busy," left the room with her brothers. Pomuchelskopp was always said to be "busy" when he was working amongst his crop of usurer's daisies.

"Mr. Pomuchelskopp," said David, "I've come about the skins, and I wanted to speak to you about the wool.--I had a letter ....."--"Why, what's all this about? wool and skins!" cried the attorney. "You can arrange that afterwards.--We've come about the business you know of."--Anyone could see that the attorney was a new-fashioned man of business who did not like to waste time with a long preface, but who always came to the point at once, and Mr. Pomuchelskopp no doubt liked a man of this kind, who grasped his nettles boldly, for he went up to him, and shaking his hand warmly made him sit on the sofa beside him.--"Yes," he said, "it's a difficult matter and will take a long time to settle."--"Hm!--That depends upon how long we hold out. And difficult?--I've done harder things before now. David has bills to the amount of three hundred and seventy-five pounds. I myself sent him a hundred and twenty-five pounds last term. Will you have the bills? Here they are."--"It's a good investment," said Pomuchelskopp smoothly, and rising he paid down ready money for the papers the attorney had brought.--"Will you have mine too?" asked David.--"Yes, I'll take them," said Pomuchelskopp as benignantly as if he were bestowing a great favour on the world at large. "But gentleman," he continued, as he counted out the money, "I have one stipulation to make. You must let him think that you owe me the full amount of these bills and must have the money. Just give him a fright, you understand, for if he is left too quiet, he'll have all his wits about him and will slip out of our hands, for he can easily raise money elsewhere."--"Yes," said the attorney, "that isn't a bad plan, I could easily do that; but David has something to tell you that you ought to know."--"Yes," said David, "I have had a letter from Mark Seelig in P---- where Mr. von Rambow's regiment is stationed, and he tells me that he can see you three hundred pounds worth of the lieutenant's bills. And if you like to have them, why not buy?"--"Hm!" said Pomuchelskopp, "it's a large sum to pay at once--but--well you can buy the bills."--"I also have a stipulation to make," said David, "you must sell me the wool."--"Why not?" asked the attorney pressing his client's foot with his own. "Why shouldn't he go and look at it now?"--And Pomuchelskopp took the hint, and civilly showed David out that he might go and inspect the purchase he intended to make, and when he returned to his seat the attorney laughed and said: "We understand each other."--"What do you mean?" asked Pomuchelskopp startled.--"I have known what you were after all along, my fine fellow, and if you'll come down handsomely you may do what you like for all I care."--How frightfully sharp the rascal was! Pomuchelskopp was breathless. "Mr. Slus'uhr, I don't deny ....."--"You needn't explain; it isn't necessary; we can understand each other quite well without that. If matters go as they ought you will be owner of Pümpelhagen before very long, and David will have his percentage, and I--well I could do the business on my own account, but the place is a little too large for me--a mill or a farm would suit me better than such an enormous estate.--It will cost you no end of money."--"That it will indeed; but never mind. It makes me miserable to see a fine property like that in such inefficient hands."

The attorney peered at him out at the corner of his eye, as much as to say: are you in earnest?--"What's the matter? Why are you looking at me?"--"Ah!" said Slus'uhr, laughing, "you amused me. Two may play at the same game. You don't really think that you can bring an estate like Pümpelhagen into the market, by buying up bills to the extent of a few hundred pounds? You'll have to do much more than that, you must get all the mortgages on the property into your own hands."--"I intend to do so," whispered Pomuchelskopp. "But how am I to get possession of the bond for a thousand and fifty pounds which old Moses holds? I'm afraid there's no hope."--"I'll have nothing to do with Moses, I can tell you; but there's David, you might get him to manage it. Still, that's nothing to what will have to be done. You ought to make up to the lieutenant, pretend to wish him well, and lend him money yourself now and then when he's in a worse fix than usual, and then you should be hard up in your turn, and be obliged to sell his bills--to me if you like--and if you do that I will touch him up a bit, and at length when the time for the crash comes--you ...."--"Yes, yes," whispered Pomuchelskopp excitedly, "I'll do it, but I should like to have him at home first, so you must give him no peace about the bills till he is forced by the state of his affairs to leave the army."--"Oh, that's easy enough to manage. If you don't want anything more difficult than that, it'll all be plain sailing."--"Ah, but there is something else," whispered Pomuchelskopp, "*there's Hawermann*; as long as he is in that puppy's confidence we shall make no way."--"How stupid you are!" laughed the attorney. "Did you ever hear of a young man confiding his money-troubles unreservedly to an old friend? No, no! And it's just as well for us that they never do. If that is all, Hawermann may stay as long as he likes at Pümpelhagen; but wait a moment--perhaps it would be better that he should go--he's too good a farmer--if he makes Pümpelhagen pay as well for the future as it has done during the last few years, it will be a long time before it slips out of the lieutenant's hands."--"Hawermann a good farmer!--He!--Why he tried it for himself once and failed!"--"You do him injustice there. It is a great mistake to think your opponent weaker than he really is. He must go."--"Yes, but how are we to get rid of him?"--"*I* can't help you there," laughed the attorney, "but you can manage it when you are providing the lieutenant with the golden sovereigns he needs so much. A well-directed hint as to the bailiff's being too old for his place would have a good effect. The devil will prompt you when the time comes."--"That's all very well," said Pomuchelskopp impatiently, "but it's slow work, and my wife is always in such a hurry."--"In this case she'll have to wait quietly," said the attorney with calm decision. "An affair of this kind can't be settled in a day. Remember how long Pümpelhagen has belonged to the von Rambow family; you can't expect to get it away from them at a moment's notice. But now--hush! I hear David coming, and he must not know what we have been talking about. You understand, he is to know of nothing but that you like taking up good bills."

When David entered the room he saw before him a couple of happy faces; Pomuchelskopp was laughing as if the attorney had been making a good joke, and the attorney was laughing as if Pomuchelskopp had been telling an amusing story. But David was not half so stupid as he looked at that moment, he knew that he had been sent out of the way, and that his colleagues were laughing at something very different from a joke.--"They have *their* secrets," he said to himself, "and I have *mine*."--So he seated himself at the opposite side of the table to Pomuchelskopp, and said with the most stupidly unconcerned expression in the world, such as only a Jewish rogue can put on: "I've seen it."--"Well?" asked Pomuchelskopp.--"Hm!" said David, shrugging his shoulders, "you say that it has been washed. Well--perhaps it has."--"What, don't you believe me? Isn't it as white as swan's-down?"--"Humph! If you ever saw swan's-down like it, perhaps it may be like swan's-down."--"What is your offer?"--"Look here! We had a better from Löwenthal in Hamburg--the great house of Löwenthal in Hamburg--the price per stone is two pounds three and sixpence."--"Yes, I know all that; you always get them to write you some scoundrelly nonsense of that kind."--"A house like that of Löwenthal never advises one of anything that is not true."--"Come, come," interrupted the attorney, "this isn't business, it's quarrelling. Suppose you send for a couple of bottles of wine, Pomuchelskopp, and then you'll both manage to strike a bargain more easily."--Mr. Slus'uhr insisted on his plan being acceded to, and the squire had to obey; he rang the bell, and when Stina Dorothy came in, he said politely and confidentially--for he was always polite to the members of his own household, above all to the women, from his Henny down to the nursery-maid:--"Bring two bottles of wine, Dorothy; the blue seal you know."

When the wine was put on the table Pomuchelskopp filled three glasses, then taking his, he emptied it at a draught, David merely smelt his, and when the attorney had finished his glass, he said: "Now, gentlemen, I've got something to say to you," and as he spoke, he winked across the table at David, and pressed Pomuchelskopp's foot under the table. "Suppose, David, you consent to give two pounds five per stone, and you Pomuchelskopp--pressing his foot again--don't want ready money, a bill to be paid on S. Antony's day would suit you better if the security is good."--"Yes," said Pomuchelskopp taking the hint, "and if you give me your father's bond on Pümpelhagen, the security is so good, that I'll give you the overplus of the wool-money into the bargain"--"There's nothing to object to in that," said David. "But how about the lumpy wool?"--No attention was paid to his remark, so he repeated: "How about the lumpy wool?"--"Oh that," said Pomuchelskopp, "of course you'll only pay me half...."--"Stop," interrupted the attorney. "You'll get the lumpy wool for nothing if you bring the bond."--"I don't see anything against that," said David. When they had finished the wine, and were going out to their carriage, the attorney whispered jocosely to Pomuchelskopp: "David might begin the attack on the lieutenant tomorrow, and next week I can look him up myself."--Pomuchelskopp pressed his hand as gratefully as if he had just saved Phil from drowning. As soon as his visitors were gone he went back to his Henny, and with her assistance they soon arranged the future to their satisfaction. The attorney sat in the carriage smiling at his good day's work, he was pleased with himself, for he saw that he was cleverer than either of the other two; and David sat by his side, and said to himself: "Let them be. They have their secrets, but I have the lumpy wool!"

But he had reckoned without his host! When he got home and told his father of the bargain he had made, and asked for the Pümpelhagen bond, Moses looked over his shoulder at him, and said: "So, you went with that cut-throat, the attorney, to visit Pomüffelskopp--who is another cut-throat--and bought his wool; then all that I've got to say is: you can pay for it with *your own* bonds, for you shall have none of *mine*. *You* may do business with rats if you like, but *I'll* have nothing to do with them."--So David's chance of getting the lumpy wool was small.

CHAPTER X

That made it worse, much worse for the poor lieutenant next morning when David was shown into his room. No one could accuse David of being softhearted--not even his own mother--but he had changed very much since Mr. von Rambow had last seen him. He had had some sort of human kindness in his expression when he was counting out the gold the lieutenant wanted in attorney Slus'uhr's office; but now that he had come to ask for his money he looked so hard and cruel that the young man was half frightened even before he knew for what he had come. And then there was nothing for it but to renew the bill, for David insisted on its either being renewed or paid at once, adding, "very well then, Sir, just sign this paper and it will do." When this was done David's face relaxed, and became what it had been on their first acquaintance.

"Thank God! that's over now," thought the lieutenant. But a few days later a carriage drove into the court, and attorney Slus'uhr was seated in it.--"Merciful Heaven!" sighed Hawermann, shaking his head, "has he got into his clutches too?"--And when the attorney was shown into the lieutenant's room, he also exclaimed: "Merciful Heaven!" on seeing his visitor. Still, this was a less painful piece of business than with David, for the attorney was a more respectable looking man, and easier to talk to; his clothes were always clean and neat, and even handsome, and he had the art of making his conversation in keeping with his dress--as long as it was his interest to do so. The lieutenant made him sit down on the sofa, and ordered coffee, and it seemed at first as if they were going to have a pleasant conversation about the weather, and the neighbourhood, and human wickedness--the attorney had a great deal to say on that head, for he had all his life been accustomed to look at the failings of others, and never at his own. "Yes," he said, in allusion to a certain tradesman in Rahnstädt, "only think, Mr. von Rambow, of the wickedness of that man. In the kindness of my heart I gave that man--that is to say, that not having so much money of my own, I had to borrow some at a large percentage--well, as I was saying, I lent him enough money to free him from his difficulties, and he was very grateful--but *now*, when I want to have it again,--*must* have it--he turns up on me, and threatens to have me tried at law for asking too high a percentage."--Naturally the attorney said no more on that part of the subject, he had only mentioned it to give the lieutenant a fright, and it did not fail in having the required effect. In order to turn the subject, the young man asked what kind of shop the tradesman had. The attorney, however, was too well up to his work to allow himself to be put off, so he answered the question shortly, and then went on: "But I have gone to law with him instead, and now he'll see what will happen---his credit is gone--and then the scandal! I never went to law with one of my clients before, but he has himself to thank for it. What do you think?"--It was thus that the attorney carried the war into Mr. von Rambow's country, and the poor young fellow prepared to receive the attack that was to be made on him. He coughed, and moved about restlessly, but said nothing, for he did not know what to say. It was all the same to the attorney, who only brought his battery a little nearer: "But, thank God, I hav'n't always such rascals to deal with. He is quite an exception. By the way, as we are talking of money," here he drew out his pocketbook, "allow me to return you your bill," and he handed the lieutenant the bill for a hundred and twenty-five pounds, and as he did so he pricked his rat-like ears, his grey eyes stood out more prominently than usual from his yellow-grey face, and he licked his dry lips in the same way as his prototype does at the sight of a nice bit of fat bacon. Our poor lieutenant took the bill, and tried to deceive the lawyer by putting on an indifferent manner. Yes, he said, he would take the bill, and would send the money; he had started for Pümpelhagen so suddenly, and the cause of his coming was so sad that he had not thought of bringing money with him to meet the bill.--Ah, replied Slus'uhr, he could quite believe that, he remembered so well when *his* father died; yes, at such a time it was impossible to think of anything but the loss one had sustained.--And as he said this he put on such a pitying expression that the lieutenant felt renewed courage--but, added the attorney, he had been obliged to look forward to the punctual payment of this bill, for he was much in want of money as he had to pay up a large sum at once--and so he must have the bill discharged.--"But this is such little money," interrupted Alick.--"Yes--yes," said the attorney slowly, and at the same time taking some more papers from his pocket-book. "These are also for small sums," laying on the table before him the bills for upwards of three hundred pounds, which David had bought in the town where the lieutenant's regiment was stationed.--Alick was startled out of his pretended indifference: "How do you come by these papers?" he cried.--"Surely, Mr. von Rambow," was the answer, "you are aware that it is the nature of bills to change hands in course of business, therefore it ought not to surprise you that I should have accepted these in lieu of money, more especially as it saved me a great deal of trouble in writing, and at the post-office."--The lieutenant felt more uncomfortable than even at first, but still he had not the faintest suspicion of the plot against him. "But, Mr. Slus'uhr," he said, "I hav'n't got the money at this moment."--"You hav'n't!" cried the attorney, glaring at him as much as to say that he suspected him of being in league with the devil to play him false. "No, no," he added, "I don't believe that."--What could the lieutenant say now. The attorney had looked him full in the face, and had told him coolly that he didn't believe what he said, that he could pay if he would. At length the beautiful old plan of putting off the evil day was agreed to. The lieutenant would gladly have arranged it so before, but the attorney would not at first consent, for he wanted to taste the full enjoyment of his position, and to make a better bargain for himself than David had done. His happiest moments were those when he could say to himself: I am far cleverer than any of my neighbours, I can set down my foot on gentle and simple, and I delight in seeing them writhing under my tread.

These were the troubles and anxieties which weighed upon Alick von Rambow, and disturbed him in his mourning for his father. The soul can fight its way through God-sent sorrows however deep and agonizing they may be. When it at length reaches port after having done battle manfully with the mighty billows of that wide and eternal sea, it is strengthened and purified by what it has gone through, and is able to face life again with a larger experience, and a greater courage. But it is otherwise with those whose trouble is caused by their own sins, they have fallen into a quagmire, and some of the mud sticks to them, so that they are ashamed to look other men in the face. This was the case with the young squire, he was ashamed of having led such a foolish and thoughtless life; he was ashamed of having allowed himself to fall a prey to usurers, whether Jew or Christian; he was ashamed of being unable to think of any plan by which he might extricate himself from the mire into which he had fallen, and of having saved himself for the moment by means that would only serve to draw him further into the slough. How easy it would have been for him to have kept out of all this trouble if he had only taken Hawermann's advice. And how willingly would the bailiff help him now that loyalty to the old squire did not stand in the way. But the human heart is very reserved and timid, and thinks it will find rest when far away from the place where it has suffered pain and mortification, so Alick left Pümpelhagen sooner than his sisters had expected.

He found everything as he had left it when he reached the barracks, but *he* himself was changed, at least he told himself so every day; but if his brother officers had been asked their opinion on the subject, they would have said that they saw no difference in him, which was quite natural, as the only change in him was that he made plenty of good resolutions, but never put them in practice. He was determined to be economical; he was determined to follow his father's advice, and read the agricultural books he had sent him, as much of them, at least, as he could; he was determined .... he was determined .... Oh, what did he not determine to do?--His economy began early in the morning with his coffee; for a whole long week he drank it without sugar, for, said he, "Take care of the pence, and the pounds will take care of themselves;" after coffee he smoked a cigar, for which he now paid at the rate of two pounds seventeen a thousand, instead of three pounds; he scolded his servant for giving him butter at breakfast; he ordered his groom to give his horses half feeds of corn instead of whole feeds as before, because, he said, oats were so dear. Of all his new regulations this was the only one that lasted--probably because he and his horses did not dine together--the rest came to an end after a week's trial. And why? Because, he said, he could not carry out his plan in everything, and to be of use it must be done thoroughly. It was not much better with his studies. He knew the first three pages of each of the books on farming almost by heart, he had read them so often. He always began at the very beginning again when he took them up, for if he did not, he lost the sense of what he was reading. To make up for this conscientiousness on his part, he sometimes amused himself by picking out the most interesting bits of the books, and when he had gone through them all in this way, reading a page about horses here, and another there, he threw them aside, and said that he knew all about it now, and indeed understood the whole affair better than the authors themselves. Ah, well--what good did all that reading do him? He knew nothing of agriculture practically, and a farmer must be *practical*, theory is worse than useless to him. He made the acquaintance of a Mr. von so and so whose estate lay near the town in which his regiment was quartered; like Mr. von so and so he asked the bailiff what they were doing to-day whenever he rode to the farm, and then he went home again understanding as much about the real state of matters as Mr. von so and so himself, for he knew as well as his friend that manure had been carted in Seelsdorf on the 15th of June, and that the young horse at Basedow was descended from Gray Momus; or else he went out to shoot over the barley-stubble with Mr. von so and so, and as they walked, found on enquiry that the last load of barley had been led in on the 27th of August; then he shot a few partridges, and when he came home at night he knew as well as Mr. von so and so whether the partridges were good.

    He liked that way of farming very much, and as people generally enjoy talking of what pleases them, our friend Alick was not behindhand in this respect, and so of course soon gained a reputation of understanding such matters, and was regarded as a shining light by his comrades. As most of his brother officers were the sons of noblemen who were possessed of large estates they knew that in course of time they would have to give up their easy comfortable garrison life and undertake the difficult task of managing a property in such a way as to gain the largest possible income from it, they therefore looked upon Alick as a miracle of diligence and imagined that he enjoyed the thought of the hard work before him. The greater number of them admired him heartily for it, but there were several foolish fellows amongst their number, who were such fine gentlemen, that they considered taking an interest in such matters beneath the dignity of an officer in his majesty's service.

Alick was always chosen as umpire in any dispute on farming matters, and as he had to defend his position by argument, he was obliged to keep his eyes open lest he should be worsted, and so his knowledge gradually increased. Great progress had been made in the science of agriculture during the last few years, for Professor Liebig had written a learned book for the benefit of country-gentlemen, which was filled with analytical observations about coal, and nitre, and sulphur, and gypsum, and chalk, and ammonia, and which explained hydraulics and irrigation--it was enough to make any sane man go mad only to read it! And yet everyone who wished to increase his knowledge of such matters, and to dip his fingers into science, bought the book, and sitting down, read and read till his brain whirled, and when he had finished the book he hardly knew whether gypsum was nutritious or otherwise--for clover, not for men--or whether he ought to attribute the odour of the farm-yard to the presence of ammonia or not.-- Alick got the book and read it diligently, but it quite stupified him, he felt as if his head were going to burst, and his mind became a blank, so he shut it up, and would soon have forgotten all about it, if he had not made the acquaintance of a good-natured chemist, who showed him the different substances specified by the professor and let him examine and smell them for himself. This was learning the thing practically, and from that moment he understood the whole matter as well as Liebig himself, and so never needed to look into the book again.

There was one branch of agriculture in which he took particular interest, viz. farming implements and machinery. He had always delighted in mechanical contrivances, and when a boy had made a little mill for himself, and although his mother hated to see him employ his hands in any useful way, he had, when at school, insisted on having private lessons in bookbinding. These little accomplishments were very useful to him now, for, with the help of drawings of the new-fashioned American plough and Scotch harrow, he found it quite easy to cut out of wood miniature ploughs, harrows and rollers, and in this occupation he found much innocent amusement.--He did not rest satisfied with this, he went further, and attempted to make whip-lashes, bird-rattles, &c. He would probably have been contented with these triumphs of mechanical skill--and it was certainly much to his credit that he did not think it beneath his dignity to use carpenter's tools--if he had not become acquainted with a half-mad old watch-maker, who had spent his life and substance in trying to discover the secret of perpetual motion for the good of his ungrateful fellow creatures. This benefactor of his species showed him his whole plan, pointed out how one wheel acted in connection with another, and showed him rollers, screws and springs, and then another wheel; he showed him machines that would not go, and some that did go, and others that would not go as they ought; he showed him machines which Alick could understand, and some which he could not understand, and one or two which he himself could not understand. The whole thing interested Alick so much that he at once joined the noble army of benefactors of mankind, and determined to invent something. His great desire was to invent a machine which would plough, harrow, roll and act as clod-breaker at the same time, and it was a touching sight to see the handsome young cavalry-officer sitting beside the weazand old watch-maker and thinking how he could by his invention be of use in his generation.

So matters might have continued for a long time, and he might have made a wonderful invention for the good of mankind, and might also in the pursuit of this object have been brought to beggary by the increasing number of his bills, for of course while thus engaged, he had neither time nor inclination to think of the payment of his debts, and though Pümpelhagen brought him in a good income he had enough to do with it. He had to pay interest on the money borrowed by his father, and to provide for his sisters, and then he lived happily on what remained without a thought of his own debts now that he had got over the first onslaught of the usurers.

But there are two spirits, a brother and sister, who at a moment's notice awake even the most indifferent of men from their dreams by the warm fire-side, and drive them out into the storm and rain, and these are Hate and Love. Hate seizes a man, by the scruff of the neck and throws him out violently, saying: Get out, you blackguard!--Love takes him gently by the hand and leads him to the door, saying: Come with me and I will show you something better than this. But it is six of the one and half-a-dozen of the other, for whichever of these spirits comes to a man he is at once obliged to leave the warm chimney corner whether he will or no.--Alick had to make acquaintance with them both, and by no fault of his own.

I do not know whether it is still the case, but it used to be the custom in the Prussian army for the colonel of a regiment to send in regular reports of the conduct of his officers to the war-office at Berlin, and King Frederic William was in the habit of looking over these reports himself just to see how everything was going on in the different companies. Now Alick's good old colonel liked his young lieutenant extremely, and that for many reasons. One of them was this; The colonel had once possessed an estate over at Länneken, near Bütow and Lauenburg, which he had farmed on the most curious and eccentric principles in the world, and now that he had an auditor who was capable of entering into the merits of the case, he launched forth in explanation. The chief peculiarity of his system was that he would allow no manure to be used on his land, because he could not see the use of it; in short he had his own little ways of doing things, and like a stage-coachman who has grown too old to drive, he found intense enjoyment in talking over his experiences. Alick listened attentively and silently, for it would not have done to contradict his commanding officer, and so the old colonel thought him an unusually clever fellow. Alick's name therefore always appeared well in the report, but unfortunately the colonel spelt very badly, and on one occasion he wrote: "Lieutenant von Rambow is a very 'fe-iger' (cowardly) officer," when he meant "fähiger" (smart). The king saw this and wrote on the margin of the report, "I do not require cowards in my army--dismiss him at once." The old colonel was in despair, he must set matters right, but he could see no help for it but to consult his adjutant as to how it should be done. The latter showed him his mistake and then not being able to hold his tongue, told everyone what had happened, and before long poor Alick became the butt of his regiment. The man who laughed loudest, and referred to the matter oftenest, was a pompous fool of "very old family," who had always disapproved of Alick's agricultural talk, not because he found it stupid or mistaken, but because he found fault with everything he did, and now he battered his comrade with his heavy jests so unmercifully that all his brother officers noticed it. Alick alone remarked nothing.

Then something else happened; Mr. von so and so from whom Alick had learnt so much farming when riding, or with his gun in his hand, had a wonderfully beautiful daughter--I am not exaggerating, she was really a lovely girl. The lieutenant of "very old family" paid her great attention, but she would have nothing to say to him, and rather showed a preference for her other admirer, Alick. Whether it was that the lady was so stupid as to dislike the lieutenant of "very old family," or whether she wanted to marry a man who was really a man, or whether Alick's good-nature and his gentle deference to women pleased her, cannot be known, but before long Alick was as happy as a king, and the lieutenant of "very old family" was left out in the cold.

It chanced about this time that the officers of the cavalry-regiment gave a great ball, and that the lieutenant of very old family got a pair of false calves made for the occasion. His own comrades scarcely recognised him-

-his nether man was so changed, and as was natural when so many young people were together, such a good opportunity for playing a practical joke could not be allowed to pass, more especially when a mischief-maker like the adjutant was amongst them. The adjutant managed, unperceived by his victim, to pin a number of butterflies on the false calves of the lieutenant of "very old family" who danced away with them quite happily. Everyone looked and laughed and pointed him out to their friends, till at last he himself caught sight of the decorations on his false calves, and turning in a rage upon the first laughing face he saw, which, as chance would have it, was Alick's, growled: "If you had not been properly described already in the colonel's report, I should have had all the pleasure in the world in characterising you in the same way."--Alick did not take in the meaning of the words, but he heard the contemptuous tone in which they were uttered, and, being an extremely fiery young gentleman, said angrily in reply to his rival, that he had not the remotest idea of what he meant, but that his tone was most insulting, and that he must answer for what he had said. He then went and asked his captain, with whom he was on very friendly terms, what it all meant, and the explanation he received was not exactly calculated to lessen his resentment. He challenged the lieutenant of "very old family," and then challenged the adjutant for making known the colonel's mistake; and the lieutenant of "very old family" also challenged the adjutant because of the butterflies. So, a few days later, on a beautiful Sunday afternoon, they all three drove out to a cool and shady wood attended by their seconds and witnesses, doctors and surgeons, and there they slashed at each other's faces with their swords, and shot at each other, and after that peace was once more established amongst them. Alick had received a cut on the nose, because he had very foolishly parried a blow with his face instead of with his sword.

    The cut did him no harm although it did not add to his beauty, for Mr. von so and so's pretty daughter heard of what had happened, and after she had put two and two together, and had guessed that their rivalry was the true cause of their disagreement, who could blame the girl for being even kinder to Alick than before.

    Now I could tell you the whole of Alick and Frida's love story if I chose to do so, and then everyone would say that I had chosen a hero and heroine such as are not to be met with every day, a lieutenant in a cavalry-regiment and a nobleman's daughter. But I will refrain. In the first place because I never give myself more to do than I can help, and who is to oblige me to give the tradesman's young daughters who may possibly read this book private lessons in the way a cavalry-officer makes love, or to show young men without position how to make love to a nobleman's daughter.--And who will guarantee its not having that effect?--Secondly, I wish to say once for all that I am not writing for the young, but for the old who take a book to fan away the flies, and to make them forget their worries as they lie on the sofa in the afternoon.--Thirdly, I have still three girls to marry before the end of my book, and just let who ever wants to know what *that* is, ask the mother of three unmarried daughters. Louisa Hawermann must of course be married, and would it not be a shame to make the twins old maids and leave them to get through the world as best they can?--Fourthly and lastly, I do not feel myself capable of describing the love-making of a lieutenant in a cavalry-regiment. Such a thing is beyond me and beyond Joseph; it would require a Shakespeare or a Mühlbach to do it justice, and indeed who knows whether Shakespeare would have succeeded either, for as far as I know he never even attempted it.--The short and the long of it is that they were married at Whitsun-tide in the year 1843, and Mr. von so and so having no other dowry to give his daughter on that momentous occasion, gave her--his blessing. Now that he is our Alick's father-in-law we will call him by his right name, Mr. von Satrop of Seelsdorf, but it is as well to mention at the same time that Seelsdorf was far more deeply mortgaged than Pümpelhagen.

Frida von Satrop was a sensible girl, and thoroughly understood, even before her marriage, that as the lieutenant's affairs were somewhat involved, and as she herself had not a farthing, it would be much better for him to leave the army, and Alick consented to do so, for he saw that the joke about his cowardice was not likely to die out for a long time to come, and that the old colonel's blunder in the report would always remain there with the red ink stroke to mark it, and besides that he wanted to try some of his farming theories at Pümpelhagen, and to see whether he could not by these means make more money out of the estate and so pay off his debts.

He therefore sent in his papers, packed up his uniform, scarf and epaulettes, took sad leave of his trusty sword before laying it in the chest beside the other things, and then nailing down the lid affixed his seal to it, and tied on to it a piece of paper on which he had written these words: "The seal is to be broken by my heir if I should happen to die suddenly," and then the chest was sent to Pümpelhagen. Alick was married in a black dress-coat, and as soon as the ceremony was performed he and his young wife set off on their wedding-tour to the Rhine.

How he arrived at Pümpelhagen on midsummer's-day 1843, must be told in another chapter.

CHAPTER XI

The three years since his father's death which Alick had spent with his regiment, and which he had filled with agricultural study, heroic deeds and a love-affair, had been equally well employed at Pümpelhagen, for these three occupations had taken as prominent a part in the life of our old friends there as they had in his. Of the farming there is no need to speak; but the heroic deeds and the love-affairs might never have become known, had it not been for Fred Triddelfitz's conduct on one of the feast-days of the church. The friendship between him and Mary Möller had changed from that of a mother and son to that of a sister and brother; but on her side there was a very tender affection, which she showed in the way she kept him supplied with ham and sausages, indeed Mary was sometimes guilty of building up insecure castles in the air about priests and rings, bridal-wreaths, farms and self-government, so that the change in her sentiments was not a little alarming. Then Fred gradually took fright lest Hawermann should discover his secret luncheons, &c., and that his aunt, and mother, and father would, when they heard of what he had been doing, lecture him by the hour, tell him how silly he was, and--in short make it very disagreeable for him, Taking his love-affairs all together it must be confessed that though he did not dislike a talk with the twins, or--if his aunt were well out of the way--with Louisa Hawermann, his greatest happiness was caused by his friendship with Mary Möller. The heroic deeds done at Pümpelhagen during these three years were all performed within his own sphere of action. At first he had only shown his courage and enterprise secretly to the farm-lads, for if Hawermann had discovered what he was about, the great glory his cane had won him on the farmboys' shoulders would have been quickly dissipated. As time went on he grew bolder from not being found out, and on Palm Sunday morning he ventured, in an evil hour for himself, to treat one of the grooms in the same way, but the man was impertinent enough to forget the respect due to him, and seized him by the collar, and beat him so hard across the back and shoulders with his own cane, that Mary Möller had to spend the greater part of the afternoon in applying damp towels to his shoulders they--smarted so terribly. The worst of it all was that every time Mary Möller laid a cool piece of linen on his back, she made his conscience prick him by recapitulating all the kindnesses she had shown him, and in spite of the pain and discomfort from which he was suffering, asked him point blank what his intentions were, taking care to assure him at the same time, that she believed in his love, and that he would be true to her. He did not like that sort of talk at all, for he himself believed far more strongly in his love for good eating than in his love for her, and as for his intentions, he would rather not tell what they were. He stammered a few words of no particular meaning, and the better his back felt, the less inclined he was to tie himself down in any way; he tried to turn the conversation to another subject, but she would not allow that to be done, and laid the damp linen on his back less gently than at first. "Triddelfitz," she said at last when she found that she could get no satisfactory answer from him, "what am I to think of you?" And then, having finished arranging the linen on his back, she came round in front of him, and putting her arms akimbo, stared him full in the face. He was rather afraid of what might follow, and said deprecatingly: "What do you mean, Polly?"--"What do I mean? Shall I have to tell you more distinctly?" she cried, her eyes losing their former sweet and loving expression, "am I always to be led by the nose?" So saying she came dose up to him, and slapped him right between the shoulders on the top of the bandages.--"Ugh!--Hang it all!" he shrieked. "That *did* hurt."--"Ah, that hurt you, did it?" she asked. "And do you think that it doesn't hurt me to see the man to whom I have shown so much kindness treating me so deceitfully?"--"Oh, Polly! What *do* you mean?"--"What do I mean? This is what I mean!"--thud, came her hand down on his back.--"Confound it! It's burning like fire."--"I'm glad to hear it. It's only what you deserve for making a poor girl believe all your fine speeches and promises."--"Bless me, Polly, I'm only nineteen!"--"What has that got to do with it?"--"And then I'd like to take a situation as bailiff somewhere first, and then----" --"Well, and then what?"--thud, came another slap on the back.--"For Heaven's sake, mind what you are about! You're hurting me frightfully."--"Mind what *you* are about with *me*. Well, and then?"--"And then I shall be ready to take a farm, and that will be in about ten years time, I suppose."--"Well, and *then*?" she asked with a determination that was dreadful to him.--"Yes--and then," Fred stammered, with a nervous dread of the consequence of what he was going to say, "you will be too old."--His Polly Möller stood for a moment as though rooted to the spot, her eyes blazing with anger, then, bending forward, she struck him on the mouth with the wet bandages she had in her hand, and as she did so, the water in the linen fell upon his neck and ears in spray: "Too *old*? You fool! Too old, did you say?" then snatching up the basin of water she dashed it over his head and shoulders, and ran out of the room. While Fred stood there puffing and blowing, she pushed the door a little open again, and cried: "You'd better never show your face in my kitchen again."

That was the end of this love-affair, at least for the present, and it was also the end of the dainty little luncheons eaten in secrecy. Fred Triddelfitz stood motionless where Mary Möller had left him, and thought over the change in his circumstances, and of how essentially this love-affair of his had differed from all his preconceptions and from all the novels he had read, and then he made use in his ill-humour of the same expression that he had used when, soon after his arrival at Pümpelhagen, he had been sent road-mending on a rainy day in November: "I never thought it would be as bad as this!--What a blessing," he added, "that the governor is out, otherwise he'd have been certain to have heard the row she made."

Hawermann and Frank had gone to church at Gürlitz that morning. The farmer walked on silently, his heart full of love and gratitude to God for all His fatherly goodness to him and to his child who was to be confirmed on that Palm Sunday morning. As he went down the dry foot-path--there had been a slight frost during the night--his eyes rested on the bright scene before him, the snow was still lying in white patches beside the ditches, and under the shade of the dark pines, while the rye-fields with their tender green carpet on which the sun poured down its golden light, announced that Easter was nigh, and quietly awaited the promised resurrection. The smoke rising from the chimneys of the small villages round about was gilded by the sun's rays, showing how little the aspect of nature is affected by the cares and troubles of man, and from the church-towers on every hand was to be heard a solemn peal ringing over woods and meadows.--"Ah, if she had only lived to see this day!" said the old man aloud, forgetting that he was not alone.--"Who?" asked Frank with some hesitation, and fearing lest he might be thought intrusive.--"My poor wife, the mother of my dear child," the old man answered softly, as he turned his honest face and looked kindly at the youth at his side, as much as to say: My face and my heart tell the same tale, as you would know if you could only read my thoughts.--"Yes," he went on, "my good wife. But what am I saying? She sees our child better than I can, she does more for her than I can, and her thoughts are higher than the blue heavens, and her joy purer than the golden sunlight."--Frank walked on in silence not wishing to disturb the bailiff; he had never before felt such a deep reverence for his dear old friend, and now as he looked at him, and saw his white hair lying on his broad forehead as white and pure as those patches of snow on the ground, and read in his expression a full assurance of hope, and a calm faith in the resurrection, such as was also to be seen in the face of nature, for while his countenance was irradiated with the sunshine of love, the earth was bathed in that of the golden sun. At last he could resist the impulse no longer, and seized the old man's hand, saying: "Hawermann, dear Hawermann, you must have had a great deal of sorrow during your life."--"Not more," was the answer, "than other people have, but enough for me to remember as long as I live."--"Will you tell me about it? It is not curiosity that makes me ask."--"Why not?" he said, and then he told him his whole story, but without once mentioning Pomuchelskopp's name; "and," he said in conclusion, "as my child was once my only comfort, she is now my only joy."

While thus talking they reached the parsonage. Little Mrs. Behrens had grown rather older and rounder in the last few years, and did not trot about the house quite so restlessly as she used to do. To-day she sat perfectly still, leaving her duster to lie idly in its drawer, where it found life as dull as a pug-dog in a toy kennel; for the solemnity of the act to be performed that day in church forbade her attending to matters belonging only to the work-a-day world, above which she was raised for the time being by reason of her position of clergyman's wife, which made her the "nearest" to those taking part in the ceremony. Still, try as she might she could not keep quite motionless, and though she did not bustle about from place to place as usual, she could not resist going to see how her pastor was getting on, and then tying his bands for him and giving him a glass of wine; after that she went in search of Louisa, straightened her ruffles and whispered words of love and encouragement in her ear, and now that young Joseph, Mrs. Nüssler, the little twins and Bräsig had come, she was just about to resume her customary ways of going on when the church-bell rang out its last peal. The twins were also to be confirmed, and when Mrs. Behrens saw the three pretty children--Lina and Mina on either side of Louisa, who was a head taller than her little cousins--walking up the church-yard path, her eyes filled with tears: "Hawermann," she said, "our child has no gold chains and brooches such as it is now the foolish fashion for girls to wear at their confirmation; and, dear Hawermann, that black silk is thirty years old, I wore it last on the first Sunday I went to church after my marriage, and a happy heart beat within it I can assure you, for it was full of love to my pastor--I never wore it afterwards for it soon grew too tight for me, I was always rather stout, and so you see it is as good as new, and no one would ever find out that a bit had been added to the bottom of the skirt to lengthen it. And, Hawermann, I have put the money you gave me to buy a new dress into Louisa's purse. You are not angry with me, I hope? I wanted so much to see my gown in all its old glory again."--When they got to the church-door Bräsig pulled Hawermann back by the coat, and then said, looking at him with great emotion the while: "A confirmation such as this is a remarkable thing, a *very* remarkable thing, Charles. When I saw the three little girls going on before us I suddenly remembered my own confirmation which put an end to that dreadful work of herding sheep which I hated so at my father's, and permitted me to do some real farming. Just as these three little girls are going to church, I went with my companions, Charles Brandt and Christian Guhl, only that we did not wear black silk gowns; no, Christian had on a green coat, Charles, a brown one, and mine was grey; and instead of the nosegay of flowers that the little girls are carrying in their hands, we had each a small green sprig in our button-holes, and then we did not walk in a row like these children, but followed each other in single file like geese on their way to the pond.--Ah yes, it was just like this."

When the congregation had sung a hymn, Mr. Behrens preached his sermon. He had grown much older looking, but his voice was strong, his thoughts were well and clearly expressed, and his words were uttered with a gentle dignity. Age is less injurious to a clergyman's influence than to that of any one else, if only the man is worthy of his office. His people not only hear his words but look back upon the course of his long, true and honourable life and see in him a living example of goodness, as well as a mere preacher of it.--And that was the case with parson Behrens.

Now was the time for the examination, and the young girls took off their shawls. Louisa clasped her arms round her father and foster-mother with tears in her eyes; and Mrs. Nüssler kissed her twin-daughters lovingly; young Joseph wanted to say something, but said nothing after all, and then the three children left the parsonage pew and took their places at the altar.--"I wonder," said Bräsig to Frank, who was standing beside him, "how the little round-heads will get through their examination, I'm afraid that my god-daughter Mina will break down completely." And then he blew his nose and wiped his eyes.

Frank made him no answer, he had lost sight of all but one face, and that face which he knew so well had a look on it to-day that he had never seen before; he saw but one form, usually so graceful and active, but now slightly bent with a feeling of solemnity and awe, and the hands which had always given him such eager welcome were now raised in devotion, and it seemed to him as if God Himself were standing by the bending figure in the simple black dress, within which Mrs. Behrens' heart had once beat so happily, and showed him the purity of the heart that was now within it and told him to see that his heart was fit to take its place by hers. He felt as if he had been accustomed to see a beautiful landscape brilliant with sunshine and had had no thought awakened by its beauty but one of careless enjoyment, but now he felt as if he had returned to the same place after a long absence, and saw it bathed in the calm, pure light of the moon, and lo, all was changed. It seemed to him as though there were a weight upon his heart, and he were begging for mercy with supplicating hands raised to heaven, and he was filled with a deep compassion for himself, for he felt what a poor, miserable gift his heart would be were he to presume to offer it to such loveliness. And this deep compassion for oneself, this secret craving for a better heart, which comes over us when our eyes are opened to see that moonlight loveliness, we children of men call "love."

Bräsig stood beside him and every now and then whispered a few words to him which he did not hear, and which, if he had heard, he would have thought great nonsense. Perhaps he might even have been angry if he had listened to what was said to him, and yet the old bailiff only spoke as he felt, for he had lost the rose coloured spectacles of youth, and saw everything through a greyer medium. Bräsig underwent a frightful martyrdom while the examination was going on; he was so terrified lest his god-daughter Mina should break down, and every time she answered a question rightly he gave vent to such a tempestuous sigh, that if Mr. Behrens had been a clergyman of the new school, he would have imagined that he had brought some miserable sinner to repent in dust and ashes.--"God be praised and thanked!" murmured the sinner, "Mina knows her catechism." Then going up to Frank: "It's coming now, only listen." And getting round to the other side of Hawermann: "Do listen, Charles. Mina will have it. Mina will have to answer the great water question. I knew it quite well, but Christian Guhl couldn't answer it, so I was made to say it instead. I've forgotten all but the beginning now: 'For water truly accomplishes nothing, but only the spirit of God.'"--While Mina gave the answer without hesitation the old man repeated it after her word for word. The churchwarden now came up with the collecting-bag, and Bräsig dropped half-a-crown into it with a bang, as though he expected his donation to buy him freedom from the weight of his anxiety. He then turned round, and seizing Mrs. Nüssler by the hand, exclaimed almost aloud: "*Did* you hear our little roundheads?" after which he blew his nose so loudly that Mrs. Nüssler had to remonstrate with him for disturbing the congregation.

If anyone had examined the tie that bound Bräsig to little Mina, a tie which was founded on the memory of his old affection for her mother, it would have been found to be quite as strong, although much calmer than that by which Frank wished to bind Louisa to himself.--Love is manifold, and reveals itself in the most unexpected forms. It flies up to heaven on rosy pinions, and walks the earth clumsily in wooden shoes; it speaks with "tongues" as the apostles did on that first Whitsunday-morning, and again it sits by our side like an innocent child; it gives the loved one diamonds and coronets, or acts like old bailiff Schecker, who paid his court to my aunt Schäning by presenting her with a fat capon.

When the confirmation ceremony was over and the Holy Communion had been for the first time received by the young people, Mr. Behrens retired to the vestry, and Samuel Pomuchelskopp, whose son Tony was one of those confirmed on that day, stalked past the clergyman's pew, in his best blue coat, and followed him there. Instead of going into the room he merely put his head in at the door--"To show everyone what a noodle he is," whispered Bräsig to Hawermann--and in a loud voice, as if he had been at market instead of in church, invited the parson to come up to the manor-house and have some broth, roast-beef and a bottle of red wine with him.--"That everyone may hear what a confounded Jesuit he is," whispered Bräsig.--The clergyman regretted that he could not accept the invitation, as he was not only rather tired, but also expected some friends to dinner at the parsonage. As Pomuchelskopp went away he glanced over his shoulder at the occupants of the parsonage pew, and was about to bow with such condescension that it would have been a pleasure to look at him, when he caught sight of the quizzical expression of Bräsig's face. Our old friend was what Mrs. Behrens, if she had seen him at that moment, would have called too bad a Christian to keep his evil thoughts from showing themselves in his face even when he was in God's own house.--How different he looked a few minutes later when the three young girls came up to receive his kiss and blessing after they had had those of their parents and foster-parents. He raised his eyebrows as high as he could, and frowned solemnly, so as to make himself look as paternal as possible. And he succeeded very well as far as Louisa and Lina were concerned, but when his little Mina came to him, he felt as if he himself were a child again, and caught her in his arms, saying so that she only could hear: "Never mind, Mina, never mind. I'll give you something nice." And because he could think of nothing suitable on the spur of the moment, and chanced to have his handkerchief in his hand, he added: "I'll give you a dozen pocket-handkerchiefs--nice bright ones too." For he wanted to do the thing well when he was about it.

All of the company had now offered their good wishes and had kissed the children, but two of their number had come off badly in this respect. Young Joseph only got half a kiss, and Frank got none at all. As far as young Joseph was concerned it was his own fault, for he had squeezed himself into a corner of the seat in such a way that the girls could only get at the small right side of his mouth, while the left, and larger half was completely hidden by the wood-work of the pew. And Frank--he had not yet come down to earth, he was raised in thought far above all sublunary things, and it was not till they had reached the church-door that he took Louisa's hand in his and said something to her, but what it was he could not have told five minutes later.--He was in love. That beautiful face with its look of rapt devotion had conquered him--and for ever.

It is possible that some punctilious matron, or perhaps some very strict maiden lady--whether old or merely come to years of discretion--may be displeasured with this part of my story, and ask me: "Why did the young man not look out for a suitable wife elsewhere if he must needs do such a worldly thing as fall in love?"--To which I can only reply: "Honoured Madam, or most respected Miss so and so, the young man was so new to those little affairs, of which you, from your earlier experience, have such a thorough comprehension, that he did not regard falling in love as at all a worldly action. And when and where ought a young man to fall in love? Is such a thing only allowable at a garden party in summer, or during the cotillon at a ball in winter? If there are many roads leading to Rome there are far more which lead to marriage, and he who can date the beginning of his journey along one of these roads from a meeting in church, is much wiser than he who sets out from a ball-room. In the first instance the altar is near at hand, and in the second there is often a long and miry lane to be traversed before the lovers can reach the altar, so that thin shoes and boots are sometimes worn and travel-stained when they enter the holy estate of matrimony. Do you not agree with me, honoured Madam. Am I not right, most respected Miss so and so?"

A simple repast was set out in the parsonage. Bräsig was in high spirits and beamed upon every one like sunshine after rain. The old clergyman was also cheerful, for like Solomon he knew that there is a time for every purpose, "a time to cast away stones, and a time to gather stones together;" but still the remembrance of what had taken place that morning was strong upon them all, and neither Mrs. Behrens nor Mrs. Nüssler recovered the full use of their tongues until they were sitting over the coffee-table. Immediately after dinner the old clergyman went to lie down on the sofa in his study to rest after his exertions, and enjoy a quiet nap. Hawermann went out for a walk with his daughter and his two nieces, for he thought that the calm beauty of the spring-day would soothe the excitement in their young hearts, and Frank went with them, his heart full of the influence of the spring of love newly awakened within him. Joseph Nüssler found a corner which was almost as comfortable as his favourite seat at home, and Bräsig paced up and down the room with a long pipe in his mouth. Since he had had his pension he had entirely changed the character of his walk, and turned out his feet far more than of old, indeed it may be said that when his face was turned to the north his feet pointed due east and west. He did it to show that he was his own master, and to prove that long years of walking over ploughed fields had not destroyed his grace of movement, or prevented his appearing worthy of his new position, that of a gentleman at large. The two ladies seated themselves on the sofa above which the pictures were hung.

"Yes, dear Mrs. Nüssler," said Mrs. Behrens, "thank God, the children have done well so far. Louisa is now sixteen and a half, and your girls are six months older than she is. My pastor says, and I know that he is right, that they are well educated, and so if ever they have to work for themselves they are quite able to do so. They might get situations as governesses any day."--Bräsig came to a standstill, raised his eyebrows, and blew such a thick cloud of smoke towards the sofa that even young Joseph was amazed.--"Ah, yes," replied Mrs. Nüssler, "and the children have to thank you and Mr. Behrens for that," here she seized her friend's hand. "Brother Charles and I have often agreed that though we were quite able to provide them with their daily bread, to see that their dresses were neat and suitable, and to teach them to be honest and truthful, and everything that relates merely to domestic life, still we were not capable of teaching them such things as make human beings worthy of the name. Am I not right Joseph?"--A comfortable grunt of acquiescence came from behind the stove, it was a sound resembling that which a faithful old dog would utter when his back was stroked by a friendly hand.--"Did you hear, Mrs. Behrens? Joseph quite agrees with me."--"Don't say that please," remonstrated Mrs. Behrens, not wishing to be thanked, "I've done very little for your girls after all, it was different with Louisa of course, for I was the nearest to her. But--what I was going to say was this--we've never spoken of it before--do you intend one of your children, Mina perhaps, to go out as a governess?"--"*What?*" cried Mrs. Nüssler, staring at the clergyman's wife in as great astonishment as if she had just announced that Mina has serious intentions of having herself elected pope of Rome, but when Mrs. Behrens began to explain her meaning more clearly, Bräsig interrupted her by bursting into a hearty fit of laughter: "Ha, ha, ha! What a joke! What a joke! Did hear, young Joseph? Our little Mina a governess! ha, ha!"--Mrs. Behrens sat stiffly back in her corner like a doll that had had its ears bored, her rosy turned purple with anger, and her lilac cap-rib vibrated with every word as she said indignantly: "What are you laughing at, Bräsig? Are you laughing at me, pray? Are you laughing because I thought that Mina might become a governess? Perhaps, Mr. bailiff Bräsig," she continued drawing herself up proudly, "you are not aware that *I* was a governess once, and that teaching children is a *very* different thing from beating farm-lads?"--"Ah, but--don't be angry, Mrs. Behrens--ha, ha!--our Mina a governess."--But Mrs. Behrens had lost her temper too completely to be able to remain silent, so she went on excitedly: "There is a great difference between educated and uneducated people; a person like *you* could never governess!"

As she uttered these words her parson, who been wakened by Bräsig's laughter, entered the room. He was struck by the comicality of the idea, and being too short-sighted to see his wife's angry face, laughing: "Ha, ha! Bräsig a governess!"--A great change came over Mrs. Behrens on her husband's entrance; although she had been boiling over with wrath the moment before, the mere fact of his presence seemed to cast oil on the troubled waters, and she grew calm and quiet. She was sometimes guilty of uttering a hasty word, or of reddening with anger when he was in the room, but she had never yet given way to a regular fit of passion in his presence, and so her honest round face, which only a moment ago was flushed with anger, now glowed with a deeper blush of shame at the thought that she, a clergyman's wife, had so far forgotten herself, and on such a day too. The feeling of shame drove away the last remnants of her anger, and when she heard her own words repeated, that Bräsig could never be a governess, she hid her face in her handkerchief and laughed heartily though silently.

Mrs. Nüssler had been sitting on thorns during the scene between Mrs. Behrens and Bräsig, and when the parson came in, she sprang to her feet, exclaiming: "Oh, reverend Sir, I am the innocent cause of the quarrel. Bräsig, have done with your stupid laughter. Bless me, if Mrs. Behrens thinks that my Mina ought to be a governess--I have no objection. If you and Mrs. Behrens really think it better for her, I will give my consent, for you've always given me good advice. Don't you agree with me, Joseph?"--Joseph came out from behind the stove as he answered: "Yes. It all depends upon circumstances; if she ought to go, let her go." As soon as he had finished speaking he left the room, most probably to consider the matter in solitude.--"What is the meaning of all this?" asked the clergyman, "are you in earnest, Regina?"--Mrs. Nüssler approached the little lady anxiously: "Never mind, Mrs. Behrens.--I hope you're ashamed of yourself, Bräsig?--Dear Mrs. Behrens, don't cry any more," and as she spoke she drew the handkerchief away from her friend's face gently, but on seeing the laughing face raised to hers she started back a step or two, exclaiming: "Why, what's all this!"--"Only a misunderstanding, neighbour," said the old gentleman smiling. "No one ever thought seriously that Mina ought to be a governess. No, our children shall never swell the number of poor unhappy girls who are knocked about from place to place in the world, and earn their bread as dependents. No, our children shall, please God, become good wives, and notable mistresses of households, and in course of time they may with our full consent become governesses--to their own children."--"Reverend Sir--dear Mr. Behrens," cried Mrs. Nüssler, looking as if she were relieved from a terrible dread, "God bless you for saying that. Our Mina shall not be a governess. Joseph--where are you, Joseph? Ah, he must have gone out to hide his grief. Yes, Mr. Behrens, she shall learn to be a good housekeeper. You shall see that I'll do my best to teach her thoroughly."--"Yes," cried Bräsig, "and she must be able to cook a good dinner."--"Of course, Bräsig. Ah, Mr. Behrens, I found all the governesses that I tried such a handful! And last week I went to call on the wife of the new deputy sheriff--she had once been a governess--and I found her a weakly sort of creature who moves about the house as listlessly as if she couldn't be troubled with anything, and then she's one of those sort of people who always wants what she can't get. She's a poor white-faced thing, and looks as if she thought herself a sweet holy martyr--interesting looking, *she* calls it."--"Bosh!" said Bräsig.--"And, Mrs. Behrens," continued Mrs. Nüssler, "she always has the eggs hard boiled, and the roasts burnt in her house. Good gracious! I'm not one of those who say that women ought not to be educated, and well educated too, so that they may be able to read the newspapers, and may know all about old Fritz and his people, and may even be able to tell in what countries the orange and quinine-trees are to be found; still, these things are only pleasant to know, they are not necessary; and, Mrs. Behrens, I always say that if any woman doesn't know that sort of thing she can always wait till she meets some one learned enough to give her the information she requires; but, Mrs. Behrens, knowing how meat ought to be roasted is a different thing altogether! There can be no question of waiting in such a case, for dinner comes at a regular hour, and, living in the country as I do, Mrs. Behrens, there is no one I can trust to look after these things, except a stupid servant who'd be sure to make some dreadful mistake if she were left to herself."--"You're quite right, neighbour," said the clergyman, "the girls must learn to be good housekeepers."--"That's what I say, reverend Sir, that's just what I say. Goodness gracious me! That poor little woman, the deputy sheriffs wife, knows nothing about housekeeping. Only fancy! She asked me how many pairs of shoes my children wore out in the year when they were seven years old; she asked me how we milked the pigs at Rexow, and she asked me what the chickens said. Ah, reverend Sir, Louisa must not be a governess either."--"No, we don't want her to be one, and as Hawermann thinks as we do on the subject, it is arranged that she should remain here and learn housekeeping. Regina is beginning to take things too easily, and," seating himself on the sofa beside his wife, and putting his arm round her waist, "she is growing too old to have so much on her hands, so she is glad to have a young girl to help her to manage the house, and besides that, she could not bear to part with Louisa."--"You would like it even less than I should, pastor. I'm beginning to feel myself quite shelved, I assure you, it's 'Louisa bring me this,' and 'Louisa get me that' from morning till night."--"Well, well, I don't deny it, I should miss the child terribly if she were to go away."

Hawermann now came back with the children and Frank. When they had nearly reached the door they saw young Joseph walking excitedly up and down the garden. As she approached him, he went up to his daughter Mina, and taking her in his arms, kissed her and said: "It isn't my fault, Mina," and when Hawermann asked him what was the matter, he merely answered: "Brother-in-law, what must be, must be." When the party was separating to go home, and Joseph was seated in the carriage, he felt as if he were driving a victim up to the sacrificial altar. Although his wife explained the whole matter thoroughly to him, and told him that Mina was not to be a governess, the conversation at the parsonage had made such an indelible impression on him, that he could never get over the idea that Mina had a sorrowful life before her. From this time forward he always made her sit beside him at dinner, and gave her all the little titbits in the dish before him, as if each meal were to be the last before her sorrows began.

CHAPTER XII

So it was that the little girls' mode of life was settled as far as it is possible for human beings to settle the future of other people. But fate often interferes with the best laid schemes which worthy white-haired elders have made, and introduces the most unexpectedly incongruous elements. The worst of making such plans is that they never succeed whether they are wise or foolish, because the good old white-haired people have forgotten to call back to their remembrance the thoughts and feelings which influenced them before their hair began to turn grey. The old clergyman never seriously thought for a moment that any young man would come and take his foster-daughter away from him, and Mrs. Behrens, who, after the manner of women, thought much and often of the probability of such an event happening at some time or other, comforted herself with the thought that Louisa knew no one she could marry. She did not count Frank because of his position in society; and as for Triddelfitz, she regarded him as mere boy, for he was continually getting into scrapes and being scolded by her. She was now to be shown that a beautiful young girl, even though she may live in a parsonage, attracts young men to flutter round her as much as a flower does a butterfly. She was to see that the caterpillar which but a short time ago had roused her wrath in a different fashion, had turned into a gorgeous yellow butterfly which delighted to hover round the sweet flower she had so long tended. She would have thought the whole affair a good joke if the butterfly had not been her sister's son, and the flower Louisa Hawermann.

A few days after the confirmation Fred came to Gürlitz, his heart full of hatred to all women. The basin of water he had had thrown over his head, and being turned out of the paradise of good things to which he had been so long accustomed, had had a chilling effect on him; and as his novels had taught him that any young man who had been deceived in the character of his lady-love as he, Fred, had been, had a right to hate all women, he made use of his right and hated them. He had not been to Gürlitz for a long time because he wanted to punish his aunt for her constant lectures by depriving her of the pleasure of seeing him. When Fred had been sitting in the parlour for some time nursing his hatred of women, and only deigning to talk to the clergyman, little Mrs. Behrens went to join Louisa in the kitchen, and told her with great glee of his quiet manner: "Fred is very much improved," she said. "Thank God, he is growing wiser as he gets older."--Louisa laughed, but made no answer. Though she had not had much opportunity of studying the ways and manners of young men, still she knew Fred Triddelfitz too well to trust to appearances. Any one who understood the boy knew that if he tried to play some part that was unnatural to him, such as pretending to be a woman-hater, the real Fred Triddelfitz would suddenly reappear in his true colours and startle every one, but more especially his dear aunt. He had not been long in the same room with Louisa before he threw overboard his hatred of women, and all remembrance of Mary Möller, the wash-hand-basin, and the larder, and took in a large cargo of romantic ideas as ballast instead; this cargo he called "falling in love with Louisa." And as he had got rid of the trammels of the old love he was able to set sail gaily and make for the open sea. At first he tacked about so much that his aunt was puzzled, but as soon as he reached the high seas "of feeling," unfurled his top-gallant-sails, and had the rudder well in hand, she discovered what he was about, and was very much frightened. She looked upon him as a daring sea-rover, a pirate, a corsair who was trying to run down the dainty little brig in which she had shipped all her motherly love and hopes.

She tried a feint or two to draw off his attention, but the pirate kept on his course unchecked. She showed her parson the red danger signal she had hoisted in her distress, but he seemed to look upon the whole affair as a good joke, perhaps because he was convinced that the brig was in no danger. He sat back comfortably in his sofa corner, sometimes laughing and sometimes shaking his head.--Little Mrs. Behrens lost all patience with her nephew and called him in her own mind: "A silly boy, a young rascal, and a little wretch." But when the pirate began to fire one broadside after another of honied phrases and poetical sentiments at the tiny craft, she gallantly steamed out to sea to defend it and opened her attack on the rover by throwing her grappling irons, taking him in tow and carrying him off with her in triumph: "Come, my boy, come. I want to speak to you, Fred. You may as well take your hat with you." When she had him safe in the still-room she manoeuvred him into a corner where he was unable to move because of the barricade of jars, tubs, &c., and then seizing a loaf of bread cut a tremendously thick slice, saying: "You must be hungry, Freddy. You have an empty stomach, sonny, and an empty stomach makes people say and do things that they had better not.--There now I've spread it with butter for you, here's the cheese, won't you have a bit--set to work, my boy, and eat a good luncheon."--Fred stood silently before her not knowing what to do; he had wished to win a heart, and instead of that he had been given a slice of bread and butter! He was about to speak, but his aunt would not allow him: "I know what you are going to say, my boy, so you needn't speak, my child. But here--just to please me--here is a bottle of beer, pray take it out to Hawermann who is sowing peas in the field below the garden. Tell him that it's some of the beer he likes so much, it comes from the mayor of Stavenhagen's brewery." While speaking she took him through the kitchen, and let him out at the back door. As he was going, she called after him through a chink in the doorway: "You won't be able to come and see us for a long time as you've begun to sow the corn and will of course have a great deal to do--no, no, my boy, it can't be helped--but when you come back, in autumn perhaps, Louisa will be seventeen, and you must give up talking such childish nonsense to her as you've been doing to-day, she'll be too old for such folly then. Good-bye now, sonny, eat your bread and butter." Then she shut the door leaving Fred outside with a great slice of bread in one hand, and a bottle of beer in the other.

He felt that his aunt had treated him very badly, and was so angry at first that he felt inclined to throw the bread and butter in at the kitchen window and the bottle of beer after it, at the same time vowing that he would never again set foot in the parsonage as long as he lived. But second thoughts are always best, so he turned and walked down the garden path glancing now at the bread and butter and now at the bottle of beer, and saying to himself: "Hang it all, I'm not a bit hungry. The old lady didn't hit the right nail on the head there. But the fact is she only wanted to get rid of me.--Wait a bit, auntie, you won't get the better of me so easily! I know when and where Louisa goes to walk.--She must be mine! Whatever happens, she must be mine!" Then he threw himself under the hedge at the end of the garden and proceeded to lay out his plan of operations in this new love affair. How angry he would have been if he had known that Louisa saw him from her garret window!--He did not know that however, and as he was afraid that his bread and butter would fall on the gravel and be spoilt, he thought it better on the whole to eat it while it was good, and when he had finished it, he said: "I don't care a farthing for my aunt and Mary Möller; Louisa is an angel! She must be mine! It's quite clear that my relations won't approve of our love.--*Bong!* No girl like Louisa is ever to be won without a struggle. I'll ...... yes, what ought I to do?"--Before he did anything else he thought it as well to drink the bottle of beer, and when he had finished it every drop, he rose and crossed the ploughed field with renewed courage, stamping his firm determination into the soft soil as he went on: "She *shall* be mine!" And when the seed had sprung up the villagers, said: "Look, do you see where the devil has been sowing thistles and nettles amongst old bailiff Hawermann's corn!"

So Fred went heart and soul into his new love affair. There was one good thing in it, and that was that he was now far more amenable to the bailiff than before, because he looked on him in the light of his future father-in-law. He sat by his side in the evening and told him how much his father would advance to set him up in business, and asked his advice as to whether, he should buy or rent a farm, or consulted him about buying a large tract of land in Livonia or Hungary. The old man gently talked him out of any of his ideas which were simply absurd, but he silently rejoiced in the change that had taken place in his pupil: "The young rascal used to be able to talk of nothing but riding, dancing and hunting, and now he speaks of sensible things however foolishly." One evening when he and Fred were alone, Frank having gone to Gürlitz, he was still more astonished by Fred's confiding to him that if he remained in Mecklenburg he would either buy or rent a place with a good house in the middle of a park--park was the very word he used, not garden--for, he said, he owed it to his future wife that everything should be done in good style, and added, that he would love and care for her nearest relations like a father, as he said this he looked at the bailiff with such a touchingly affectionate gaze that the latter felt quite uncomfortable. "Triddelfitz," remonstrated Hawermann, "you are surely not so foolish as to think yourself in love at your age?"--Fred answered that it might be so, or it might not be so, but he could at least say with certainty, that he intended his old father-in-law to have a whole wing in his house for his sole use, and that as he had always been accustomed to plenty of fresh air and exercise, he should keep a couple of horses for him to ride or drive. Having said this, he rose and began to walk up and down the room with long strides, waving his hands as he went, so that Hawermann, who was sitting in the sofa corner, had to move his head about from side to side in his efforts to keep his eye on his pupil's movements. When he was saying good-night that evening, Fred pressed the old gentleman's hand as warmly and emphatically as if it were a matter of life and death, and a moment later when Hawermann suspected no evil, he was startled to feel a warm hand stroking his white hair, then a head bent over him and a hearty kiss was pressed on his brow. Before the old man had had time to recover from his consternation, Fred had left the room.

Fred was a very good-hearted young fellow and wished the whole world to be as happy as he was himself. His intentions were good but his actions were foolish. He had never gone back to see his aunt at Gürlitz. It made him cross to think of the wretched day when he had been forbidden to show his feelings to Louisa, and yet he daily lived over again all that had passed on that occasion. Bitter as the thought was, it was not long before gall was added to the draught he had to drink--And by whom was this added?--By Frank!--During the whole of that spring Frank went to Gürlitz whenever he had time, and in summer when the three Miss von Rambows came to Pümpelhagen, Louisa used to go and see them very often, and when she was there Frank was never far away, while he--our poor Fred, was not with them, and had to content himself with envying them from a distance.

I did not mean to say, and I am sure that no one who reads this book would ever imagine that Fred was mean and wicked enough to be spying and prying into what did not concern him, but he would have been very stupid if he had not suspected what Frank was about. And this was quite right and proper, a young man who is really in love ought to feel the pangs of jealousy, for jealousy is a necessary ingredient in the tender passion, and I always look upon any man the course of whose love is utterly unruffled by anxiety or by the presence of a rival as very like my neighbour Mr. Hamann, who is in the habit of riding with only one spur. Frank was the rival in this case, and Fred regarded him as such, and before long had put him in the same category as his aunt and Mary Möller, he never addressed him and kept all his conversation for his future father-in-law.

No human being can stand more than a certain amount of pain, after that it becomes unbearable and a remedy must be found; now the only remedy a lover finds effectual is an interview with his sweetheart. Matters had come to such a pass with Fred that he could no longer exist without seeing Louisa, so he began to lie in wait for her in all sorts of holes and corners. Every hollow-tree was a good hiding-place from which he could watch for her coming, every ditch was of use in concealing his advance, every hill was a look-out from which he could sweep the country with his gaze, and every thicket served him for an ambush. He was so much in earnest that he could not fail to succeed in his attempts to see her, and he often gave Louisa a great fright by pouncing out upon her, when she least expected him, and when she was perhaps thinking of ..... we will not say Frank. Sometimes he was to be seen rearing his long slight figure out of a bush like a snake in the act of springing, sometimes his head would appear above the green ears of rye like a seal putting its head above water, and sometimes as she passed under a tree he would drop down at her side from the branches when he had been crouched like a lynx waiting for its prey. At first she did not mind it much, for she looked upon it as a new form of his silly practical joking, and so she only laughed and talked to him about some indifferent subject; but she soon discovered that a very remarkable change had taken place in him. He spoke gravely and solemnly and uttered the merest nothings as if they had been the weightiest affairs of state. He passed his hand meditatively across his forehead as if immersed in profound thought, and when she spoke of the weather, he laid his hand upon his heart as if he were suffering from a sudden pain in the side. When she asked him to come to Gürlitz he shook his head sadly, and said: Honour forbade him to do so. When she asked him about her father, his words poured forth like a swiftly flowing stream: The bailiff was an angel; there never was, and never would be such a man again on the face of the earth; *his* father was good and kind, but *hers* was the prince of fathers. When she asked after Miss Fidelia, he said: He never troubled himself about women, and was utterly indifferent to *almost* all of them; but once when, as ill luck would have it, she asked him about Frank, his eyes flashed and he shouted: "Ha!" once or twice with a sort of snort, laughed scornfully, caught hold of her hand, slipped a bit of paper into it, and plunged head foremost into the rye-field, where he was soon lost to sight.--When she opened the paper she found that it contained the following effusion:

TO HER

"When with tender silvery light
Luna peeps the clouds between,
And 'spite of dark disastrous night
The radiant sun is also seen,
When the wavelets murmuring flow
When oak and ivy clinging grow,
Then, O then, in that witching hour
Let us meet *in my* lady's bow'r.

"Where'er thy joyous step doth go
Love waits upon thee ever,
The spring-flow'rs in my hat do show
I'll cease to love thee never.
When thou'rt gone from out my sight
Vanished is my sole delight.
Alas! Thou ne'er canst understand
What I've suffered at thy hand.

"My *vengeance* dire! will fall on him,
The foe who has hurt me sore,
Hurt *me*! who writes this poem here;
Revenge!! I'll seek for ever more."

Frederic Triddelfitz.

Pümpelhagen, July, 3d, 1842.

The first time that Louisa read this effusion she could make nothing of it, when she had read it twice she did not understand it a bit better, and after the third reading she was as far from comprehending it as she had been at first; that is to say, she could not make out who it was on whom the unhappy poet wished to be revenged. She was not so stupid as not to know that the "Her" was intended for herself.

She would have liked to have been able to think that the whole affair was only a silly joke, but when she remembered Fred's odd manner she was obliged to confess that it was anything but a joke, and so she determined to keep as much as possible out of his way. She was such a tender-hearted little creature that she was full of compassion for Fred's sufferings. Now pity is a bridge that often leads to the beautiful meadows stretched on the other side of it full of rose-bushes and jasmine-hedges, which are as attractive to a maiden of seventeen as cherries to a bird, and who knows whether Louisa might not have been induced to wander in those pleasant groves, had she not been restrained by the thought of Fred riding amongst the roses on the old sorrel-horse, holding a great slice of bread and butter in one hand and a bottle of beer in the other. In spite of her compassion for him she could not help laughing, and so remained safely on this side of the bridge; she liked best to watch Fred from a distance, for the sorrel might have lain down in the pond again, and Fred might have smeared her with the bread and butter. The stupidest lads under the sun may often win the love of girls of seventeen, and even men with only an apology for a heart are sometimes successful, but alas for the young fellow who has ever condescended to wear motley, he can never hope to win his lady's affection, for nothing is so destructive to young love as a hearty fit of laughter.

Louisa could not restrain her laughter when she thought of the ludicrous scene that had just taken place, but she suddenly stopped in the midst of her merriment, for she felt as if a soft hand had just taken hers, and as if a pair of dark eyes were looking at her affectionately. Perhaps this thought may have come into her head because she caught sight of Frank coming towards her from the distance. The next moment it flashed into her mind that it was Frank on whom Fred wished to be revenged, and so when they met a deep blush overspread her face, and feeling that that was the case made her so angry with herself that she blushed even deeper than before. Frank spoke to her in his usual courteous manner about indifferent things, but she was strangely shy, and answered him at cross-purposes, for her mind was full of Fred and his vows of vengeance.

"Heaven knows what's the matter," thought Frank as he was returning home after having walked a short way with her, "she isn't at all like herself to-day. Is it my fault? Has she had anything to vex or annoy her? What was that piece of paper she was tearing up?"--Meanwhile he had reached the place where he had met her. Some of the bits of paper were still lying on the ground, and he saw on one of them, without picking it up: "*Revenge!* I'll seek for evermore Frederic Triddelfitz." This made him curious for he knew Fred's handwriting, so he looked about and found two more bits of paper, but when he put them together he could make nothing more out of them but: "clinging grows ... that witching hour .... meet in my lady's bow'r ..... Spring flowers .... I'll cease to ... from out my sight .... my sole delight ... *Alas!* thou ne'er ... my *vengeance* dire! .... The foe ... *Revenge!!* I'll seek for evermore Frederic Triddelfitz." The wind had blown away all the rest.

There was not much to be made out of it, but after a time Frank came to the conclusion that Fred Triddelfitz was in love with Louisa, dogged her footsteps, and wanted to be revenged on her for some reason only known to himself. It was a ridiculous affair altogether, but still when he remembered that Fred Triddelfitz was as full of tricks as a donkey's hide of grey hair, and that he might easily do something that would be of great annoyance to Louisa, Frank determined to keep watch, and not to let Fred out of his sight when he went in the direction of Gürlitz.

Fred had broken the ice, he had spoken, he had done his part, and it was now Louisa's turn to speak if anything was to come of it. He waited, and watched, and got no answer. "It's a horrid shame," he said to himself. "But she isn't up to this sort of thing yet, I must show her what she ought to do." Then he sat down and wrote a letter in a feigned hand.

> Address: "To Her that you know of.
> Inscription: "Sweet Dream of my soul!

"This letter can tell you nothing, it only contains what is absolutely necessary for you to learn, and you will find it in the *third* rose-bush in the *second* row. I'll tell you the rest by word of mouth, and will only add: Whenever you see a *cross* drawn in *white chalk* on the garden-door, you will find the disclosure of my sentiments under the flower-pot beside the third rose-bush in the second row. The *waving* of a *pocket-handkerchief* on the *Gürlitz* side of the house will be a token of your presence, and of your desiring an interview; *my* signal, on the other hand, will be *whistling* three times on the crook of my stick. (Our shepherd taught me how to do it, and love makes everything easy to learn). *Randyvoo*: The large ditch to the *right* of the bridge.

> "Ever thine!!

> "From Him whom you know of."

"P.S. Pardon me for having written this in my shirt-sleeves, it is such a frightfully hot day.----"

This letter fell into the wrong hands, for it was Mrs. Behrens who found it when she went out to water her flowers, whilst Louisa, who was now a notable little housekeeper, was busy indoors making gooseberry jam. The clergyman's wife had no scruples about opening and reading the letter, and after she had done so she was quite convinced that it was intended for Louisa, and had been written by her nephew Fred.

She could not tell Louisa of her discovery, for that would simply have been playing into Fred's hands, she had therefore to content herself with talking of letters in general, and trying to find out in a round-about kind of way whether Louisa had received any epistles such as she had in her pocket, but as the girl did not understand what she meant, she determined not to tell her pastor what had happened. For, she thought, why should she make him angry by telling him of the foolish boy's love troubles, and besides that, it would have been very painful for her to have to give evidence against her own flesh and blood--and unfortunately Fred was her sister's son. But she wished with all her heart that she could have have had a few minutes quiet talk with the culprit himself, and that was impossible, for she never saw him by any chance.

She was very silent and thoughtful for a few days, and took the entire charge of watering the flowers into her own hands. It was just as well that she did so, for soon afterwards she found a letter drenched with rain under the third rose-bush in the second row. This letter was still more to the point than the last:

Address: "To *Her*, the *only* woman I adore.
Inscription: "Soul of my existence!!

"We are surrounded by pitfalls; I am aware that our foe watches my every step.--Cowardly *spy*, I *scorn* you!--Have no fear, Beloved, I will conquer all difficulties.--One bold deed will bring our love *recognition*. At two o'clock to-morrow afternoon, when the *Dragon* is asleep that guards my *treasure*, I shall expect to see your signal with the pocket-handkerchief. As for myself, I shall then be hidden behind the manure heap on the bank beside the large ditch, and shall whistle three times on the crook of my stick to entice you to come to me. And--even though the powers of hell should fight against me--I have sworn to be ever

Thine."

Mrs. Behrens was furious when she read this letter. "The ....! The ....! Oh you young rascal! 'When the dragon is asleep!' The wretch means me by that! But wait a bit! *I'll* entice *you* to come to *me*, and though the powers of hell won't touch you, if once I get hold of you, I'll give you such a box on the ear as you never had before!"

About two o'clock next day, Mrs. Behrens rose from her sofa and went into the garden. The parlour-door creaked and the garden-door banged as she went out, and the parson hearing the noise, looked out at the window to see what it was that took his wife out at that unusual hour, for as a general rule she did not move from her sofa till three had struck. He saw her go behind a bush and wave her pocket-handkerchief.--"She's making signs to Hawermann, of course," said he, and then he went and lay down again. But the fact of the matter is that she only wanted to show her sister's son how much she longed to get within reach of his ears. But he did not come, not yet were his three whistles to be heard.--She returned to her room very crossly, and when her husband asked her at coffee time to whom she had been making signals in the garden, she was so overwhelmed with confusion that in spite of being a clergyman's wife--I am sorry to have to confess it-- she told a lie, and said that she had found it so frightfully close she had been fanning herself a little.

On the third day after that she found another letter:

> Address: "To *Her* who is intended for me by *Fate*.
> Inscription: "*Sun* of my *dark* existence!!

"Have you ever suffered the *pains of hell*? I have been enduring them since two o'clock in the afternoon of the day before yesterday when I was hidden behind the manure-heap. The weather was lovely, our *foe* was busy in the clover-field, and your handkerchief was waving in the perfumed air like one of those tumbler pigeons I used to have long ago. I was just about to utter the three *whistles* we had agreed upon, when that stupid old *ass* Bräsig came up to me, and talked to me for a *whole hour by the clock* about the farm. As soon as he was gone I hastened to the ditch, but, *oh agony!* I was terribly disappointed. The time must have seemed very long to you, for you were gone.--But now, *listen*. As soon as I have finished my curds and cream this evening I shall start for the place of *Randyvoo* where I shall be hidden *punctually at half-past eight*. This is Saturday, so the parson will be writing his sermon, and the *Dragon* will be busy, so it is a favourable *opportunity* for us to meet, and the *alder-bushes* will screen us from every eye, (Schiller!) Wait awhile-- thy rest comes presently (Göthe) in the *arms* of thy *adorer*, who would *sell* all that is dear to him, if he could *buy* what is dear to thee with the proceeds.

> "Again to meet! again to meet!
> Till then I fain would sleep;
> My longings and my thoughts to steep
> In Lethe's waters dark and deep.

My loved one I again shall see,
There's rapture in the thought!
In the hope to-morrow of thee,
My darling, I fear nought.

("The *beginning* is by myself, the *middle* part by Schiller, and the *end* by a certain person called Anonymous who writes a great deal of poetry, but I have altered his lines to suit the present case.)

"*In an agony of longing to see you,*

Ever Thine."

"No!" cried little Mrs. Behrens when she had read the letter. "This is really too much of a good thing! Ah, my dear sister, I'm sorry for you! Well, it's high time for *other* people to interfere, and I think that being his aunt, I am the proper person to do so. And I will do it," she exclaimed aloud, stamping her foot emphatically, "and I should like to see who'd dare to prevent me!"

"I promise not to interfere with you, Mrs. Behrens," said Bräsig, coming from behind the bee-hives.

"Have you been listening, Bräsig?" asked Mrs. Behrens rather sharply.--"'Listening!' I never listen! I only keep my ears open, and then I hear what's going on; and I keep my eyes open, and see what passes before me. For instance, I see that you are very cross."--"Yes, but it's enough to drive an angel wild."--"Ah, Mrs. Behrens, the angels are wild enough already in all conscience, but we don't need to speak of them just now, for I believe that the devil himself is going about Pümpelhagen."--"Goodness gracious me! Has Fred ....?"--"No," answered Bräsig, "I don't know what it is, but certainly there's something up."--"How?"--"Mrs. Behrens, Hawermann is in a bad humour, and that is enough to show you that something unpleasant is going on. When I went to Pümpelhagen last week I found him busy with the hay and rape-harvest, and said: 'Good-morning,' I said.--'Good-morning,' said he.--'Charles,' I began, and was going to have said something when he interrupted me by asking: 'Have you seen Triddelfitz anywhere?'--'Yes,' I answered.--'Where?' he asked.--'Sitting in the large ditch,' I said.--'Did you see young Mr. von Rambow?' he asked.--'He's sitting in the next ditch close behind Fred,' I replied.--'What are they doing?' he asked.--'Playing,' I said.--'You don't give me much comfort,' he said, '*playing*, when there's so much to be done!'--'Yes, Charles,' I said, 'and I played with them.'--'What were you playing at?' he asked.--'We had a game at "I spy," Charles. You must understand that your grey-hound was peeping over the edge of the ditch towards Gürlitz, and your young nobleman was watching the greyhound, so I hid myself in the marl-pit, and watched them both. When ever one of them turned the others ducked, so there we sat peeping and ducking till at last I found it a very tiresome amusement, and, leaving my hiding-place, went to join Mr. von Rambow.' 'Good-day,' I said.--'Good-day,' he replied.--'Pardon me,' I said, 'but which of your farming-operations is it that is occupying your attention just now?'--'I,' he stammered, 'w--wanted to see how the peas were getting on!'--'H'm!' I said. 'Ah!' I said. 'I understand.' Then I bade him 'good-bye,' and went to have a look at the grey-hound. Don't be angry, Mrs. Behrens, but that's what I always call your nephew."--"Not at all, not at all!" cried the little lady, though her own name for him was different.--Then Bräsig continued: "'Good-day,' I said, 'may I ask what you are doing here?'--'Oh, nothing in particular,' he said, looking rather foolish, 'I'm only looking at the peas.'--'Now, Charles,' I said, 'if you can get the peas staked by setting those two lads to look at them, why all that I can say is that you're a deuced lucky fellow.'--'The devil take it!' he said, 'they're both up to some folly. Mr. von Rambow is quite changed this summer, he isn't like the same person. He goes about in a dream, forgets all that I tell him, and so I can't rely on him as I used to do. And as for that other stupid dolt, he's worse than ever.'--Now, Mrs. Behrens, pray don't be angry with Hawermann for calling your nephew a 'stupid dolt.'"--"Certainly not," replied Mrs. Behrens, "for that's just what he is."--"Well, you see that all happened a week ago, but this morning I went out early with my fishing-rod to try whether I couldn't catch a few trout, when just as I was coming in this direction I caught sight of your nephew, the greyhound. He slipped cautiously into the garden, and after remaining there for a few minutes, came out again. Meanwhile I perceived that the young nobleman was watching him from amongst the thorn-bushes by the side of the ditch; but what was my astonishment when I saw that my good old friend Charles Hawermann was following them on the hill-side. I brought up the rear, and so we all went on in single file quite round the village, and I couldn't help laughing when I thought that each of us only knew of the presence of the game he was stalking, and was totally unaware that he himself was being stalked in his turn. We're all to be at it again to-morrow I believe, for Hawermann, who has followed them twice already, is determined to get to the bottom of the mystery; so if either you or the parson has a fancy to join us in the hunt, you can follow me."--"Thanks very much," said Mrs. Behrens, "but I've got my part to play already. Bräsig, can you keep a secret?"--"Like a safe when the padlock is on," he answered.--"No, no. Do be serious. Can you be silent?"--"I beg your pardon," he said gravely, and clapped his hand on his mouth in token of shame at his ill-timed jesting, though had anyone else done it, he would have given him a black eye for his pains.--"Why well then, listen," said Mrs. Behrens, who now proceeded to relate all that she knew of the affair.--"Wheugh!" whistled Bräsig, "what a fool that nephew of yours is."--Mrs. Behrens then read him the letters she had found. "Hang it," cried Bräsig, "where did the young rascal get that grand way of expressing himself. Stupid as he is in other matters, he can write much better than one would expect."--When she came to the bit about the dragon Bräsig laughed heartily, and said: "That's you, Mrs. Behrens, that's you!"--"I know," she answered sharply, "but the ass in the third letter is intended for you, so neither of us need laugh at the other. But now, Bräsig, you see that it's quite necessary that I should get hold of the little wretch, and box his ears well for him."--"You're quite right, and it's easily managed. Listen. You and I must hide at the bottom of the garden at eight o'clock this evening; at half past eight, Louisa must take her place in the ditch, and you'll see that he'll come like a bear to wild honey; and then we'll spring out upon him, and take him prisoner before he knows where he is."--"That won't do at all, Bräsig. If I were going to act in that sort of way I shouldn't require your help. It would be a great misfortune if Louisa were ever to know anything about this, and I'd rather that neither Hawermann nor even my pastor should hear of it."--"H'm, h'm!" said Bräsig. "Then .... then .... Stop! I have it now. Mrs. Behrens, you must make yourself as thin as possible, put on Louisa's clothes, and go to the *randyvoo* in her stead. Then, as soon as he is seated by your side, and is on the point of kissing you, you must seize him by the scruff of the neck, and hold on till I come."--"Nay, Bräsig, that would never do!"--"Don't you think so, Mrs. Behrens? You understand that if he doesn't see his sweetheart in the ditch, you'll never manage to inveigle him there; and if we don't nab him unexpectedly, we'll never succeed in catching him, for he's a long-legged, thin-flanked grey-hound, and if it came to a race, we'd be nowhere with our short legs and round bodies."--It was quite true; but no! she go to a *rendezvous*? And Bräsig was very stupid, how could she ever get into Louisa's gown?--But Bräsig would not be convinced; he maintained that it was the only way in which she could get the interview she wanted with her nephew, and assured her that all she had to do was to put on Louisa's shawl and Leghorn hat, and then go and sit on the edge of the ditch: "You must remember to sit down," he continued, "for if you remain standing he will see at once that you're a foot shorter, and at least a foot broader than Louisa."--At last--at last Mrs. Behrens allowed herself to be persuaded, and when she went out at the back-door about eight o'clock that evening, wearing Louisa's shawl and hat, the parson who was standing at his study-window thinking over his sermon, said to himself wonderingly: "What on earth is Regina doing with Louisa's hat and shawl? And there's Bräsig coming out of the arbour. He must want to speak to me about something--but it's a very odd thing altogether!"

Mrs. Behrens went down the garden path with Bräsig feeling ready for anything that might befall. She opened the garden-gate and went out alone, leaving Bräsig squatted under the hedge like a great toad, but no sooner was she by herself than her courage oozed away, and she said: "Come to the ditch with me, Bräsig, you're too far away there, and must be close at hand to help me when I've caught him."--"All right!" said Bräsig, and he accompanied her to the ditch.

Canal-like ditches such as this are no longer to be found in all the country-side, for the thorough system of drainage to which the land has been subjected has done away with their use; but every farmer will remember them in the old time. They were from fifteen to twenty feet wide at the top, but tapered away till quite narrow at the bottom, and were fringed with thorns and other bushwood. They were generally dry except in spring and autumn, when there was a foot or a foot and half of water in them, or in summer for a day or two after a thunder-storm. That was the case now.-- "Bräsig hide yourself behind that thorn so that you may come to the rescue at once."--"Very well," said Bräsig.--"But, Mrs. Behrens," he continued after a pause, "you must think of a signal to call me to your help."--"Yes," she said. "Of course! But what shall it be? Wait! when I say; *'The Philistines be upon thee'* spring upon him."--"I understand, Mrs. Behrens!"

"Goodness gracious me!" thought the clergyman's wife. "I feel as if I were quite a Delilah. Going to a *rendezvous* at half past eight in the evening! At my age too! Ah me, in my old age I'm going to do what I should have been ashamed of when I was a girl."--Then aloud. "Bräsig don't puff so loud anyone could hear you a mile off." Resuming her soliloquy: "And all for the sake of a boy, a mischievous wretch of a boy. Good gracious! If my pastor knew what I was about!"--Aloud. "What are you laughing at, Bräsig? I forbid you to laugh, it's very silly of you."--"I didn't laugh, Mrs. Behrens."--"Yes, you *did*, I heard you distinctly."--"I only yawned, Mrs. Behrens, it's such frightfully slow work lying here."--"You oughtn't to yawn at such a time. I'm trembling all over.--Oh, you little wretch, what misery you have caused me! I can't tell anyone what you've made me suffer, and must just bear it in silence. It was God who sent Bräsig to my help."--Suddenly Bräsig whispered in great excitement, his voice sounding like the distant cry of a corn-crake: "Mrs. Behrens, draw yourself out till you're as long as Lewerenz's child;[15] make yourself as thin as you possibly can, and put on a pretty air of confusion, for I see him coming over the crest of the hill. His figure stands out clearly against the sky."--Little Mrs. Behrens felt as if her heart had stopped beating, and her anger waxed hotter against the boy who had brought her into such a false position. She was so much ashamed of herself for being where she was, that she would most assuredly have run away if Bräsig had not laughed again, but as soon as she heard that laugh, she determined to stay and show him that he was engaged in a much more serious undertaking than he seemed to imagine.--

It was quite true that Bräsig had laughed this time, for he saw a second and then a third black figure following the first down the hill. "Ha, ha, ha!" he chuckled in his hiding-place in the thorn-bush, "there's Charles Hawermann too! I declare the whole overseeing force of Pümpelhagen is coming down here to see how the peas are growing in the dusk of evening. It's as good as a play!"--Mrs. Behrens did not see the others, she only saw her sister's son who was coming rapidly towards her. He hastened over the bridge, ran along the bank, sprang to her side, and threw his arms round her neck, exclaiming: "Sweet angel!"--"Oh you wicked little wretch!" cried his aunt trying to seize him in the way Bräsig had desired her, but instead of that she only caught hold of the collar of his coat. Then she called out as loudly as she could: "The Philistines be upon thee!" and immediately Bräsig the Philistine started to his feet.--Confound it! His foot had gone to sleep!--But never mind! He hopped down the bank as quickly as he could, taking into consideration that one leg felt as if it had a hundred-and-eighty pound weight attached to the end of it, but just as he was close upon his prey he tripped over a low thorn-bush and tumbled right into the foot and a half of water.--And there he sat as immovably as if he had gone back to the hydropathic establishment, and were in the enjoyment of a sitz-bath! Fred stood as if he had been turned to stone, and felt as though he were suffering from a douche-bath, for his dear aunt was clutching him tightly and scolding him to her heart's content: "The dragon has caught you now my boy! Yes, the dragon has caught you!"--"And here comes the ass," shouted Bräsig picking himself out of the water and running towards him. But Fred had now recovered from his astonishment. He shook himself free from his aunt, and darting up the bank would have escaped had he not at the same moment encountered a new enemy--Frank. In another second Hawermann had joined them, and Mrs. Behrens had scarcely recovered from the shock of seeing him, when her pastor came up, and said: "What's the matter, Regina? What does all this mean?"--The poor little lady's consternation was indescribable, but Bräsig, from whose clothes the water was running in streams, was too angry to hold his tongue, and exclaimed: "You confounded rascal! You greyhound!" giving Fred a hearty dig in the ribs as he spoke. "It's all your fault that I shall have another attack of gout. But now, I'll tell you what, everyone shall know what a d--d Jesuit you are.

Hawermann, he ....."--"For God's sake," cried Mrs. Behrens, "don't attend to a single word that Bräsig says. Hawermann, Mr. von Rambow, the whole thing is ended and done with. It's all over now, and what has still to be done or said can quite well be managed by my pastor alone; it's a family matter and concerns no one but ourselves. Isn't that the case, my dear Fred? It's merely a family matter I assure you, and no one has anything to do with it but we two. But now, come away, my boy, we'll tell my pastor all about it. Good-night, Mr. von Rambow. Good-night, Hawermann, Fred will soon follow you. Come away, Bräsig, you must go to bed at once."

And so she managed to disperse the assembly. The two who were left in ignorance of what had happened, went home separately, shaking their heads over the affair. Hawermann was indignant with his two young people, and put out because he was to have no explanation of their conduct. Frank was mistrustful of everyone; he had recognised Louisa's hat and shawl in spite of the darkness, and thought that the mystery must have something to do with her, though how, he was unable to conjecture.

Fred was much cast down in spirit. The clergyman and his wife went on in front of him, and the latter told her husband the whole story from beginning to end, scolding her hopeful nephew roundly the whole time. The procession moved on towards the parsonage, and as the evil-doer guessed that a bad half-hour awaited him there, he had serious thoughts of making his escape while it was possible, but Bräsig came as close up to him as if he had known what he was thinking of, and that only made him rage and chafe the more inwardly. When Bräsig asked Mrs. Behrens who it was that had come up in the nick of time, and she had answered that it was Frank, Triddelfitz stood still and shaking his fist in the direction of Pümpelhagen, said fiercely: "I am betrayed, and *she* will be sold, sold to that man because of his rank and position!"--"Boy!" cried Mrs. Behrens, "will you hold your tongue!"--"Hush, Regina," said her husband, who had now a pretty good idea of what had taken place, "now please go in and see that Bräsig's room is prepared, and get him sent to bed as quickly as you can. I will remain here and speak to Fred."

This was done. The parson appealed to Fred's common sense, but his sense of injury far exceeded that other, and his spirit seethed and boiled like wine in the process of fermentation. He put aside all the clergyman's gentle arguments, and declared passionately that his own aunt had determined to destroy the whole happiness of his life, and that she cared more for the rich aristocrat than for her sister's son.

Within the house matters were going on in the same unsatisfactory manner; uncle Bräsig refused to go to bed in spite of all Mrs. Behrens' entreaties. "I can't," he said, "that is to say, I can, but I mustn't do it; for I must go to Rexow. I had a letter from Mrs. Nüssler to say that she wanted my help." The same yeast which had caused Fred to seethe and boil over was working in him, but more quietly, because it had been a part of his being for a longer time. At last, however, he was persuaded to go to bed as a favour to Mrs. Behrens, and from fear of bringing on an attack of gout by remaining in his wet things, but his thoughts were as full of anxious affection for Mrs. Nüssler, as Fred's were of love for Louisa when on leaving the parsonage he exclaimed passionately: "Give her up, does he say! Give her up!--The devil take that young sprig of the nobility!"

CHAPTER XIII

Next day--it was Sunday morning--when Bräsig awoke, he gave himself a comfortable stretch in the soft bed. "A luxury," he said to himself, "that I've never before enjoyed, but I suppose one would soon get accustomed to it." Just as he was about to get up the housemaid came in, and taking possession of his clothes, placed a black coat, waistcoat and pair of trousers over the back of a chair in their stead.

"Ho, ho!" he said with a laugh as he examined the black suit; "It's Sunday, and this is a parsonage; but surely they never think that I'm going to preach to-day!" He lifted one article of clothing after the other curiously, and then said: "Ah! I see now, it's because mine were wet through in the ditch last night, so they've given me a suit belonging to his Reverence. All right then!--here goes." But it did not go so easily after all! And as for comfort, that was totally out of the question. The trousers were a very good length, but were frightfully tight. The lower buttons of the waistcoat could neither be coaxed nor forced into the button-holes, and when he put on the coat, there was an ominous cracking somewhere between the shoulders. As for his arms, they stood out from his body as if he were prepared to press the whole world to his faithful heart on this particular Sunday.

After he was dressed he went down stairs, and joined Mrs. Behrens in the parlour. As to his legs, he looked and walked very much as he had done ever since he had received his pension; but as to the upper part of his body! Mrs. Behrens burst out laughing when she saw him, and immediately took refuge behind the breakfast table, for he advanced with his arms outstretched as if he wished to make her the first recipient of his world-embrace.--"Keep away from me, Bräsig!" she laughed. "If I had ever imagined that my pastor's good clothes would have looked so ridiculous on you I'd have let you remain in bed till dinner-time, for your own things won't be washed and dried before that."--"Oh, ho!" laughed Bräsig, "that was the reason you sent me these things, was it? I thought perhaps you wanted to dress me up for another *randyvoo* to-day."--"Now, just listen to me, Bräsig!" said little Mrs. Behrens, blushing furiously. "I forbid you to make such jokes. And when you're going about in the neighbourhood--you have nothing to do now except to carry gossip from one house to another--if you ever tell any one about that wretched *rendezvous* of last night--I'll never speak to you again."--"Mrs. Behrens, you may trust me not to do that," here he went nearer the clergyman's wife with both arms outstretched, and she once more retreated behind the table. "Indeed, you've nothing to fear. I'm not a Jesuit."--"No, Bräsig, you're an old heathen, but you ar'n't a Jesuit But if you say anything about it .... Oh me! Hawermann must be told, my pastor says so. But if he asks about it, don't mention my name, please. Oh, dear! If the Pomuchelskopps were ever to hear of it, I should be the most miserable of women. God knows, Bräsig, that what I did, I did for the best, and for the sake of that innocent child. I've sacrificed myself for her."--"That's quite true," answered Bräsig with conviction, "and so don't let fretting over it give you any grey hairs. Look here. If Charles Hawermann asks me how you came to be there, I'll say--I'll say--h'm!--I'll say that you had arranged a *randyvoo* with me."--"*You!* Fie, for shame!"--"Nay, Mrs. Behrens, I don't see that. Am I not as good as the young grey-hound any day? And don't our ages suit better?" And as he spoke he looked as innocently surprised at her displeasure as if he had proposed the best possible way out of the difficulty. Mrs. Behrens looked at him dubiously, and then said, folding her hands on her lap: "Bräsig, I'll trust to you to say nothing you ought not to say. But Bräsig--dear Bräsig, do nothing absurd. And .... and .... come and sit down, and drink a cup of coffee." She took hold of his stiff arm and drew him to the table, much as a miller draws the sails of a windmill when he wants to set it going.

"Thank you," said Bräsig. He managed to get hold of the handle of the cup after a struggle, and lifted it as if he were a juggler and the cup were at least a hundred pounds in weight, and as if he wanted to make sure that all the audience saw it properly. Then he tried to sit down, but the moment he bent his knees a horrible cracking noise was heard, and he drew himself up again hastily--whether it was the chair or the trousers that cracked he did not know. He therefore drank his coffee standing, and said: it didn't matter, for he hadn't time to sit down, he must go to Mrs. Nüssler at once because of her letter.--Mrs. Behrens implored him to wait until his clothes were dry, but in vain; Mrs. Nüssler's slightest wish was regarded by him as a command, and was inscribed as such in the order-book of his conscience. So he set out for Rexow along the Pümpelhagen road, the long tails of his clerical garment floating behind him. His progress was as slow and difficult as that of a young rook learning to fly.

As he passed Pümpelhagen, Hawermann saw him, and called him to stop, adding: "Bless me, Zachariah, why are you dressed so oddly?"--"An accident, nothing but an accident. You remember that I fell into the muddy water in the ditch last night. But I haven't time to stop now, I must go to your sister."--"My sister's business can wait better than mine, Bräsig. I've noticed lately that a great many things are going on behind my back, that I'm not wanted to know. It wouldn't have mattered so much, but that I saw last night that both the parson and his wife are better informed than I am, and that these good people want to hide the true state of the case from me out of the kindness of their hearts."--"You're right, Charles. It is out of kindness."--"Certainly, Bräsig, and I am not mistrustful of them, but I can't help thinking that it's something that concerns me very nearly, and that I ought to know. What were you doing yesterday evening?"--"I, Charles? I was just having a *randyvoo* with Mrs. Behrens in the ditch."--"And the parson?"--"We knew nothing of what brought him, Charles. He took us by surprise when he came."--"What had Mr. von Rambow to do with it?"--"He caught your grey-hound by the scruff of the neck, and perhaps threw me into the water by accident."--"*What had Fred Triddelfitz to do with it?*" asked Hawermann impressively, "and what had Louisa's hat and shawl got to do with it?"--"Nothing more than that they didn't fit Mrs. Behrens at all, for she's far too stout to wear them."--"Zachariah," said Hawermann, stretching his hand towards his friend over the low hedge, "you are trying to put me off. *Won't* you tell me what is the matter, we are such old friends--or is it that you must not tell me?"--"The devil take the *randyvoo* and Mrs. Behrens' anxiety," cried Bräsig, seizing Hawermann's hand and shaking it vehemently over the hedge and amongst the tall nettles that grew there, till the smart of the stings made them both draw back. "I'll tell you, Charles. The parson's going to tell you himself, so why shouldn't I? Fred Triddelfitz fell in love with you sometime ago, most likely because of the good fatherly advice you have often given him, and now it seems his love for you has passed on to your daughter. Love always passes on, for example with me from your sister to Mina."--"Do be serious, Bräsig!"--"Am I not always in earnest, Charles, when I speak of your sister and Mina?"--"I am sure you are," cried Hawermann, seizing his friend's hand again in spite of the nettles, "but, tell me, what had Frank to do with it?"--"I think that he must have fallen in love with you too, and that his love has also passed on from you to your daughter."--"That would be a great pity," cried Hawermann, "a very great pity. God only knows how it's to be stopped."--"I'm not so sure, Charles, that you're right in thinking it a misfortune, for he has two estates ...."--"Don't talk about that Bräsig, but come in and tell me all that you know."

As soon as Bräsig had told as much as he knew of the affair, he set off down the foot-path that led to Rexow. Hawermann stood and watched him till he was out of sight, and then said to himself; "He's a good man, his heart's in the right place, and if I find that it is so, I will .... but .... but ....!"-- He was not thinking of Bräsig when he said this, but of Frank.----

On this Sunday morning young Joseph was sitting in his easy chair beside the parlour-fire waiting to be called to breakfast. Lina and Mina had spread the cloth and arranged dishes of ham, sausages, bread, and butter neatly on the table, and now that everything else was ready, Mrs. Nüssler came in carrying a skillet with hot buttered eggs: "Come along, Joseph," she said, "don't let the eggs get cold," and then she left the room again to see that all was going on rightly outside.

The eggs were still bubbling and sputtering in the skillet--but young Joseph did not move. Whether it was because he had not yet finished his pipe, and felt that he ought not to be deprived of his customary smoke before breakfast, or whether it was because he had fallen into a brown study over the two letters which were lying open on his knee, cannot be known with any certainty. But whatever the cause may have been he did not move, and kept staring straight before him at one particular spot under the stove. And on that spot at which he was staring lay young Bolster, who was staring back at him. Young Bolster was the last descendant of the Bolster family, and had been born and brought up in, the house since old Joseph's time; When he was spoken to he was called "Bolster," but he was always spoken of as the "crown-prince," not for his own sake, no, but for Joseph's sake, for this was the only joke--if indeed it might be called one--that he had been able to make on the dog after long consideration.

So, as I have just said, the two young people, young Joseph and young Bolster, stared hard at each other. They were both plunged in deep thought, the one about the letters, and the other about the savoury smell of the eggs in the skillet. Joseph never moved a hair's breadth; but the crown-prince sometimes rubbed his paw gently over his thoughtful face, and raising his pointed nose in the air, refreshed himself with a sniff at the good things on the table. At last he crept out from under the stove, put on a look of polite entreaty, and tried to attract Joseph's attention by wagging his tail. But young Joseph never moved a muscle, and young Bolster saw that he was not conscious of his presence, so he advanced to the table, looking round slyly out of the corner of his eye as he did so; but more from fear of Mrs. Nüssler's coming than of young Joseph's seeing what he was about. He then rested his head on the breakfast-table, and indulged in the pleasures of hope, like a great many other young people. But though hope is all very well for a time, every one likes his hope to be realized after having shown a proper amount of patience. The crown-prince, therefore, placed his feet--only his forefeet--on the chair, and so got a little nearer the object of his desire. His nose touched the plate on which the rosy slices of ham were lying.--Ah! young people!--And then he snatched a bit as quickly as we used to steal a kiss from sweet red lips when we were young.

"Bolster!" cried young Joseph as reproachfully as a mother could have done when she saw her daughter kissed so unceremoniously. But still he did not move, and Bolster--either because he thought he had a right to kiss all the sweet red lips in his kingdom, or because he had grown a hardened offender--looked at him impudently, wiped his mouth, and licked his lips for more. Joseph stared at him without moving, and in another moment Bolster was standing on the chair, this time with his hind legs also, and had set to work to finish the dish of sausages.--"Bolster!" cried young Joseph. "Mina, Bolster's eating up the sausages!" but still he did not move.--The crown-prince moved, however; as soon as he had finished the plate of sausages he went to the principal dish, the skillet containing the buttered eggs.--"Mother, mother!" cried young Joseph, "he's eating up all the eggs now!"--Meantime young Bolster had burnt his nose in the hot skillet; he started back, and in so doing upset the skillet, and knocked the bottle of kümmel over with his tail. The whole table shook, but still young Joseph did not move. He contented himself with shouting: "Mother! Mother! That beast of a dog is eating up all the eggs!"

"What are you bellowing at in your own house, young Joseph?" cried a voice at the door, and then some one came in who frightened Joseph considerably. He was so much startled that he let his pipe fall out of his mouth, raised both his hands, and exclaimed: "All good spirits praise God, the Lord!--Is that you reverend Sir, or is it you, Bräsig?"

Yes, it was Bräsig, or at least it was very like him, as Joseph would have seen if he had had time to look. But he had not time, for the newcomer had caught Bolster in the very act of pilfering, and was now rushing about the room, looking in every corner for a stick with which to chastise the delinquent, his long black coat tails streamed behind him as he ran, and his angry red face showed between the high collar of his black coat, and his tall black hat which had fallen half over his eyes with the violence of his exertions. He looked for all the world like one of those terrible bogies with which nurses frighten naughty children. Young Joseph was no longer a child, but he was really alarmed; he started up from his chair, and holding on to the back of it tightly, kept shouting: "Reverend Sir!--Bräsig!--Bräsig!--Reverend Sir!"--But the crown-prince was still very young and so he was frightened out of his wits. The door was shut so that he could not make his escape that way. He rushed wildly round the room, till at last, springing at the window, he dashed right through it into the road, carrying a great part of it along with him.

The noise was enough to waken the dead, so why did Mrs. Nüssler not come in from the kitchen? She did not appear till Bräsig shoving his hat out of his eyes with one hand, and pointing at the broken window with the other, said: "It's all your fault, young Joseph! That poor creature the crown-prince didn't know that he was doing any harm. All the good kümmel spilt!"--"Good gracious!" cried Mrs. Nüssler, letting her hands fall limply by her side. "What's the meaning of all this, Joseph? Law, Bräsig! How very odd you do look to be sure!"--"Mother," said young Joseph, "the dog and Bräsig ..... What could I do?"--"For shame, young Joseph," cried Bräsig, beginning to walk up and down the room, the long tails of his coat almost sweeping the pool of kümmel as he passed it, "Who is master in this house? Is it you or young Bolster?"--"But, Bräsig, whatever induced you to make such a guy of yourself?" asked Mrs. Nüssler.--"Ah!" replied Bräsig, looking at her reproachfully, "what was to be done? I fell into the water yesterday evening during a *randyvoo* with Mrs. Behrens, and my clothes were still too wet to put on this morning. And then the letter I got from you yesterday telling me that you wanted to consult me about family matters! How else could I have come?--And is it *my* fault that the parson is as long as Lewerenz's child, as thin as a mere slip of a girl, and has a larger head than I happen to have got? Why did Mrs. Behrens lend me her husband's clothes, and why did all the stupid labourers, who saw me in the distance on the path leading to Gürlitz church, call out: 'Good-morning, reverend Sir' when I was coming here in the kindness of my heart to help you out of your family difficulties?"--"Bräsig," said young Joseph, "I swear ....."--"Swear not at all, young Joseph, for you will go to the bad place if you do. Do you call it a family council when the kümmel is lying in a pool on the floor, and I have to go about in the parson's clothes?"--"Bräsig, Bräsig," said Mrs. Nüssler, who hardly recognised the friend of her youth in the angry little man, and who had been busily engaged in picking up the bits of broken glass, and straightening the table-cloth, &c., "that's a small matter. See now, I've got everything neat and tidy again."--Bräsig could not keep up his anger when Mrs. Nüssler spoke so kindly to him, so he merely growled out in a low voice: "Hang it, young Joseph, I used to hope that you'd grow wiser in time and cease to need leading strings, but what's bred in the bone comes out in the blood! Well now, tell me what's the matter?"

"Yes," said Mrs. Nüssler ...... "Yes," said young Joseph, and his wife stopped thinking that Joseph was really going to explain, but he only added: "It all depends upon circumstances!" So she went on: "You know that Godfrey Baldrian, who is Joseph's nephew, is a very religious young man and has been working hard preparing to become candidate for a living--but you must often have seen him here?"--"Yes," said Bräsig with a nod, "he's a very good young man, a sort of Methodist, and wears his hair combed straight down behind his ears to make him look like the pictures of our Lord. He tried to convert me once when he saw me going out to fish on a Sunday morning."--"That's the very man I mean. Well, he hasn't quite finished with the university yet, and his father, the school-master, wants us to let him come here for a time that he may study without interruption. And we wanted to ask you whether we ought to consent to this arrangement."--"Why not? Methodists are quiet, well-behaved people who only care about the conversion of others, and you, Mrs. Nüssler, will provide them with an object, and young Joseph is--thank God!--not to be converted by me and young Bolster."--"That's all very well, Bräsig, but the thick end of the wedge is coming. You see that Rudolph Kurz, another nephew of Joseph's, is also studying for Holy Orders, and we have had a letter from his father to say that as he understands that Godfrey is going to lodge with us for a time, he would like us to take his son too. Now Rudolph has been amusing himself in Rostock instead of working, and his father thinks he'll be able to read better in a quiet place like this. But I just ask you how that's possible? If he didn't learn in Rostock where he had all sorts of learned professors to help him, do you think that he'll do any better when there's only Joseph and me?"--"I know him too," answered Bräsig, "he's a very nice young fellow. Before he went to the university he caught me half-a-dozen perch in the black pool, the smallest of which weighed a pound and a half."--"Yes, of course, you know him. It was he who brought Mina safely down to us, when she was a silly little thing of six years old and had climbed up the ladder to the roof to see the stork's nest. I remember yet how she stood up there clapping her hands with glee while we stood below in an agony of fright. He could do that sort of thing quite well, but as for book learning, he never took kindly to that! Rector Baldrian tells me that he has been fighting a great deal in Rostock. Only fancy they fought with swords, and he, Rudolph, was one of them. The duels were about the daughter of a rich merchant at Rostock."--"Do you really mean to tell me that!" cried Bräsig. "Bless me! So they really fought a duel for the sake of a merchant's pretty daughter! Ah, young Joseph, women are the cause of all the mischief that goes on in the world."--"Yes, Bräsig, that's quite true; but what's to be done now?"--"I don't see much difficulty in answering," replied Bräsig. "If you don't want the two young divinity students, write and say so; but if you want them, write and tell them to come. You've plenty of room for them, and can easily provide them with enough to eat and drink. As for their books, you'll have to look out a place for them to be stowed; and I should think they'd have a great number. If you are only going to take one of the young men, I advise you to choose the fighter, for I'd much rather be fought with than converted."--"That's all very fine, Bräsig, but you see we have consented to take Godfrey Baldrian, and the Kurzes would be angry if we were to refuse to receive their son."--"Very well then, take them both."--"But, Bräsig, the two little girls .... they've just been confirmed .... Come, Joseph, speak."--And Joseph began: "It all depends upon circumstances. Look here, Bräsig, Mina was--as you know--brought up to be a governess, and my old mother always used to say that it never did to have a governess and a divinity student in the same house."--"Ha, ha! Young Joseph! I understand you now. You mean that they'd fall in love. Pooh! nonsense! Little round-head in love!"--"Nay, Bräsig, don't think it such a ridiculous idea!--I am their mother and so I ought to know. I wasn't as old as the twins when ...."--Mrs. Nüssler stopped abruptly for Bräsig's face grew very long, and he looked at her enquiringly.--Fortunately Joseph came to the rescue by saying: "Give Bräsig something to drink, mother. Bräsig, you see it might quite well happen, and what are we as their parents to do?"--"Let them alone, young Joseph! Why does God send young folks into the world, if He doesn't intend them to love each other? But the little round-heads!"--"It's easy for you to talk, Bräsig," said Mrs. Nüssler quickly, "but you shouldn't speak of a serious matter so lightly. Hatch a common looking egg and perhaps a basilisk creeps out!"--"Let it!" cried Bräsig.--"Let it, do you say?" exclaimed Mrs. Nüssler, "then I don't agree with you. Joseph isn't of a nature to be anxious about anything. He wouldn't care if all the maids in the house were to fall in love, throw up their places and marry; while I--good gracious!--I have my hands full in trying to keep everything straight, and in holding my eyes open to see what they want to hide from me, for I know that a good deal goes on behind my back that ought not to be."--"But why not consult me?" asked Bräsig.--"*You*," said Mrs. Nüssler smiling, "you don't understand that kind of thing."--"What!" cried Bräsig. "*I* not understand, and yet I was once engaged to three women ...."--He got no further, for Mrs. Nüssler's face lengthened as much as his own had done a short time before, and she looked at him so enquiringly, that he swallowed his glass of kümmel at a single gulp to hide his embarrassment--"It's a silly affair altogether," he said after a pause, "and it's all young Joseph's fault."--"Mine, Bräsig! What had I to do with it?"--"What! I'll tell you. You let the crown-prince eat up your breakfast before your very eyes; you allow two divinity students to come and live in your house, and then you don't know how to get out of the scrape you've got yourself into. I--I give in--about the little round-heads, and the devil take the students! I'll watch the duellist; do you keep your eye on the Methodist, for he's the worst of the two."--"That's all that can be done," said Mrs. Nüssler, getting up from her chair.

The two divinity students took possession of their new quarters at Michaelmas, and at the same time Frank went to the agricultural college at Eldena. As Frank walked down the path outside the parsonage garden for the last time, a lovely face peeped through the hedge at him, from the same place where Fred had disposed of the bread and beer.

When Louisa went into the parlour that evening, Mrs. Behrens took the tall handsome girl upon her knee, kissed her, and pressed her to her heart.--Women never can let well alone!

FOOTNOTES

Footnote 1: *Note*. Stemhagen, properly Stavenhagen, Reuter's birthplace.

Footnote 2: *Note*. The feudal-system was kept up longer in Mecklenburg than elsewhere, the peasantry belonged to the estate, and always continued to work on it. A Mecklenburg squire often beat his labourers when he was angry with them.

Footnote 3: *Note*. In Mecklenburg the cows are always milked in the fields.

Footnote 4: *Note*. The Kammer is the chief government office in Mecklenburg, and Mr. von Rambow was a member of it.

Footnote 5: A mortgage or lien.

Footnote 6: *Note*. "ing" is used instead of "chen" as a diminutive in Mecklenburg.

Footnote 7: *Note*. I have changed Thou and You into Christian name, &c., as it sounds better in English.

Footnote 8: *Note*. Daring the spring cleaning.

Footnote 9: *Note*. "It is the custom in Scandinavia, as with us, for friends to exchange presents, good wishes, and visits on Christmas-day and New-year's-day..... If 'St. Nicholas' in the Rhenish Provinces, 'Knecht Ruprecht' in Northern and Central Germany announce the arrival of these holidays to children, whom they reward or punish according to circumstances, the 'Julklapp,' takes their place in Pomerania, bestows welcome gifts, and recalls the memory of the highest god of our forefathers." From "Unsere Vorzeit" by Dr. W. Wagner, vol. I. part II. page 138.

Footnote 10: *Note*. Knecht Ruprecht.

Footnote 11: *Note*. Bad Stuer. Stuer belongs to the von Flotow family, one of the oldest families in Mecklenburg, and the hydropathic establishment was put up by Rausse who has written a number of well known books on hydropathy. J. Duboc's "Auf Reuter'schem Boden."

Footnote 12: *Note.* "Quey," Scotch for heifer, used here because it was the only word of that meaning into which "fée" could be changed. Caroline makes "kleine Fée"--"lütt Veih."

Footnote 13: *Note.* This story is founded on fact, and during Reuter's last visit to Stuer (from the 13th of December 1868 till the 29th of January 1869) he discovered to his great amusement that he had been given the very room in which the director of the establishment told him the hero of the tale had been attacked by a neighbour's bees while he was lying helpless in the "packing" sheets. Sec Duboc's "Auf Reuter'schem Boden" in Westermann's "Monats-Hefte."

Footnote 14: *Note.* A yellow flower.

Footnote 15: *Note.* A common saying in Mecklenburg, the origin of which is unknown.